More Than a Song

A COMPANION PUBLICATIONS BOOK

In memory of our beloved Buddy (June 8, 2004 – April 17, 2017)
You brought love and laughter to our lives... more than you'll
ever know.

We love you and miss you, pumpkin.

More Than a Song

A COMPANION PUBLICATIONS BOOK

by

Chris Paynter

This is a work of fiction. All characters, locales and events are either products of the author's imagination or are used fictitiously.

MORE THAN A SONG

Cover design by Stephanie Solomon
Editor: Nann Dunne

Published by Companion Publications

www.ckpaynter.com

ISBN: 978-1-942204-14-5

First edition: June 2017

Printed in the United States of America and in the United Kingdom.

Acknowledgements

First, I'd like to thank my editor, Nann Dunne, who always improves each book I write. Thank you for catching my overabundance of "-ing" words in this one, plus some overused phrases. Like most authors, there's always at least one phrase that pops up waaay too many times in the first draft. I look forward to working with you on the next one, Nann.

Thank you, Toni Whitaker and Patty Schramm, for your awesome prowess in formatting my ebooks and print copies, respectively. Thank you, too, to my cover artist, Stephanie Solomon. This one really rocks!

A big thank-you to my wife, Phyllis, who supports me in everything I do, who nudges me to get back to my writing, and who is so patient with me when I zone out thinking about plots and characters. I am so proud of all she does to help others in her volunteer work and in her everyday life. She is the kindest human being I know, and I am blessed to call her my wife. I love you, sweetheart.

More Than a Song is a bit of a departure for me, and it was a book I went back to after much encouragement from Phyllis. She loved the story and frequently gave me many ideas for the character of C.J. James. I had fun with the humor and dialogue. I hope you, the reader, will also have fun with the story.

There is one character in this book based upon someone who was very close to us. Frodo the beagle mirrors our Buddy. This is the first book that will be published without Buddy to share in the joy of the release. Sadly, we lost him this year to kidney failure. His death has hit us hard. He was our best friend, our constant companion. But he lives on, not only in our hearts and minds, but as the "face" of Companion Publications. It is his image you see for our logo. We love you and miss you, little guy.

And, Buddy, may there be lots of toast and a recliner in the happy place you now call home. God's peace to you... until we meet again.

Chapter 1

"I think you'll enjoy this," Dani Roberts said as she slid the newly purchased book into a "Dani's Den of Books" bag. "It's one of the author's best."

"Oh, yeah?" The blonde gave her a cocky grin, her dark eyes appraising Dani. "You know something about romance?"

Dani willed her body not to respond to the woman's blatant flirting.

"I know something about good writing. I hope you enjoy the read." She held out her hand for the next customer's book.

The blonde took the hint and left. Dani was completing the other customer's purchase when she felt the presence of her assistant, Tina Dewey. Never subtle, and certainly hard to ignore, Tina was polite enough to wait until the customer walked away.

"What is it, Tina?"

"Uh, have you checked Twitter today?" Tina shifted her short, stocky frame, obviously nervous about something.

Dani forced herself not to roll her eyes. Although she was well aware of how important marketing and social media were to the success of her store, it didn't mean she had to like what she felt was an invasion of her privacy.

"You know I don't read that shit unless I have to. You do most of our twitting."

"Tweeting."

"What?"

"It's called tweeting."

"All right, tweeting." Dani scrutinized her friend a little closer. Tina's Atlanta Braves hat was slightly askew with her curly brown hair sticking out at all angles. Yeah, something was definitely off. "What is it? Did someone diss our shop?"

Tina glanced down at her smartphone.

Dani held out her hand. "Let me see it. It can't be that bad." She grabbed the phone, but Tina didn't loosen her grip. "T, you need to let go if you want me to read the tweet." Dani still found it hard to believe that adults freely used the word "tweet." She felt like a second-grader. Tina relinquished the phone.

Dani saw it wasn't the bookstore's Twitter account. It was her personal account, the one Tina had talked her into opening. The tweet was from her girlfriend, Katie:

I hate to break up on Twitter. It's the only way you'll take me seriously. I'm moving back to Indiana. I don't love you anymore, D. I'm sorr

"Oh. My. God. She did not just break up with me on Twitter." Dani sank onto the padded stool behind the register. "And couldn't she have left some of this other crap out and at least finish her apology?"

"Well, you only have 140 characters."

Dani glared at Tina.

"Sorry. Look, the woman isn't right in the head." Tina raised her hands when Dani started to speak. "She's not." Tina thrust her finger at the phone. "That proves my point. What kind of sick bitch breaks up on Twitter?"

Dani stared down at the words again. "I guess the woman I've lived with for the past two years." She tried to feel sadness over the loss, but what she really wanted to do was hit something. Hard. Maybe that gave a clue about the state of their relationship.

Tina gently pried the phone out of her hand. "I don't want my phone to become a casualty. You looked like you were about to spike it, and this thing ain't cheap."

"I knew there was a reason I hated social media," Dani mumbled. She walked to the large, plate-glass window overlooking the street and watched as couples, straight and gay, strolled hand-in-hand in front of her store. A quaint, gay-friendly town, Francis, Georgia, lay on the outskirts of Atlanta. She and Katie had moved there two years earlier.

Tina joined her at the window. She draped her arm around

Dani's shoulders. "It'll be okay."

Dani didn't answer. What was there to say? Tina moved away to greet another customer. Dani spent the remainder of the day in a fog, alternating between anger and sadness. Tina seemed to sense her need for privacy. At least she didn't broach the subject of Katie anymore.

When closing time came, Tina volunteered to shut down the register and drive the day's deposit to the bank. She clapped her hand on Dani's shoulder. "Why don't you go home? If you want, Barb and I can drop by later to check on you."

Although Tina and her partner, Barb, were her best friends, Dani felt the need to be alone—well, alone with her two-year-old beagle, Frodo. He always seemed to make things a little better. Even when they'd gone to shit, as they had today.

"Thanks, T. I think I'll be okay tonight."

"You're sure?" Tina looked worried.

"I'm not really sure of anything right now, but I think tonight I'd like to be alone."

"Well, call us if you need us."

Dani left by the back door, slid behind the steering wheel of her red MINI Cooper, and headed home. Usually, she felt pumped up when driving her car, as if she were a different person behind the wheel. Today, she felt none of that. Her anger from earlier had dwindled into a lingering sadness.

She flipped on the radio and searched for something to drown out the voice in her head that berated her for staying in a relationship that ended with a breakup on Twitter. Maybe she should've seen it coming, but how could she possibly think it would end this way?

A song came on that seemed to be written for just this moment in her life. The singer, C.J. James, had a raspy voice that reverberated in Dani's brain as she reached the chorus of the song:

You kissed me, then said goodbye. I thought you were mine.
Now all I have left are your lies.
Yeah, all I have left are your lies.

Dani pulled into the drive of her modest brick home. Normally, she hopped right out to let Frodo in from the backyard. But today, she sat in her idling car, still listening to the song, as the tears fell.

"Shit." She slapped at her wet cheeks, upset that she let Katie get to her this way. A part of her wanted to reach into the console and throttle this C.J. James who tapped into Dani's every emotion—especially when a mournful guitar solo accompanied the words.

Dani thought back to Tina telling her it would be okay, but she doubted Tina's logic. She didn't have much choice in how to handle this. She either wallowed in self-pity or she moved on, and wallowing in self-pity had never been her style.

Chapter 2

One year later...

Dani opened the shop a little before nine a.m. She stepped outside to breathe in Georgia's fresh spring air and stretched her body to her full, five-six height.

The streets were still wet from a rainstorm that whipped through Francis the night before. Dani loved this time in March when temperatures averaged in the mid- to upper-sixties. The almost unbearable humidity would descend with a vengeance later in the summer.

"Hey, Shelly." Dani waved at the bakery owner across the street.

Shelly was picking up some loose trash the storm had deposited at the bakery's doorstep. She straightened and waved back. "Hey, Dani. How you doing this morning?"

"Good. You?"

"Great."

Shelly gave another wave before entering her shop.

A soft breeze riffled Dani's short, dark hair. At the age of twenty-eight, she was starting to get some gray. Katie had harped on her to dye it, but considering her ex wasn't even in the picture anymore, Dani was glad she'd resisted.

After Katie had so publicly dumped her, Dani took a long break from dating and concentrated on her business, despite Tina's heartfelt attempts to hook her up with any lesbian she thought was suitable for her "boss."

Dani would reply she'd just as soon go home, climb into her pajamas, and curl up with a good book—especially something that involved the Civil War. She could get lost in the intricacies of the third day in the Battle of Gettysburg or in General Lee's decision to split his army and flank Joe Hooker's troops at Chancellorsville. That was much more enjoyable than a drink-filled night out with a woman whose first thought was how she was going to get Dani into bed.

Lord, I'm too young to be so cynical. She reentered her shop. She needed to set up a display of a writer's debut novel, a book Dani had read in two nights. It promised to be a great summer read, and she thought it would go over with the lesbians who ventured to Francis and frequented her shop.

Dani carried out a box of the books from the storage room. She took down copies of a novel that hadn't been selling so well to make room for the new books. She'd prepared a display board with information about the author and a short synopsis of the novel. Tina had jokingly told her, "You need to put on there that even I enjoyed the book, and considering my attention span, that's saying something."

As Dani neatly stacked the books onto the table, in her mind's eye she could still see that clear, hot, summer day when she found the small corner shop with a "For Sale or Lease" sign in the window. Dani had a bachelor's degree in business and had been savvy with her investments. She used that money to purchase this place.

She stocked the store with gay and lesbian publications—mainly lesbian. In the past years, she'd included a children's section and was pleased with how popular it was, especially with some of the lesbian moms. Although Francis was both gay- and lesbian-friendly, the town cultivated its image as a lesbian mecca. A couple of lesbian musical artists had gotten their start here.

The bell to the door jingled, and two women entered. They parted and perused different sections of the store, but Dani thought they were a couple. Eventually one of the women, the short petite one, arrived at the display Dani had set up. She silently read the information board on the author and book. She picked up a copy and flipped through it.

"Excellent book," Dani said.

The woman looked up at Dani. "You've read it?"

"Yes. I highly recommend it. And, no, the author and I aren't related, and she's not my girlfriend."

The woman laughed. "You've sold me. Looks interesting." She added it to the books she held under her arm.

Thirty minutes later, the women approached the counter to purchase their books. Between the two of them, they spent a little over $100. A very nice sale.

The rest of the day passed slowly. It would pick up the following week, the last week of the month, when the "Women in Music" series started at Carl's Cavern. It ran through the summer. Carl, the gay owner, had musicians in throughout the year, but starting the last week of March, he focused on lesbian artists.

At six, Dani locked the front door while Tina balanced the register.

"Hey," Tina said, "remember it's poker night."

"Is everyone going to show?"

"As far as I know. My girl, Barb, will be there, of course. Shelly, Betty, and Monica said they'll be there, too. I don't know if Monica will be bringing her girlfriend. Most of the time, she doesn't want to play. She just sits there." Tina made a face. Monica's girlfriend, Estelle, wasn't one of her favorite people.

Dani entered the office and opened the safe. She lifted out the moneybag and carried it to the register. She counted the money and handed it to Tina to check her total. "You know we need to be open-minded about Estelle."

"If she breaks Monica's heart, I'll be open-minded while I kick her ass. How's that?"

"As long as we're watching over Monica, I think she'll be okay. You have to remember she's a big girl."

"Whatever." Tina handed the money over to Dani, who filled out the deposit slip and slid everything into the moneybag.

"I'll run this to the bank and get a quick shower at home, first. Are we ordering a pizza?"

Tina stepped into the office and slipped on her jacket. "Definitely. No mushrooms for you, as usual."

"Right."

"See you about seven-thirty?"

"Seven-thirty it is." Dani shrugged on her lightweight jacket. She left by the back door and locked it behind her. She approached her MINI Cooper parked in the alley behind the building. She slid into the driver's seat, swung by the bank, deposited the money, and drove the short distance to her home. Pulling into the drive, she spotted her beagle, Frodo, sticking his nose between the slats of the gate in the backyard. Soon, she wouldn't be able to leave him outside because of Georgia's thick heat and humidity.

"Hey, Frodo, I'll be there in a minute, bud."

She heard Frodo scraping his claws against the screen door. "Okay, okay, little guy, I'm coming."

When she opened the screen door, Frodo bounded in and circled in front of her in the kitchen. With his head up, he wagged his tail and waited for her to pet him. Dani leaned down and stroked his ears. He lapped it up as his tail thumped against the cabinets.

"So, how was your day, boy? Did you guard the house? Chase any squirrels?"

Frodo cocked his head as if trying to understand what Dani said. Dani had a friend once who, after she observed Dani converse with Frodo, said, "You realize what he hears is 'blah, blah, blah,' right?"

"But he knows it's directed at him," she answered.

Dani gave Frodo some treats. After changing the water in his bowl, she dropped a cup of food in his dish.

"You know this is poker night, right, bud?"

At those words, he lowered his tail and flattened his ears against his head. He gave her a mournful look.

"Sure, you can't understand me," Dani mumbled as she went upstairs to the bathroom and started the shower. She stripped down and stepped into the warm water. Washing her hair, she thought of the women who'd be at the poker party tonight. They were either business owners or worked in the shops around town.

Poker night was one night that she allowed herself to let loose a little and hang out with the "clan." Since she'd drink a few bottles of beer, she always walked over.

Dani stepped out of the shower and toweled off. She pulled out some jeans and a denim shirt from her closet and quickly dressed. She trounced back downstairs, slipped on her jacket, and gave Frodo one more ear scratch before leaving.

* * *

Cars filled Tina's drive, and a couple more were parked in front of her house. Great, Dani thought, a full house for poker.

She chuckled at the play on words and tapped on the door.

"Get your ass in here!" Tina shouted from her kitchen at the back of the house.

Everyone called out a greeting when Dani entered. Betty got up from her chair in the living room to give her a hug. She was about Dani's height with blonde, curly hair, a pug nose, and a bright smile.

Monica waved at Dani from the couch where she sat next to Estelle. Monica was beautiful. Tall, with a model's features—light-brown, shoulder-length hair, and expressive blue eyes—she was the only lesbian Dani knew who looked like any of those actresses on *The L Word*. Estelle, on the other hand, was the complete opposite. She was about five-two with mousy brown hair that seemed to take on a life of its own, usually tangled looking. Dani was never sure whether that was on purpose.

Dani greeted Monica and Estelle and headed into the kitchen to see if Tina needed any assistance with preparing the table.

"Hey, Dani. Come help me with the goodies." Tina had her back to Dani while she dumped potato chips and pretzels into two separate bowls.

Dani yanked off Tina's Braves hat and smacked her over the head with it.

"Ow!" Tina yelled in mock protest.

Dani put the hat back on her but turned it around backwards. "Sometimes, T, you're such a baby. I know that didn't hurt. I'll help with the goodies, all right." Dani grabbed a potato chip and munched down on it. "There. I helped."

"Gee thanks."

Shelly entered the kitchen from the sliding glass doors that led to the backyard. In her late forties, she was the oldest of the clan.

"Hey, I thought I heard Ms. Dani come in." Shelly slid her arm around Dani's waist and gave her a peck on the cheek.

"Hi, Shelly." Dani returned the kiss. "When I saw you earlier today, I spaced about tonight until I got back in the store."

"Me, too. Must be a Tuesday thing."

"Okay! Let's get this show on the road!" Barb's booming, husky voice summoned everyone to the dining room table where the cards and chips were waiting for the poker game to begin. She handed out beer from the refrigerator. Barb styled her dark hair into a crew cut. A tattoo of the U.S. Marine emblem on her right biceps peeked out from her T-shirt. A few years before and, as she liked to say, about twenty pounds lighter, Barb was honorably discharged from the Marines after an investigation of "homosexual conduct," back in the days before the "Don't Ask, Don't Tell" policy was revoked. She rarely talked about the incident. Now, she worked as a bartender at Carl's Cavern.

The women took their seats around the large, dining room table. Tina put a CD in the stereo. The opening notes of the Indigo Girls' latest release drifted into the dining room. Dani sat down next to Betty.

"How was work today?" Betty asked her.

"It was good. We had some nice sales."

Tina scooted in her chair and started shuffling the cards. "Okay, let's play us some poker. I'm ready to kick y'all's asses like I do every poker night."

Everyone laughed as Tina dealt the cards. Everyone except for Estelle, of course. God forbid she should actually look like she was having fun. They only played with the chips—money wasn't involved. The winner claimed bragging rights and went home with a trophy that was passed on to the next poker night's winner.

No one said anything for the first few hands, each focusing on the game. Dani had won the first two hands and was holding three sevens. She took two cards and picked up a pair of tens. A nice full house. She threw in five more $100 chips.

"Jeesh, Dani, it's only the third frigging hand." Tina sported her "dealer" hat with the green plastic bill.

"Hey, you worry about your money, and I'll worry about mine."

"That's too rich for me." Monica threw her cards on the table. The other women did the same. It was down to Dani and Tina.

"All right. For that, I'll see you and raise you $300." Tina tossed in her chips.

"Be ready to lose, sister," Dani said as she matched the $300. She slapped down her full house with confidence. "Beat that." She gave Tina a smug smile.

Tina frowned. "Damn." Dani started to reel in the chips. "Not so fast, my friend." Tina slowly laid down her royal flush.

"Well, fuck you."

"Bwaa haa haa." Tina made a big show of raking in the chips.

Barb shook her head. "Now, girls. Tsk tsk."

Laughter rang out again—except for Estelle, who merely rolled her eyes.

"Anybody know anything about this C.J. James coming in next week for the 'Women in Music' series?" Tina asked. "I hear she's really good. Saw her pic, too, and whoa." She let out a low whistle. "If she can't sing, she sure as shit will look good sitting there."

Barb stared at her across the table.

"Now, darling," Tina told her, "you know you're the only one for me."

Barb snorted.

"I've heard she has a hell of a voice," Tina said. "Any of you going to hear her?"

The name startled Dani. "I heard one of her songs last year." She didn't bring up exactly when she heard the song. She didn't want to think about that infamous day of her life. "You're right. She's good. I'd like to see her perform."

Monica spoke up, too. "Estelle and I are up for it."

Estelle swung her head around and glared at Monica.

"Do you think it'd be a good idea for me to contact this C.J. and get some of her CDs for the shop?" Dani asked as she arranged her next hand.

Tina nodded. "I really do from what others have told me. I've yet to go to her website to check her out."

"I'll do that when I get home. Maybe we can do a display highlighting her music and get a jump on the others."

The pizza arrived, and the rest of the night passed quickly. Tina managed to keep her title as "World's Greatest Poker Player" for two more weeks. She barely beat out Dani on the last hand. After they added up their chips, Tina came out on top with $100 more than Dani's total.

Everyone grabbed their jackets and shared hugs while saying their goodbyes. Dani noticed that Estelle had already stepped outside to light up a cigarette. As they were walking to the door, Tina took down the trophy that sat on top of the mantel. She dramatically polished it with the tail of her shirt and then set it back on the mantel. "Looks good up there, doesn't it?" she asked.

"Oh, shut up!" everyone yelled in unison.

"Hey, see you tomorrow, boss," Tina said as Dani headed out the door.

"See you in the morning."

Dani slipped on her jacket on and started her walk home. She stared up at the starlit Georgia sky. With the lack of city lights, the stars were very visible. It was a gorgeous night. Dani took a deep breath of fresh air. This was when she loved the seasons here. She still missed the snow on occasion—that was until she heard of ten inches of it falling in her hometown of Peabody, Indiana.

It didn't take her long to make it to her house. She unlocked the door. Frodo greeted her as if she'd been gone for weeks.

"Hey, boy, how was your night?"

Frodo jumped on her leg until Dani scratched his head and patted his side.

"Come on, time to go out." She pushed open the back screen door.

The home was perfect for Dani. It was a four-bedroom brick with an open front porch. Two bedrooms were on the main floor. Dani had turned one of the first-floor bedrooms into her den where she kept her bookcase and desk with a computer, while she kept the other as a spare bedroom. The master bedroom and another spare bedroom were upstairs. There was one full bath on the main floor and one on the second. Hardwood floors ran throughout the home. Large throw rugs added to the warm feel of the house.

Frodo barked loudly out back like he'd spotted a critter. Dani sighed. She'd better get him in. She didn't want to piss off the neighbors around her who tended to go to bed earlier than she did.

"Man, Frodo, did you get him?" Dani asked when Frodo flew into the house. He stood by his bowl and waited for his nighttime food. She dropped a half a cup into his dish. She really did keep an eye on his weight. Beagles were notorious for overeating. After he finished gobbling down his food, he lapped up his water, exaggerating as if he'd gone without water all day and was just now getting his first taste.

Dani climbed the stairs, and he followed on her heels. After changing into boxer shorts and a tank top, she went into the bathroom to brush her teeth. He was right behind her and sat in the doorway, watching her every move. This was his way of letting her know he was ready for bed, but she wanted to check out this C.J. James before she called it a night.

She bounced back downstairs with Frodo hot on her heels. She flipped on the computer and logged onto the Internet. On a whim, she typed in "cjjames.com" to see if it was that easy.

The screen turned black, and "C.J. James" was spelled out in turquoise blue script. Then the screen dissolved into a photo of the singer, and her music drifted out from the speakers. It was similar in sound to the first song Dani had heard James sing.

Dani sat back in her chair when she saw the photo. Wow. She could definitely see what everyone was talking about. C.J. James had short, light-blonde hair, cut so the strands feathered away from her face. With her hypnotic, light-blue eyes and a smile that dazzled, she was gorgeous. Her music had a folk-blues sound to it, sung with a husky, sultry voice.

Dani quickly decided she'd call the number listed on her website tomorrow and inquire about purchasing some of her CDs for the store in time for her arrival the next week. Dani happened to look down to see Frodo beside her. He cocked his head as he listened to James's voice.

"Yeah, pretty good, huh, boy?" She stroked his head for a while. The song playing now was about losing a lover to a best friend. It was the song Dani couldn't get out of her head for weeks after her breakup:

You kissed me, then said goodbye. I thought you were mine.
Now all I have left are your lies.
Yeah, all I have left are your lies.

C.J. then started the mournful guitar solo.

Dani waited until the songs began to repeat before logging off. She double-checked the locks, turned off the lights, and headed back upstairs. Frodo raced up the stairs before her, made it to the bedroom, and hopped effortlessly onto the bed.

Dani swore she'd never let him sleep in bed with her, but he'd learned since he was a puppy to stay at the foot of the bed. Her ex had helped train him to do this. He dutifully kept to his territory. Of course, when she and her ex made love, Frodo found himself on the other side of a closed door.

The only thing he insisted on was one good-night lick on the side of Dani's face, a few pets of his head, and then he'd wander to the end of the bed. He'd "fluff up" his area, scratch at the comforter with his front paws, do his three or four circles, and finally curl up in a ball, letting out a big sigh.

Dani stared up at the shadows that the tree branches cast on the ceiling. As she started to drift off to sleep, C.J. James's sultry voice floated into the deep recesses of her brain.

You kissed me, then said goodbye...

Chapter 3

The next day, Dani stood at the window, anxiously awaiting the UPS delivery. She hadn't told Tina about her special package arriving that day, mainly because she didn't want to be teased incessantly. When Dani spotted the UPS truck rounding the corner, she practically jumped the driver as he entered the store. She signed off on the delivery and barely refrained from kissing him on the cheek as he left.

She carried the box to the counter and caressed it like a lover. She was almost afraid to open it. She felt like a kid on Christmas day, anticipating a present she'd longed for, but perhaps finding disappointment once she tore off the wrapping.

But she knew what was inside. Something she'd saved all year to buy. She'd convinced Brenda, the seller, to accept her $1,000 down payment twelve months ago. Brenda would've been ruthless with anyone else, but she and Dani were mutual bookstore owners and good friends.

Dani grabbed a letter opener from the drawer under the counter and carefully slid it along the tape.

"Jesus, Dani. Are you ever going to open the damn thing?"

Dani started at Tina's voice. Tina leaned against the doorway that stood between the front of the store and the office.

"How did you know I even had anything to open?"

"I heard the driver enter the store and saw you almost tackle him to get to the package."

"Funny. You have no clue what this is." Dani put a protective arm around the box as if it were her kid brother.

"Whatever," Tina said over her shoulder as she walked back into the office.

Dani pulled the paper out of the box and removed the bubble wrap from its precious contents. When she laid her hands on the dust jacket of the book, tears sprang to her eyes. She gingerly pulled the dust jacket aside and brushed her fingers over the blue writing and scroll on the gray cloth cover: *Gone with the Wind.* The copyright page read: "Published May, 1936." She flipped to the back where the book ended on page 1037. These were all proof of the jewel she held in her hands, just as they were twelve months before. But the ultimate thrill was the first inside page, the fly page. She opened the book again. There, staring back at her, was the neat scrawl of Margaret Mitchell's autograph. The book was a first printing of the first edition of Mitchell's Pulitzer Prize-winning novel. It had cost Dani $7,500, which, as a collector, she recognized was a major bargain—especially considering its excellent condition.

Dani felt Tina behind her.

"Oh, wow. I see why you're treating this thing like it's the Gutenberg Bible." If anyone knew about Dani's infatuation with *Gone with the Wind,* it was Tina. She laid her head on Dani's shoulder. "I'm sorry for being so insensitive."

Dani playfully shoved her away. "Go back to the office and check those invoices."

"Seriously, I'm glad you did something for yourself. You don't do that enough." Tina returned to the office, took her seat behind the desk, and shuffled through some papers.

Dani carefully rewrapped her "new" book and carried it to the office until she left for home. The only place this treasure was going was behind glass in her special bookcase. She'd collected a few rare first editions over the years, but nothing would ever top this.

With that memorable task out of the way, Dani concentrated on greeting customers until lunchtime, a typically slow time as shoppers and tourists made their way to the various eateries in the area. Tina had already stepped out to buy them both sandwiches at the deli down the street.

While Tina grabbed them lunch, Dani decided to call the number from C.J. James's website. The phone kept ringing on the other end with no answer. Dani was about to give up when a husky voice came on the line.

"Hello?"

"Hello. I was calling to inquire on purchasing a bulk order of C.J. James's CDs."

"This is C.J."

"Oh, great. Hi, Ms. James, my name is Dani Roberts. I'm a bookstore owner in Francis, Georgia. I know you'll be coming here next week for the 'Women in Music' series at Carl's Cavern. I heard about your music and checked out your website. Your songs are very impressive." *Jesus. Will someone please find the Off switch to my mouth?*

"Yeah? Thanks. And it's C.J., by the way."

"Oh, okay," Dani said. For some reason, she blushed. "I'd like to order twenty copies of your newest release."

"Twenty? Then we're definitely on a first-name basis, Dani."

"I'd like to get the jump on everyone in the area and showcase your CD in my store. We have a stereo system set up in the shop, so the customers can hear it, too."

"Sounds good to me."

"I'll send you a check this afternoon. Is that okay?"

"Sure. I can get those out to you as soon as possible, probably by the middle of the week."

"Okay."

"I'd like to meet you when I get to town. Would you like that?"

Again, Dani felt her face get hot. "I can come over to Carl's Cavern when you get here. I'd like to hear your music in person anyway."

"It's a deal. Hey, thanks again for the order, Dani. Have a great day."

"Yeah, you, too, C.J."

As she hung up the phone, Tina walked through the front door of the store with the sandwiches.

"They didn't have any green peppers for your veggie sandwich. Sorry." Tina set the bags on the counter. "Hope you're not too disa—" She stopped in mid-sentence. "What the hell's wrong? Your face is all red."

Which made Dani blush even more. "Nothing. I made that call to C.J. James and—"

"And she has that kind of effect over the phone?" Tina asked with a sly grin. "Imagine what effect she'll have in person. Are we rethinking our 'I'm going to remain celibate for a year' thing now?"

"Shut the hell up and give me my sandwich. I never said I

planned to be celibate for a year. I simply said I wasn't ready to date."

"Touchy, touchy." Tina handed over the bag. "I have to say I'm immensely curious about this chick now." She hopped up on one of the stools and opened her bag.

"I liked the music from her website," Dani said. "I'm purchasing twenty copies of her latest CD for the store." She didn't say she'd heard C.J. James's voice for the first time the evening of her breakup with Katie. She just hadn't known at the time that C.J. would be playing at Carl's.

Tina munched on her ham sandwich. "Maybe I'll check out her website on the computer in the office when I'm done here."

Dani tried to understand why she'd gotten so flustered. She almost missed Tina had asked her a question.

"What do you like about the songs?" Tina asked.

"They have a great blues sound to them and a folk sound, too. She reminds me a little of Bonnie Raitt. I think they'll definitely sell here."

Tina stared at her and put her sandwich down. "That does it. The way you're acting has convinced me that I definitely need to meet this chick. If you plan to go to Carl's to hear her sing, like you said you were last night, I'm joining you."

There was that protective side of Tina that she loved so much. Dani took a bite of her sandwich. "Sure, Tina, you can join me. God forbid I do something for myself," she said between bites.

"You love me, and you know that I'm always looking out for you. That's not a bad thing."

"No, it isn't. You're a good friend."

The front door jingled, and Monica and Estelle strolled into the shop.

"Hi, guys," Monica said as she walked up to the counter. Estelle began wandering around the store. Dani glanced over at Tina who rolled her eyes—she really did need to show some restraint, Dani thought.

"How's it going, Monica?" Dani asked.

"We're good." Monica glanced beside her to find that Estelle was no longer there. The two had been dating now for three months, which was about ten weeks longer than Dani had given it. "Do you have that new book in stock that you raved about?"

"*Summer on the Cape*, right?" Dani asked. She put down her sandwich and came around the counter.

"I'm sorry. I didn't mean to take you away from your lunch."

"My sandwich can wait." Dani picked up the book from the display. "This is what you're looking for."

"Thanks."

"How's business at your shop?" Dani asked as she rang her up. Monica owned an antique store about three blocks down the street.

"It's picking up. You know how the tourists usually start coming into town right now. I've especially had good luck with some older lesbians who travel down from the north."

Dani agreed. They seemed more apt to spend money in her store, too. The younger women typically came in and browsed but usually left with maybe one book, if that.

"Estelle? Are you ready? I had the 'Out to Lunch' sign set for us to be back in fifteen minutes," Monica said.

"Why don't you head on back. I think I'll take a walk around town after leaving here." Estelle hadn't even bothered to pop her head around the bookshelves when she was speaking.

Monica sighed. "Thanks, Dani. I'll let you know what I think of the book." Monica waved it in the air on her way out the door. She glanced once more in Estelle's direction as she left the store.

Tina glared at the bookshelf Estelle was behind as if Estelle could see her. It was good she couldn't. Tina would have bored holes through her with that look. Not even two minutes after Monica walked out, Estelle left and headed in the opposite direction. She smirked at Dani and Tina through the window as she passed by.

"Man, I could just throttle that little weasel," Tina snapped. "Fucking bitch."

It was Dani's turn to sigh, but this time she didn't offer up any protest. "Let's hope Monica ends this soon. For her sake."

Tina stomped off to the office, red-faced. Dani knew better than to go after her. Soon, Dani heard C.J. James's voice coming from the computer speakers. Dani waited for Tina's critique. When she didn't come out right away, Dani figured she still needed to stew.

Since it was slow, Dani pulled out the latest *Advocate* magazine and caught up on the news around the country. The rest of the day went by quickly. Business picked up right before closing with four sizeable sales at five-thirty.

Tina was balancing the register when she said, "I have to agree. C.J. James has a hell of a voice. She's one nice-looking chick, too." She paused. "I'm still going with you and the others to Carl's."

Dani entered the office and shut down her computer. "Tina, you have nothing to worry about." She carried the deposit slip to the front counter. As she filled it out, she said, "Do you think you can take this to the bank tonight? Frodo has an appointment with the vet for his shots, and I need to get him there by six-thirty."

"Not a problem. I can even close shop before I leave."

"Thanks. Remind me to give you a raise!" Dani shouted as she headed out the back door.

"I do!" Tina shouted back. "Every freaking week!"

As Dani drove to her house, she thought back to her very public breakup with Katie. They'd been drifting apart for months. Katie hit the bars with their friends more often, not caring that Dani begged off. What Dani dubbed "The Twitter Incident," when Katie said she was moving back to Indiana, really shouldn't have been that much of a surprise. Still, breaking up on social media and keeping the apology to less than 140 characters was cold. She hadn't talked to Katie since and had no intention to contact her.

Dani pulled into the drive. First things first, she thought. She lifted the box out of the backseat and carried it into the house. As she placed the book in her bookcase and closed the glass door, she thought back to Tina's words. Yeah, to Dani this was her Gutenberg Bible.

She retraced her steps outside, picked up her mail, and went back into the house. As she walked toward the back door to get Frodo's leash, Dani checked her phone and noticed she had a voicemail. It was from Brenda in New York.

"Hey, Danster. I wanted to double-check that the package arrived there today. 'Package.' Lord, it sounds like I'm talking about drugs or something. If you could give me a call sometime tomorrow, I'd appreciate it. I got notification that it arrived there, but you know me. I worry about everything."

Dani hung up the phone and made a mental note to call Brenda when she got back from Frodo's trip to the vet. With leash in hand, she approached Frodo.

At sight of the leash, Frodo's tail thumped loudly against the door.

"No, Frodo, no w-a-l-k. It's off to the vet." Dani wasn't sure whether it was her tone or the word "vet" he had somehow learned for his vocabulary, but he immediately stopped wagging his tail, and it drooped behind him. "It's okay, bud. You like Dr. Patterson, right?"

She led him outside and lifted him into the MINI Cooper. He placed his paws on the dash while he watched her every move around the front of the car. He hopped over the gearshift to jump up on the driver's side door. She gently pushed him away as she got in. "Give me some room, boy." She situated him in the passenger seat.

He sat straight up in his seat, appearing every bit like a "fur person," as Dani backed out of the drive. The vet's office was a few miles outside of town. As he occasionally did on these trips, Frodo pushed his nose hard under Dani's arm and laid his head under her chin.

"Frodo, you won't have to stay there," Dani soothed. She'd boarded Frodo at the vet's kennel twice. Since then, Tina and Barb had volunteered to watch him. They adored him and didn't want to see him traumatized. Dani informed them the only way he was traumatized was by all the attention the staff gave him.

They pulled into the parking lot, and Frodo spun around in his seat as he watched Dani's progress around the car. She led him into the office.

"Frodo Roberts here to see Dr. Patterson," Dani told Mary, the desk attendant. She felt silly about giving Frodo her last name, but that was how they identified their clients. Mary leaned up and peered over the counter.

"Aww. Hi, Frodo. How have you been?" He wagged his tail in response. Mary carried his chart to the counter and asked, "Did you get my message that I left for you about Dr. Patterson not being in this evening?"

"No." She sometimes had trouble with the voicemail feature from the phone company. Apparently, this was one of those times when the message didn't take. She was disappointed. Dr. Patterson, a practicing veterinarian for over forty years, was Frodo's vet since he was a puppy. Dani was always fearful he was going to retire—he had mentioned it a few times.

"Dr. Springer is able to see him, though, to give him his check-up and shots. She's new to the practice, but you and Frodo will love her."

Dani vaguely remembered receiving a flyer in the mail from their office about their new hire. They'd held an open house to welcome her, but Dani had been unable to attend because of work.

"That's fine."

"If we can get a weight on Frodo first," Mary said as one of the other technicians approached the counter. Frodo adored Jake and pulled hard on his leash to get to him as Dani led Frodo to the scales.

"Hey, Frodo, buddy. How you doing? Been keeping that weight off?" Jake asked. Between the two of them, they were able to settle down Frodo long enough to get a weight.

"We've been watching it as much as possible." Dani held her breath, waiting for the electronic readout to stop on a number. She breathed out a sigh of relief when the red numbers stopped on "36." It was only a pound over his ideal weight.

"Great job, Frodo." Jake knelt down and rubbed his ears. Frodo jumped on Jake's leg. "Did you miss me, boy?" Frodo licked him on the face. Jake laughed. "I'll take that as a yes."

He gave the leash back to Dani. "You're in Exam Room 2." When Jake shut the door, he took out his pen and scribbled down Frodo's weight on the chart. "Good to see he's maintaining that weight. I know it's hard."

"You have no idea." Dani thought back to the numerous times she said no to Frodo's mournful gaze while she ate at the dining room table.

He clicked the pen and set it by the closed chart. "Dr. Springer will be in shortly." He reached down and gave Frodo one more pet before he left.

Alone now, Dani let go of Frodo's leash so he could roam the office to smell to his heart's content. He was busy tracking by the other door that led to the back when it opened. Dani saw Jake enter, but she couldn't see the doctor because the exam table blocked her as she leaned down to pet Frodo.

"How are you, little fella?" a soft, melodic voice inquired. "Investigating are we?" When she rose, Dani almost stopped breathing. She was of slender build, a little shorter than Dani, with shoulder-length, dark-brown hair and bright green eyes accentuated by long lashes. The overhead fluorescent light brought out the color in her eyes even more. The kindness Dani saw there was unmistakable.

"Hi." She extended her hand to Dani. "I'm Liz Springer."

Dani shook her hand. She seemed close to Dani's age. Perhaps she'd gone directly to veterinary school after earning her undergrad degree.

"Hi, Dr. Springer. I'm Dani Roberts, Frodo's mom."

"Please, call me Liz." She leaned down and greeted Frodo again. "Do you mind if Jake picks you up, so I can get a better look at you?"

Frodo wagged his tail and almost did a little dance in response. Jake swept his arms around Frodo's legs and easily lifted him up on the exam table. Liz ruffled his ears some more as she talked to Dani.

"I'm sorry Dr. Patterson was unable to see you tonight. There was an emergency with a pregnant Lab at one of the farms nearby. The family didn't have time to bring her in. It was supposed to be a hard labor, so he wanted to be there."

"I know these things come up. Besides that, it seems Frodo has taken a liking to you already." Which he had. He licked Liz's hands while she talked to Dani and pushed his head under them so she'd continue to pet him.

Liz laughed. "He has, hasn't he?" She opened his chart. Frodo turned his head and nosed the file. Liz rubbed his ears as she read the paperwork. "He's in for his annual with his shots?"

"Right." Dani couldn't stop staring as Liz concentrated on Frodo's file. Dani's "gaydar" had pinged the minute Liz had locked eyes with her. Or was it only wishful thinking?

Liz raised her head and caught Dani's stare. She smiled. Dani's heart skipped a beat, and her face warmed. *Is that smile for me or my dog?*

"It's good to see that Frodo keeps his weight down." Liz grabbed the scope and peered in Frodo's ears. "Has he had any problems with his ears?"

"No. I know most hounds do, but I've been lucky with him."

Liz probed his sides, which Frodo didn't seem to mind. He usually jumped a little when Dr. Patterson did this. Jake held Frodo as Liz put on latex gloves to examine his hind quarters. He didn't flinch, which surprised Dani. Normally, he hated this part of the exam.

Liz removed the gloves and tossed them into the large metal receptacle. "Good boy," she said as she patted his side. "I know that's not your favorite thing." She had her back to Dani and Frodo while she prepared the shots. She turned around, and as Jake continued to hold Frodo, she grabbed the nape of Frodo's neck in one smooth motion and quickly administered the shots. Frodo seemed blissfully unaware of what was going on.

Liz rubbed Frodo's ears. "That's it. You were such a good boy, too." She lifted a treat from a glass jar in the corner of the table, handed it to him, and kept rubbing his ears. Frodo stared up at her like he'd found a new best friend.

"I'd say you've definitely made an impression on him, Liz." It surprised Dani how easily the name rolled off her tongue. Normally, when a doctor asked her to call them by their first name, she stumbled over it like it was a foreign language.

"Think so?" Liz asked, glancing at Dani. A few seconds passed before Liz said, "Well... uh... I guess we're done here. Jake, you can put him back down from the table." As he did that, she reached for Frodo's chart and knocked it to the floor. Some of the paperwork spread out from the chart. Dani knelt to help her gather it up. They both grabbed the same paper, and their fingers touched. They slowly rose together as their eyes met once again.

Dani realized they were holding the same piece of paper. She quickly let go, and stammered, "S-sorry. I'll let you take that."

Liz's face reddened, as well. Okay, Dani thought, maybe this isn't just me.

"I've enjoyed meeting you and Frodo." Liz slid the papers back into his chart. She petted Frodo, rose to her feet, and offered her hand again to Dani.

Dani took it and squeezed. "The pleasure has been ours." She inwardly cringed. *The pleasure has been ours?* It sounded like something from a BBC show. The only thing missing was a British accent.

"Take care." Liz backed up to the other door leading out of the exam room. She kept eye contact as she groped behind her for the door handle. She gave up and with a nervous smile, turned, grabbed the handle, and hastily left the room with Jake following her.

Dani stood there for a few seconds, staring at the door. She glanced down at Frodo who also stared at the door where Liz had exited. Which was odd. He normally was at the other door that led into the office area, ready to head home immediately after his annual exam. He wagged his tail.

"Yeah, I know, Frodo. I thought so, too," Dani said quietly as she opened the door to leave. She walked up to the counter to pay. Liz brought Frodo's chart to Mary and gave Dani another smile before turning away. Dani paid the bill and led Frodo to her car. She glanced back at the vet's office and caught Liz watching her from the window. *She came back to the window to watch us leave.* Dani gave a little wave, which Liz returned.

As she drove, Dani couldn't get Liz's beautiful face out of her mind.

* * *

Liz walked back to her office to write down her notes on Frodo—at least that's what she told herself. Instead, she pictured Dani Roberts's soft, brown eyes. Her short, thick, dark hair was the kind she'd love to run her fingers through.

"Jesus, what's wrong with me?" she said soft enough that no one could hear. She wouldn't want the staff to think their new doctor had any emotional issues. After all, she'd tried to leave those behind in Ithaca, New York. She'd managed to leave her ex there, thank God. That was a year ago.

Liz was the only one in her family to graduate from college, let alone go on to further her education. Her two older sisters, Laurie and Lacey, were happy to marry shortly out of high school and raise families of their own. Liz received a scholarship to attend Cornell, one of the top veterinary schools in the country, right out of high school. With her grades, she set lofty goals. And she'd reached them. When she met and fell in love with a fellow student in veterinary school, she thought she'd achieved all of her dreams. That had all come to a crashing halt that fateful day when Liz came home early, after completing the last of her exams.

She'd walked in on Therese in bed with Liz's now ex-best friend, Rachel. Despite Therese's desperate pleas that it "meant nothing" and Rachel's frequent calls and texts to apologize, Liz had moved back home to some place safe since her family still lived in Francis.

After giving herself a couple of months to lick her wounds and clear her head, she took her state licensing exam. When she'd passed the exam, she'd applied at the one veterinary clinic where she'd volunteered in high school. Dr. Patterson hired her on the spot.

Dani Roberts was the first woman who'd turned Liz's head since she'd left Therese.

Just what I need, she thought as she gazed out her office window to the tall pine trees behind their clinic. Another dark-haired, handsome woman who might be nothing but trouble.

"Dr. Springer?"

Mary's voice startled her out of her thoughts.

"Sorry. Didn't mean to sneak up on you. Your next patient is here." Mary handed Liz the chart.

Right. Work. Work is good.

Chapter 4

"You like your new vet?" Tina carried two bowlfuls of popcorn to the living room and set one of them down on the coffee table in front of the couch. She handed Dani the other. Scooping up a handful of popcorn, she plopped down next to Barb on the couch.

"She's not my new vet. We happened to see her because Frodo's regular vet had an emergency." Dani had held off telling Tina until Saturday night about Dr. Liz Springer. She'd needed the remainder of the week to sort out her feelings. Barb and Tina invited Dani over to watch the latest *Star Wars* installment. She grabbed some popcorn and shoved it in her mouth.

"That's two women in one week that you've shown an interest in. I'm not sure how to take this," Tina said. Barb nudged her with her elbow and shook her head slightly.

"What? That thing with C.J. James? She just has a nice voice." *That, and she managed to invade my brain for weeks with that damn song of hers.*

"And she's good looking. *And* you got flustered talking about her," Tina reminded her.

"I haven't even met the woman."

"Maybe you shouldn't. We'll simply sell her music at the store and let it go at that. Seeing her on the website, I have to say she looks like a heartbreaker."

"I'm meeting her as a courtesy."

"I'm just saying—"

"Hon, do you ever know when to keep your mouth shut?" Barb asked.

"You know you love me, darling." Tina leaned over to kiss Barb on the cheek. "Anyway, let's get back to this vet. In all seriousness, your face lights up when you talk about her, Dani. That's only from one meeting. Is there a way to get to know her better? Can't Frodo develop a hangnail or something?"

Dani laughed. "I don't think dogs have hangnails. Nails maybe. Hangnails, no. T, you're too much."

"I know I joke a lot, and I give you a hard time. But I—" Tina turned to Barb. "We want to see you happy."

"I know you do, and I love you both for it." Dani cleared her throat. "As for the vet, maybe I'll be lucky and see her in town sometime."

"Maybe we can make it hap—"

Barb smacked Tina on the leg. Tina held up her hands in surrender. "Okay. I'll shut up."

Dani patted Tina on the knee. "You both have always looked out for me, and don't think I don't know that." She grabbed some more popcorn. "Now how about seeing some Jedi kick butt?"

* * *

The CDs arrived in the store on Wednesday of the following week. Dani priced them $2.00 more than C.J.'s price. The store wouldn't make a large profit, but that was okay as long as she was advancing music she believed in.

Dani discovered C.J.'s first opening night at Carl's Cavern was tomorrow. She gave everyone in the clan a call to see if they'd like to go. Barb was working behind the bar, so she'd be there. Tina said of course she'd come. Monica agreed to go as well. She said Estelle had something else going on that night. Shelly was the only other one who could make it.

The bar was already turning smoky by the time Dani arrived there with Tina and Monica. They spotted Shelly at a table close to the bar.

Dani sat down in the chair facing the bar. Music from the amplifiers drifted lazily into Dani's brain as she slowly downed her beer Barb had brought over. Through the mirror's reflection, she observed the women at the tables behind them.

The crew started hauling out the equipment for C.J. Dani leaned over to hear something Monica had said but had a hard time with the loud bar music. The sound of someone tuning a guitar caught Dani's attention. She turned around to see C.J. had stepped onto the stage. The women at the tables behind them glanced C.J.'s way, then chattered amongst themselves like school girls spotting the cute, new kid in class. Watching them, the line from "You're So Vain" ran through Dani's mind about the girls dreaming that they'd be the partner.

C.J. set her guitar aside and strode over to their table. Before Dani could even think to react, C.J. was standing beside her.

"C.J. James." She stuck out her hand for Dani to take. "You're Dani Roberts, the owner of Dani's Den of Books, right? We talked on the phone."

"Yes." Dani was at a loss as to how C.J. knew her.

"I asked around about you when I got into town. Joe, one of the crew, pointed you out to me just now." C.J. motioned at Barb. "I'll take a shot of Jack when you have time."

"You're very talented." Dani took a sip of her beer as she tried to recover from C.J. James's striking good looks. "I think your music will take off here."

Barb came to the table with the bottle and a shot glass. She poured the shot and handed it to C.J. who downed the whiskey in one big gulp and set the glass down on the table. Tina squinted at C.J., as if trying to read her. The fact Tina had her hat turned around backwards made her appear even more skeptical.

"Another?" Barb asked, holding the bottle of Jack Daniels over C.J.'s glass expectantly.

C.J. shook her head. She turned back to Dani. "I haven't made it to your store yet but plan to soon."

"We're open nine to six during the week, longer on Friday and Saturday. Depends on how I'm feeling if I'm open on Sunday."

C.J.'s light-blue eyes captured Dani's. "I'll come in this week sometime. Maybe we can do lunch."

"Sure. There are a lot of great restaurants here in town."

"Sounds perfect." C.J. glanced over at the women at the table behind Dani and gave them a nod. Dani watched their reactions in the mirror. *I bet each one of them thinks, "she's only looking at me."*

C.J. offered her hand again to Dani. "Good meeting you."

"Nice meeting you, too." This time C.J. held on a little longer and ran her index finger across Dani's palm before letting go.

Dani followed C.J.'s progress as she stepped back onto the stage and started tuning her guitar again. Her photo on her website didn't do her justice, if that was even possible.

Tina leaned over so only Dani could hear her. "She seems pretty slick, if you ask me."

Dani nodded absently, still unable to take her eyes off C.J. She took a couple of big gulps of her beer until the glass was empty.

"Whoa there, missy," Tina said. "You don't usually down those that fast."

"What?" Dani was a little surprised she'd finished her beer. "Oh, that. You drove, right? I think I'll have a couple more than I normally do tonight." She got up and headed to the bar.

"I'll take another, Barb."

Barb poured her a beer from the tap. She set it in front of Dani, but before Dani walked away, Barb grabbed her arm.

"Be careful, Dani," Barb said with some concern in her voice.

"It's okay. Tina drove over, and it's been awhile since I drank more than two of these at a time." Dani held up the glass.

"I'm not talking about the beer." Barb stared pointedly at the stage then back at Dani.

Dani bit back her irritation. "Thanks. I'll keep it in mind." She left for her seat.

C.J. finished tuning her guitars, leaned them against their stands, and went backstage. An hour later, the bar was packed wall-to-wall with women—some standing in the back. With help from Tina, Barb hurried to find some chairs in the storage room.

Finally, Carl Griffith, the owner, walked on stage. The women hooted and hollered. He stood in front of the microphone, his bald scalp glistening with sweat in the spotlight.

"Ladies!" he shouted. "How y'all doin'?"

The women screamed in response.

"I said, 'How y'all doin'?!'" he yelled even louder.

The place shook with noise.

"We have a special treat tonight at the Cavern and for the next three weeks. C.J. James from Cincinnati is here. She's got an amazing voice, and her expert guitar playing has been compared to Bonnie Raitt's. Let's give a big Francis, Georgia, welcome to C.J. James!"

Dani clapped loudly with everyone else—except for Tina. She

barely clapped and dropped her hands in front of her on the table.

C.J. walked out. Still dressed in the baggy blue jeans she had on earlier, she'd changed into a blue Atlanta Braves T-shirt that looked to be about two sizes too small. And she no longer wore a bra.

Dani's gaze drifted to C.J.'s full breasts. Her nipples pushed tight against the T-shirt material. Some of the women let out wolf whistles.

"Hey, everybody." C.J.'s voice was even huskier. "What are you guys looking at in the front tables here?" she asked with a sly grin, shading her eyes from the spotlight. "You like my T-shirt?"

The women screamed even louder.

"Even though I'm from Cincy, I wore this T-shirt just for you."

More whistles rose up from the crowd.

C.J. strummed her guitar a few times. "I'm not sure how many of you know my music."

Some in the audience applauded.

"Really? That many?" C.J. said, grinning. The place erupted in laughter. "I'll play mostly my new stuff tonight, but I have some oldies, too." She started expertly picking her twelve-string acoustic guitar. "This is the first song I ever wrote, and appropriately, it's about my first love."

It was a slow, sad song. One that had Dani feeling C.J.'s pain—that is until she realized C.J. was talking about her first guitar:

I knew it wouldn't last 'cause I couldn't caress your neck like
I used to.
And when your strings broke with my lightest touch,
I knew we were through.
Through... through... through.

C.J. flashed her dimples, and her eyes danced mischievously as she sang. Although the song was a play on words, C.J. still put a lot into it. The women clapped appreciatively when she was done.

"You like that?" She switched guitars and placed a glass pill bottle on her left middle finger. Definitely like Bonnie, Dani thought. "How about some blues?"

"Yeah!" one woman yelled out.

"Alrighty then." Sliding her finger expertly over the bridge of the guitar, she picked out a tune. Dani recognized it—a song from C.J.'s website she couldn't get out of her head. It was a big hit with the crowd.

C.J. slowed it down again and sang about meeting someone new:

I saw in your eyes what you wanted.
And what you wanted was me.
So come over here, let me love you.
Let me set your spirits free.
Yeah, let me set your spirits free.

C.J. held onto the last note.

Dani was lost in the song. Her head spun from the alcohol she downed a little too fast. It was also spinning from the voice of the woman on the stage. She felt like she was in a trance. C.J. seemed to look right at her. Or was it simply Dani's imagination? Wasn't she just laughing about other women doing that?

C.J. sang a few more songs before taking a break. The lights flicked on in the bar.

"She's good," Monica said. Her words were slurred. Dani hadn't noticed how much Monica had been drinking, but she was on to mixed drinks. Dani was glad that Monica rode to Carl's with Dani and Tina. Neither Dani nor Monica needed to be driving.

Shelly spoke up. "She definitely has a fantastic voice and stage presence."

Tina quietly sipped her beer, saying nothing.

Suddenly, Dani felt a hand on her shoulder. It lightly slid down her back, causing Dani to shiver. She looked up to see C.J. beside her.

"Hi again. Do you mind if I get a chair and join you between sets?"

"N-no. I don't mind."

C.J. grabbed a chair from a nearby table and flipped it around to straddle it. She motioned again at Barb for a drink. Barb brought over a shot glass, poured a drink for C.J., and left the bottle of Jack Daniels on the table.

C.J. addressed the other women. "Hey, everyone. Are you enjoying the music so far tonight?"

Shelly and Monica nodded and smiled.

C.J. downed her whiskey and poured herself another. The alcohol didn't seem to have much of an effect. She glanced at Tina and smiled, but Tina didn't smile back.

"Dani, why don't you introduce us?" C.J. said while still staring at Tina.

"These are my friends Monica White, Shelly Martin, and Tina Dewey."

"Nice to meet all of you," C.J. said.

"You, too," Monica and Shelly chimed in. With her arms crossed in front of her, Tina acknowledged C.J. with a nod.

C.J. leaned forward so only Dani could hear her. As she did, she slid her leg closer to press it against Dani's. "We talked about lunch. How about tomorrow?"

"I don't think I have anything going on." Dani's stomach did a couple of flip-flops, and her leg warmed next to C.J.'s.

"Where's your store?" C.J. asked.

"The corner of Main and Third. About six blocks from here."

Dani felt C.J.'s hand on her knee and had to keep from jumping. She hadn't even noticed that C.J. had dropped it below the table.

"Twelve-thirty okay with you, Dani?"

"Yeah."

"Perfect." C.J. stood, poured herself one more shot of whiskey, and downed it. She gave a mock salute to all the women at the table. "Hope you enjoy the rest of the show."

When she walked away, Dani felt relief. Her pounding heart slowed down to its normal rate. She glanced over at Tina who was giving her a look. Shelly and Monica got up to go to the bathroom.

After they did, Tina scooted her chair closer to Dani's. "You okay?"

"I think so."

"Do we need to go?" Tina asked, infusing the question with hope.

"I'd like to hear the rest of her show."

"I noticed you slowed down on your beer there." Tina nodded at Dani's full glass.

Dani hadn't realized it, but once C.J. started her show, all of Dani's attention was on the stage and nothing else. "I guess I did."

C.J. came back onto the stage, and the houselights dimmed

again. She played for another hour. A standing ovation greeted her when she finished. She waved her hand to the crowd before leaving the stage.

Shelly said her goodbyes. Tina, Dani, and Monica started for the parking lot. Tina and Dani steadied Monica between them as they walked to the car. They helped her into the backseat and slid into the front.

They drove awhile in silence before Monica spoke up. "You guys are the best," she said, slurring her words again. She sat up and leaned her elbows on each of their bucket seats. "You really are."

Dani smelled the alcohol on her breath "You're the best, too, Monica."

They pulled up to Monica's house first. Dani noticed that Estelle's car wasn't in the driveway. She shot a glance over at Tina whose jaw tightened. They both got out to help Monica to her front door. Tina took the keys from her swaying hand and pushed the key into the lock.

"Do you need us to get you to bed?" Tina asked as they helped Monica inside.

Monica shook her head hard. "Nope. I'm fine." As the words left her mouth, she stumbled over a stool and fell onto the floor. Dani and Tina rushed to her and lifted her to her feet. They led her back to her bedroom and helped her into bed. They removed her shoes and clothes except her underwear. Tina pulled the covers up. Monica's eyes filled with tears.

"You both really are the best," she repeated.

Right at that moment, seeing Monica's vulnerability, a surge of anger shot through Dani's body. She really wanted to hurt Estelle.

Tina leaned over and kissed Monica's forehead. Dani did the same.

"Remember we're here if you need to talk," Tina said in a gentle voice.

"I love you guys." Monica rolled over onto her side and quickly passed out. Dani scooted over the wastebasket and set it beside the bed in case she felt sick during the night.

They didn't talk as they walked out to the car and drove away. They were almost to Dani's house when Tina spoke. "I'm offering the same to you, Dani," she said softly.

Dani looked at her in confusion.

Tina pulled into Dani's drive. "I'm always here if you need to talk."

Dani hesitated before answering. "I know, T." She patted Tina's leg before she got out. She leaned back into the car. "I'll see you tomorrow."

"See you then."

Dani shut the door and headed into her house with images of the night racing through her mind. She still saw the sadness that seemed to pour from Monica's eyes. And then there were C.J.'s playful, light-blue eyes that caused Dani's heart to flutter.

Tina's voice echoed in her head as she let Frodo out back. Heartbreaker.

Chapter 5

"Oh. My. God. This singer at the Cavern was so hot last night," Liz overheard Mary tell another technician at the vet clinic. "Damn, Rita. The woman had sex oozing from her pores. I'm surprised she didn't melt down in a big ol' puddle of it right there on stage." Liz glanced up from her paperwork. Between a gap in the charts on the bookshelf to her left, she watched as Mary fanned her face. "I sure as hell was about to from where I sat in the front."

Rita, one of the youngest employees at the clinic, giggled. "Oh, Mary. You say that about any hot, new lesbian artist who plays there."

"This was different. I know you're straight, Rita, but trust me. This woman would've gotten to you, too."

Liz heard more murmuring and giggling. The desk where she sat working on her notes wasn't exactly concealed, but it was parked behind the towering stack of client charts. She couldn't believe she was straining to hear the rest of their conversation.

"And oh, my Lord, could she play that guitar. Just like Bonnie Raitt, I tell you. I'd love to have been the neck of that damn thing, the way she rode that pill bottle up and down it. Woo-wee!"

Rita barked out a full laugh at the comment.

Liz shook her head. Rita was diminutive. Liz marveled every time she heard that unique laugh bursting forth from her.

The employee on the phones for the morning hollered from her perch out front. "Hey, Mary. Can you check if Dr. Springer got that prescription ready for Clover York? Her mommy's on the line."

Mary rounded the corner and stopped short. "Dr. Springer. I didn't know you were back here." Her cheeks glowed with an adorable full blush.

Liz gestured to the notes she was working on. "Catching up on some paperwork until my first appointment. Clover's prescription is on the second shelf."

"Right. Okay." Mary quickly grabbed the prescription bottle.

"Be sure to tell Ms. York to have Clover take it with food."

"Will do." Mary hastened around the files. "I didn't know she was back here. Why didn't you tell me?" Mary whispered to Rita, probably not knowing Liz could still hear her.

"I thought you knew."

After that, their voices grew more hushed. Liz smirked, then her smile slid from her face. A part of her wanted to be included in the gossip, a part of her held back. In her limited time at the clinic, she'd been accepted and treated well. But she still felt a little apart from the other doctors and how they interacted with the staff. Maybe in time, she'd have that.

* * *

Dani woke up the next morning with a hangover. She slowly sat up on the side of the bed. Frodo, still curled up in his usual spot, quietly snored, oblivious to the world. Dani's mouth felt like an entire bag of cotton swabs had taken residence inside.

"I knew there was a reason I didn't drink like this," she mumbled as she rose. Her bare feet slapped heavily onto the hardwood floor on her way to the bathroom, jarring her already throbbing head.

She opened the medicine cabinet, pulled down the aspirin bottle, and dropped two onto her palm. She twisted the tap, threw the pills back into her throat, scooped the water into her hand, and shoveled it into her mouth. She swallowed hard and had that inevitable and involuntary shudder run through her when the bitter taste of the aspirin hit her palate.

Dani started the shower. While the water warmed, she went to the bedroom to rouse her beagle.

"Frodo, wake up. Time to face the world."

In response, he barely raised his head to blink at her. He stretched out his legs and yawned. Then he promptly plopped his head back on his front paws.

"Come on, dude." She tugged on the covers to make him move. "Mommy has to get ready for work."

He stood up, stretched once more, and hopped down to the floor. She followed him downstairs and let him out. Dani flipped on the Keurig machine in the kitchen and headed back upstairs. She undressed and stepped into the hot shower. As she shampooed her hair, she suddenly remembered she was meeting C.J. James for lunch.

What the hell do I wear? "Wait," she said out loud. "What does it matter what I wear?" But she knew the answer. She was attracted to C.J. James. Dani rinsed her hair. She closed her eyes while she stood under the water and let it cascade over her face. Warning bells went off in her head when she met C.J. She exuded danger—like a late-night walk alone in a rough part of town.

Dani quickly finished up. She pulled out a pair of khakis and a navy-blue cotton shirt from her closet. There, she convinced herself. That's not dressing up too much.

She checked the weather on TV to make sure no storms were forecast for the day. The weathercaster promised it would be clear and in the upper sixties, so she left Frodo outside. As she drove to the shop, she replayed the previous night in her mind. When C.J. placed her hand on Dani's knee, Dani had felt lightheaded.

She was so lost in thought that she didn't realize she'd made it to Main Street. She turned onto Main then into the alley that ran alongside the store. She saw Tina's Malibu already in the lot. *Damn, am I that late?* Dani glanced at the clock on her dash, relieved to see she was only ten minutes later than her normal time.

She entered the store through the back door.

"Hey, Tina!" she shouted.

"Glad to see you could make it."

Tina, dressed in her typical "Dani's Den of Books" T-shirt and faded blue jeans, was cleaning the windows with a squeegee. And of course her Braves hat perched on her head. Did she ever *not* have the thing on? Wait, Dani thought, she didn't wear it at her commitment ceremony with Barb, but only because Barb had a conniption fit when Tina pushed to wear it.

"Very funny, T. I'm not that late."

"How do you fe—" She stopped and gave Dani a once-over. "Damn, woman, where the hell are you going today?"

"I'm not dressed up."

"Riiight. You always wear khakis and that L.L. Bean shirt to work. Hell, the only time I've seen you wear that is when you went out on your first date with Katie." Tina's expression changed. "Wait. Are you going out with *her* today?"

Her. Tina had already reduced C.J. James to a "her."

"C.J. and I are going to lunch, but that's all it is. Lunch." Dani was trying to convince herself at the same time.

Tina didn't say anything. She turned back to what she was doing. Dani decided to drop it. She understood Tina's concerns. Hell, she had the same misgivings. Even so, she wanted to see C.J. again one-on-one without a roomful of women with admiring eyes.

Dani walked to the back and slid C.J.'s CD into the CD player. Her voice filled the store. Definitely easy on the ears, too.

Tina had finished cleaning the windows and stepped around the counter to grab the keys to open the front door. "Don't suppose we can listen to something else this morning, can we?"

Dani raised her head from the inventory list she was poring over. "What is it that you don't like about her?" She wasn't angry about Tina's reaction anymore. She really wanted to know.

Tina stared down at her shoes. "It's that... Oh hell."

Dani got up from her stool and stood in front of Tina. She held Tina's hand. "I hope you know you can tell me anything."

Tina looked up. The concern written on her face touched Dani. The fact she didn't automatically go into a tirade about C.J., but was carefully weighing her words, meant something to Dani.

Tina took a deep breath. "I don't know what to say, other than I have a bad feeling about her. Yeah, she's gorgeous. Yeah, she has a great voice. But there's something about her that's off."

Dani nodded. She couldn't deny what Tina was saying.

"You're my best friend, Dani. I don't want to see you hurt."

Dani pulled Tina into a hug. "That's why I love you. But I'm a big girl. I think I can handle Ms. James." Dani wondered if she sounded as unsure as she felt.

Tina gave Dani a squeeze and ended the embrace. "Just be careful, okay?" she said softly.

"I will."

Dani busied herself with the inventory. She patrolled the store and noted any books she needed to order. She didn't know what time it was when she heard the bell jingle at the front door. Bent over and checking books on the bottom shelf, she felt someone beside her. Dani glanced up and saw C.J. Was it already lunchtime? She rose to her feet.

C.J., wearing a pair of faded old jeans and a long-sleeved denim shirt with tears in the elbows, gave Dani a crooked grin. Dani felt foolish in her khakis and L.L. Bean shirt. What the hell had she been thinking this morning?

C.J.'s crystal-blue gaze raked over Dani's body from head to toe. "Damn. You look great."

"Th-thank you," Dani stammered. She held the inventory list in front of her like C.J. had X-ray vision, and somehow this ten-page inventory list would protect Dani from scrutiny.

"Want to get out of here?" C.J. asked.

"Let me tell Tina I'm leaving." Dani turned to walk the other way so she wouldn't have to brush past C.J.

Dani dropped the inventory list onto the counter. Tina was at the computer.

"C.J.'s here. I'll be back in a few."

Tina nodded.

C.J. waited for Dani at the front door. She motioned with her chin to the speakers positioned throughout the store. "You're playing my music."

"I thought it'd help sell the CDs," Dani said as they went outside. "Although I think once it gets out how great you sounded last night, it won't be hard at all to sell them."

"Thanks." C.J. ducked her head. *She actually seems humble about how good she is,* Dani thought. *Let's chalk that up as a good sign.*

"Where are we chowing down at?" C.J. asked.

"There's a pub about four blocks down on Main. They serve great burgers and deli sandwiches. Is that okay with you?"

"Can't go wrong eating at a pub."

They kept quiet the rest of the way to the restaurant. When they walked through the door, the booming voice of the owner, Freddie, greeted them.

"Ms. Dani Roberts, it's about time your ass came back in here to visit!" he shouted from the back of the room. He made his way to the front. Freddie was a large man with dark wavy hair and a bushy mustache.

"Freddie, this is C.J. James. She's the first artist for the 'Women in Music' series."

Freddie offered his meaty hand. C.J. reached out and shook it.

"It's a pleasure. If you're a friend of Dani's, you're a friend of mine." He motioned to the room packed full of diners. "I have a booth in the back. Is that okay with you?"

"That's great," Dani said. They walked to the booth and sat down across from each other. Freddie dropped off water and menus at their table.

"So what's good, Dani?" C.J. studied the menu. Dani peered at her over hers. C.J. caught Dani's stare. They sat like that until Freddie returned.

"Have we decided?" he asked. Neither of them spoke. He glanced back and forth at them, then caught Dani's eye. "Okay. I take that as a no." He gave Dani a knowing smile before walking away.

Dani found her voice. "The hamburgers are excellent, like I said."

"I trust you implicitly on your choices." C.J. gave her a wink and one of her cocky grins.

Dani's stomach fluttered, and her heartbeat throbbed in her throat. She broke the stare. She caught Freddie's attention across the room, and he hustled over.

"Y'all ready now?"

C.J. handed him her menu. "Sounds like your burger and fries are what I want. Medium well on the burger."

"I'll have the same, Freddie, but—"

Freddie interrupted. "Well done, right?"

"Thanks."

He scribbled her order and took her menu.

Neither of them spoke for a few seconds. Dani got the courage to say something.

"C.J., I have to tell you. I first heard your music last year. Unfortunately, it was right after a breakup. You really hit me with 'Your Lies.' It's like you tapped into everything I was feeling. It shook me up, to be honest."

C.J. took her hand. Dani jumped at the touch. Whatever this was, it sure as hell wasn't going away.

"You're not going to tell me I've already scared you off are you? Or that my music has?" She lightly stroked Dani's hand with her fingers.

Dani found her voice to answer. "I'd like to get to know you better."

C.J. smiled and sat back in her seat. She squeezed Dani's hand and let go. "Why don't we start tonight? My show should be ending about ten. Would you like to come see me perform again?"

Dani wasn't sure she was up for another night of listening to C.J.'s intoxicating voice. She wanted to at least be thinking clearly.

"If it's okay, I'll catch up with you after your set tomorrow night. I'll wait for you at the bar."

"Sure. Although I'd love to have you sitting there in the first row of tables so I could look at you all night."

Jesus, Dani thought. Is she really this smooth? "You're too flattering."

"It's the truth."

Freddie brought burgers and fries. Dani kept her head down and concentrated on her food.

C.J. broke the silence. "What's with your friend Tina?"

Dani almost choked on a fry. Is Tina that obvious?

"What do you mean?"

"She doesn't seem to care for me much."

"It's not that at all. She's my best friend and is a little protective of me. She knows it's been a year since I've been with—" Dani stopped when she realized what she was about to say.

C.J.'s eyebrows shot up, and her eyes danced with that same mischievous light Dani saw when she sang. "Since you've been with a woman?"

Dani took a deep breath to try to settle her emotions. "The relationship I was in before, the one I told you ended a year ago. I decided to stay away from dating for a while."

"And I'm your first?" Again, C.J.'s tone was playful, and she had an incredibly sexy smile cross her lips.

Dani swallowed hard. "You're my first date. Correct."

C.J.'s grin grew wider. "I feel honored."

Dani flagged down Freddie for the check. She needed to get back to the store and clear her head. C.J. snatched the check from her. Dani started to protest.

"I want to do this if this is our first date." C.J. laid a twenty on the table. "I'm definitely treating."

Dani stepped out of the booth. C.J. stood up in front of her.

"I need to get back," Dani said.

"I'll see you tonight then?"

"I'll be there."

"Good." They headed out the door and made it to the street. "I need to get back to Carl's to rehearse. I enjoyed our lunch."

"Me, too."

C.J. started walking toward the bar but turned to wave and flash a smile.

Dani gave a weak smile in return. "What are you getting yourself into, Roberts?" she said under her breath.

* * *

Liz entered her small bungalow and dropped her purse on the table beside the front door. She heard her dog's scratches at the back door. It'd been cool enough to leave her out in the backyard today. Soon, the heat would get almost unbearable. Scratches quickly morphed into a full-out banging on the screen door.

"I'm coming, Melanie. I'm coming."

Liz opened the screen door, and her blonde cocker spaniel hustled into the kitchen. Melanie's tail was a blur as she circled excitedly at Liz's feet. With her tongue lolling out to the side, she looked up at Liz with such adoration, Liz's eyes welled with tears.

"Oh, Mel." Liz scooped her up into her arms and rubbed her nose against Melanie's. "What would I do without you?"

Melanie gave her a little lick.

Liz set her back down on the floor, made sure she had a full bowl of water, and dropped some kibble in the other bowl. "Mommy's pretty tired tonight, sweetie. I'll take a quick shower, and then I'll join you in eating dinner." Melanie was already tearing through her food as if she hadn't eaten in weeks. "I know I left enough food out there for you today. Quit acting like you're starved."

Liz left the kitchen and walked down the hall to her bedroom. She stripped down and ran the shower until the water was nice and warm. After her shower, she dressed in her cotton-shorts-and-tank-top PJ combo. She reentered the kitchen, opened the freezer door, and stared inside. She pushed around some of the frozen dinners and settled on a Lean Cuisine lasagna. As it thawed in the microwave, she grabbed the open bottle of red wine from her refrigerator and poured a healthy glass. She raised the glass to Melanie who sat in the kitchen, staring up at her with her big brown eyes. "Cheers, little girl."

The microwave dinged. Liz grabbed a fork out of the drawer and poked around at the lasagna to check if it was done. A couple more minutes should do it. Once the lasagna finished baking, Liz sat down at the small dining room table and dug in.

As she sipped her wine, she thought back to Mary and Rita's conversation from earlier in the day. A part of her wanted to check out this singer; the other part of her, the practical side of her who was still hurting from her breakup, shut down that idea. From Mary's description of the singer, she sounded a lot like her ex. Therese had also oozed sex appeal. Liz had fallen for Therese's magnetism without any thought. There had been danger signs. Liz had plowed through them like an out-of-control car plows through pylons at a closed-off construction site.

She stared down at the wine and swirled the liquid around in her glass. "Come on, Liz. Not every woman is Therese." Tell that to my heart, she thought, as she took a big sip.

Suddenly, her client Dani Roberts's face popped into mind. Dani was so gentle with her dog. Liz could often tell what kind of person someone was just by how they treated their pet.

"Frodo." Liz smiled. It was such a cute name for a beagle. "Must be a *Lord of the Rings* fan."

Seeing the two of them together had stirred something in Liz. Something she tried to shake and play off as nothing. But she kept returning to how she and Dani had locked gazes. She'd felt her heart beating double-time in her chest. She shook her head.

"Don't need to even think about it."

Melanie, after her feeding, sat beside her at the table and nudged Liz's leg with her nose.

"You agree, right, Mel? We're happy here on our own."

But she couldn't deny that a part of her secretly hoped that she'd see Dani again... soon.

Chapter 6

Frodo sat on the floor beside Dani while she put on her third shirt for the night. He cocked his head when Dani threw it on the floor on top of the other two and dug into the closet again. She returned to the full-length mirror with a red denim shirt. She held it in front of her before putting it on. Smoothing down the tails, she glanced at her reflection. This one seemed to flatter her the most. Someone had once told her that red looked good on her. Who was that, she wondered vaguely. It was... oh, hell. It was her ex. Dani sighed, unbuttoned the shirt, and threw it on the pile. She rifled through the hangers and stopped when she got to a worn denim shirt. *This is it. I'm going to be comfortable.*

As she stood there eyeing her baggy blue jeans with scraggly hems, she ran her fingers through her still-damp hair. She had just stepped out of the shower and realized she had a little time to worry about her clothing for the night. She glanced at the clock. Now that time was up. It was nine-thirty.

"What do you think, Frodo? Does Mommy look like a hot lesbian, or do I look like someone who's trying too hard?"

Frodo wagged his tail and jumped up on her leg, gazing at her with his expressive brown eyes. She reached down and rubbed his head.

"What would I do without you, bud?" she asked. He licked her hand in response. "I know. I love you, too."

* * *

Dani opened the door to Carl's Cavern. A crowd of women still packed the bar. C.J.'s set had ended for the evening, so the houselights were up. Dani spotted Tina at the bar having a conversation with Barb. Tina waved Dani over.

"Hey, boss. How's it going?"

Dani settled onto a stool beside her. "Good. I'll take a Bud when you have time, Barb."

Barb poured the beer from the tap. She put down a napkin and set the glass in front of Dani. "What's this I hear about you going out with Ms. Sexpot?"

Dani was taking a sip of beer and almost spit it out. "C.J.?" She wiped her mouth with the back of her hand.

"Who else?"

"We're supposed to meet up here. I'm not sure where we're going."

Barb smirked. "I don't think C.J. has that problem."

"What problem?"

"A sense of direction. She knows exactly where she's going."

Dani turned to Tina. "Did you two rehearse this routine?"

"Hey, Barb's got a mind of her own."

Dani was about to say something witty when, out of the corner of her eye, she caught C.J. walking over. C.J. had on a blue T-shirt that matched her eyes. She wore a bra this time, but Dani couldn't help but notice that the T-shirt still accentuated her breasts. Her black jeans hugged her hips just right. She moved close enough to Dani so that her left breast brushed against Dani's arm. There was that jolt of electricity again. Dani only hoped that she hadn't outwardly flinched.

"Ready?" C.J. asked.

"Yeah." Dani set a five on the bar.

Barb handed it back to her. "You know where you can put that."

"Keep it for your tip then." She slid the five across the bar. "I'll see you Monday, Tina."

C.J. and Dani walked out into the cool spring air. "I'm not sure what you had in mind," Dani said. "Did you know where—" Dani didn't get to finish her question. C.J. gripped her arm and yanked her into the alley between Carl's bar and the building next door. She pushed Dani against the brick wall and pressed their bodies together, while placing her hands flat on the bricks beside Dani's face.

"What I have in mind," C.J. whispered in Dani's ear, "is to do this." C.J. slid the tip of her tongue across Dani's lips until Dani felt her mouth open almost involuntarily, inviting C.J. in. C.J. captured

Dani's tongue with her own, and her mouth opened wide. She felt a sensation between her thighs that she hadn't felt in quite some time. She was on fire.

C.J. dropped her lips to Dani's neck and then back up to her ear. "I have an apartment that I'm renting from Carl for the next three weeks. It's not even a block from here. Come with me."

Dani knew the apartment well. All the women who performed at Carl's Cavern for any lengthy period stayed there. Many a night, after a show, while walking out to the parking lot, Dani would spot the performer pulling another woman along with her as they headed to the upstairs apartment. Their giggles would drift down to the parking lot until the door shut. A cold fear shot through her. *Was she one of those women? Was she simply a conquest for C.J.?* C.J.'s mouth pressed hard on her neck. Dani's mind was getting foggier with each flick of her tongue.

"I don't kn—"

"Don't say no," C.J. said hoarsely. Her voice penetrated Dani's last wall of resistance. "God, please don't say no."

C.J. pulled back and Dani could see the raw want in her eyes. The streetlight cast her face in shadow, but there was enough light to see that C.J.'s eyes were now a dark, smoky blue. Dani couldn't find her voice to speak. She nodded. C.J. took her hand and walked her down the alley to the two-story apartment building behind Carl's. Dani allowed C.J. to lead her up the stairs. One thought flickered through Dani's mind when they got to the top—at least I'm not a giggling mess.

C.J. unlocked the door and tugged Dani inside. As soon as she shut the door, C.J. spun Dani around and slammed her into the door. She gripped Dani's hair as she dropped her mouth to Dani's and pressed her tongue inside. Dani became so lost that she didn't even feel C.J. unbutton her shirt until C.J.'s hand captured Dani's breast. Her nipple hardened with each stroke of C.J.'s thumb. A moan involuntarily vibrated in her throat.

C.J. undid the rest of the buttons and pulled the shirt off Dani's shoulders. She reached behind Dani and unsnapped her bra. Pulling it aside, she leaned over to capture Dani's nipple with her lips. Dani's knees began to buckle when C.J.'s tongue flicked back and forth against the very tip. C.J. must have sensed Dani was about to collapse onto the floor. She held onto Dani tighter and stood up again. She grabbed Dani's hand and pressed it to her own breast.

"Do you feel what you're doing to me?"

C.J.'s nipple hardened against Dani's palm. Dani yanked off C.J.'s T-shirt and unsnapped the front clasp of her bra. Dani had to catch her breath when she saw C.J.'s breasts in the streetlight streaming through the blinds.

"Oh, God, C.J." Dani leaned forward and captured one nipple in her mouth while she enveloped C.J.'s other breast with her hand. It was so full, it barely fit in her palm. C.J. gripped Dani's hair as Dani continued to flick her tongue back and forth across her nipple. C.J. let out a low moan. She pulled Dani away from her and pushed her back onto the couch. She unzipped Dani's jeans and slipped her hand inside. Dani wiggled until C.J. had room to press into Dani's crotch. C.J. moved Dani's panties aside and plunged her fingers into Dani's wetness. Dani gasped.

C.J. dropped her mouth to Dani's breast as she moved her fingers into Dani's wet folds. C.J. ran her tongue around one nipple, giving it lavish attention. She trailed her tongue over to the other breast. All the while, her hand moved in rhythm with the flick of her tongue. She licked her way up Dani's chest to her neck until her mouth reached Dani's ear.

"What do you want, Dani?" she whispered. "Tell me."

Dani's breathing was ragged now. She was incapable of speaking.

"Is it this?" C.J. asked as she pushed hard inside of Dani. "Is this what you want?"

Dani cried out as the pleasure began to mount. C.J. thrust her fingers deeper inside as she kissed her way down to Dani's breast and recaptured her nipple. She sucked greedily. C.J.'s hand moved faster and faster, and Dani's hips bucked wildly. *Oh, my God. This has never happened to me before.* Dani's whole world was that one spot on her body. She cried out again as she climaxed.

C.J. slowly kissed her way up to Dani's mouth. Dani was breathing so hard she felt like she was going to hyperventilate. The veins in her neck throbbed with each heartbeat, but the throbbing between her legs outpaced it.

Before she knew what was happening, C.J. yanked down her

jeans, then her panties. This time, she was gentle and slow. She kissed Dani softly on her neck and began a slow descent. She sucked on Dani's left nipple then the right. She licked down Dani's stomach, causing Dani to quiver uncontrollably. C.J. kissed the inside of Dani's thigh down to her knee and her ankle and back up to her thigh. C.J. looked up to her and smiled before she brought her mouth to Dani's other thigh. Please don't make me beg, she thought. Please. She opened her legs to C.J. willingly.

Dani closed her eyes as she held her breath in anticipation. She wasn't disappointed. C.J. planted a light kiss onto Dani's mound, pushed Dani's legs apart even farther, and spread Dani's lips with her fingers. Dani felt C.J.'s tongue where she most desired. She pushed herself up to C.J.'s mouth and felt C.J. smile before she plunged her tongue even farther into the wetness. C.J. placed her hands under Dani's ass and pulled her closer. Once again, Dani moved her hips in a steady motion. C.J. quickly joined her in perfect rhythm. Dani felt her second orgasm building as she gripped C.J.'s hair. C.J. prolonged it as long as possible until she pushed her tongue into Dani's opening then moved up to suck Dani's clit fully between her lips. White-hot explosions went off behind Dani's tightly shut eyelids as her whole body gave into her release. C.J. kissed the inside of Dani's thighs again. She moved beside Dani on the couch, draped an arm around her, and pulled her close.

Dani leaned her head against C.J.'s shoulder. She took in a deep breath and let it out as a shiver ran through her body.

"Cold?" C.J. asked.

"A little," Dani whispered.

C.J. leaned down and tugged a blanket at the foot of the couch over them. She pulled Dani tighter.

"That's nice. Soft like you," Dani murmured as she felt the blanket against her body. C.J. kissed the top of Dani's head, and Dani sank into a gentle slumber, feeling C.J.'s breath brush against her cheek.

Dani woke up with a smile on her face. She reached beside her, expecting C.J. to be there but only feeling the cushion of the couch beneath her fingers. She sat up and peered in the darkness. Eventually, her eyes adjusted to the little light in the room. C.J. sat in a chair in the shadows, now clothed again in her shirt.

"Are you okay, C.J.?"

"I'm fine." C.J.'s voice was quiet in the darkened room.

"How long have I been sleeping?" Dani wanted to add, "And why aren't you here with me?" but she thought better of it.

"A little over an hour."

Dani wanted to see C.J.'s face. She wanted to understand this mood. She suddenly felt naked—and not just because she was without clothes. She felt raw, like she was revealing too much.

Dani couldn't hold back. "Why don't you come over here?"

"I'm good, Dani."

Dani sat up and covered her body with the blanket that had slipped down while she slept.

"What? Now you're shy?" C.J. asked. Dani thought she could detect a sly grin even in the shadows of the room.

"No, it's just that—"

C.J. laughed. "I'm teasing you."

Dani wanted to shout, "This isn't the time!" What Dani needed was some warmth, some affection. Something that she shouldn't have to ask for. Instead of speaking, she stood up and walked over to grab her clothes. She was self-conscious as she began to dress.

"I'd better get home," she said.

"You don't have to go." But there was no passion in C.J.'s voice. It sounded like something she'd said to other women before, never meaning the words, only trying to appease the feelings of her lover.

"No, I need to go. My dog has been alone long enough."

"I'll see you again soon, right?"

"Right," Dani said a little too quickly. She turned to leave.

"I enjoyed this." C.J. stood by the chair now.

Dani only nodded. She opened up the door and almost sprinted down the stairs. She didn't turn back to see if C.J. was watching her from the window. She made it out to the parking lot behind the bar.

"What the hell did I just do?" she whispered in the hushed sanctuary of her car.

Chapter 7

Dani tossed and turned in bed, so much so that the impossible-to-wake Frodo popped his head up to see what the problem was. Dani glanced at the glowing red numbers of her alarm clock: 3:00 a.m.

"Shit," she muttered.

Her mind kept spinning back to being in C.J.'s arms just hours before. She had felt so alive when C.J. made love to her. It almost frightened her. But then the coldness afterward—it was as if Dani wasn't even in the same room with her. It was like finding yourself outside in a heavy blizzard seconds after basking in the heat from a cabin fireplace.

Dani sat up on the side of her bed. With as fast as her mind was racing, she knew sleep was hopeless. She put on her robe and stomped heavily downstairs. Frodo hit the floor behind her. He quickly caught up and joined her on the steps. He walked with her to the back door, and she let him out.

Dani opened the refrigerator door and ducked her head inside. The only thing that sounded halfway decent at this hour was a glass of milk. Frodo was already banging at the back door. He sprinted into the house straight to his bowl.

"Little guy, it's not morning yet." His ears fell, and his eyes became even sadder than they normally were. "Okay. Okay." How could she resist that? She set down her glass of milk, scooped out a cup of his dog food, and dropped it into his bowl. "Just don't tell Dr. Springer."

As the words left her lips, a vision of the doctor in her white lab coat planted itself in Dani's brain. A tingle ran down her body. "What the hell?" She shook her head. Nothing like going from one woman to the next in her mind. While Frodo munched happily on his kibbles,

Dani picked up her milk and carried it to the den. She pulled a book from the others tightly stacked together on the bookshelves. She had picked out the fattest non-fiction Civil War book she could find in the hope that it would help her drift off to sleep, even if it was in her favorite overstuffed chair.

Dani opened the book to the first page and began reading. She only made it to the fourth paragraph before she started thinking about C.J. again. Dani sighed. Not even the Civil War could erase the memories of what had happened.

She shut the book, leaned her head back, and closed her eyes once again. Frodo licked her hand that rested on the arm of the chair. She didn't open her eyes but petted his head. With each stroke of her hand, she felt her eyelids getting heavier and heavier. Eventually, she drifted off to sleep.

She awoke with a stiff neck. Standing and stretching, she tried to work out the kinks. She looked down to see Frodo was doing the same thing. Dani smiled. At least Frodo was a constant in her life, no matter what else was happening.

"I'll let you out again and take a shower. Then, why don't we go for a walk?"

Frodo's ears perked up, and he ran over to where his leash hung on the wall by the back door.

"Not yet, buddy. Shower first, then walk."

Dani let him out and trotted up the stairs. As she showered, she allowed herself to think about C.J. again. Had Dani made a terrible mistake in judgment? She wasn't the type to jump into bed on a first date. Hell, it wasn't even a date, she thought. It was more like a let's-make-out-in-the-alley-before-taking-it-to-my-place-where-I-can-fuck-you kind of thing. Did this woman have some kind of spell over her?

Dani stepped out and dried off. She pulled on some old sweats and her "best" worn sneakers. She hustled back downstairs to get Frodo. He about tore her arm off as they headed to the front door. No matter how many episodes of *The Dog Whisperer* Dani watched, she could never get Frodo to let her through the door first to show who was the alpha dog. She would shut the door and pull him back, but as soon as she opened it again, he'd jump ahead of her. After about the tenth try, with him looking up at her with an expression of "what the hell are you doing?" she gave up. He was, however, much better behaved after they made it outdoors.

They began their stroll down the tree-lined street. The morning air was brisk, so Dani had put on her jacket. At seven a.m., only a few people were up and out that early on a Sunday. A few typical fitness-nut joggers in their spandex pants ran by and an occasional neighbor was out walking their dog.

Dani wasn't paying much attention when Frodo yanked her ahead.

"Hey! Hey!" Dani yelled as she tried to reel him back in. What the hell had gotten into him? A woman walked toward them with a blonde cocker spaniel. Frodo was doing his best to dislocate Dani's shoulder and make it over to them. As the woman got closer, Dani recognized her—it was Dr. Liz Springer. Dani stumbled along behind her determined beagle. She instantly was self-conscious about her appearance.

Dani didn't think it could be possible, but Liz looked even better out of her white lab coat from the office. She was dressed in a dark-green turtleneck, jeans, and a black leather jacket.

"Dani, right?" Liz said as she stopped on the sidewalk. Dani nodded.

Frodo managed to pull Dani close enough so he could do his tail-to-nose inspection of Liz's dog. Then he jumped on Liz's leg to get her attention.

"Frodo! Down!" Dani said in her best "I'm in charge" voice. Of course, Frodo totally ignored her—especially when Liz laughed, leaned over, and rubbed his ears. He looked back at Dani as if to say, "See. She loves me."

"He really does like you."

Liz kept smiling as she petted him. She rose up, and when Dani looked into her eyes, she felt like she was standing on a hillside overlooking an emerald field of green in Ireland. Without even thinking how sentimental that sounded in her muddled mind, Dani tried to remember where she'd seen those beautiful eyes before. She couldn't place it the first time she'd met her. Suddenly, it hit her. Scarlett O'Hara. Well, more to the point, Vivien Leigh who brought the character to life. How could Dani miss that?

"I see he's none the worse for wear from his trip to our office," Liz said. Dani hadn't noticed her dimples at their first meeting.

"He survived." Dani returned the smile. She reached over to let Liz's dog sniff the back of her hand. "She doesn't mind being petted by strangers?"

"What do you think?" The cocker spaniel's tail was a blur. "Besides that," Liz added in a soft voice, "I don't consider you a stranger."

Dani's heart fluttered. She didn't feel the nervousness or even the trepidation she had when she was around C.J. "Thanks. I feel the same way." She glanced down at the cocker spaniel again to keep from getting lost in Liz's eyes. "What's her name?"

"Melanie. I know that's a silly name for a dog, but I named her after one of my favorite characters from *Gone with the Wind*."

The answer startled Dani. Liz noticed her reaction.

"What? Please don't tell me you're one of those people who thinks *Gone with the Wind* is so terribly outdated. I mean, it's meant to be in the heart of the Civil War and—"

Dani cut her off with a laugh before she continued. She could tell Liz was passionate about the film. "No, no. It's just that *Gone with the Wind* is my favorite book of all time. I also make my friends watch the movie with me at least once a year and drag them to the Fox Theatre in Atlanta when they have their special showings."

"Really? How wonderful. I've had to defend myself against criticism before, and it's kind of a knee-jerk reaction on my part. Hattie McDaniel was truly remarkable in her role as Mammy. In fact, if not for Vivien Leigh's performance, she would've stolen that movie."

"Have you ever heard her acceptance speech at the Academy Awards for Best Supporting Actress?" Dani asked. "It's one of the most heartfelt and touching speeches you'll ever hear. What's really sad, though, was she wasn't even allowed to sit with her co-stars."

"Even though she earned and won that award, bigotry was still prevalent in Hollywood. Some could argue it still is."

"I can't believe I've found someone who loves my favorite movie as much as I do. I thought we were a dying breed." Dani was curious. "Do you live nearby?"

"Over on Aspen."

"That's just seven blocks from where I live. We're on Elm." Dani was overwhelmed with comfort as she talked so easily with Liz. She didn't want to end the conversation and thought of a way to prolong it.

"We were headed over to the park," she said. Which was a small lie. She'd thought about it but decided she'd walk Frodo around the block. Running into Liz changed her mind. "Would you and Melanie like to join us?" Dani held her breath as she waited for Liz's answer.

"We'd love to."

They started in the direction of the park but grew quiet. *Think of something to say.*

"What made you become a vet?"

Liz pushed a lock of fallen hair behind her ear. "My parents raised beagles when I was a kid, and I always assisted when a litter was born. I learned how to care for the ones who were sick. One time, I sat up all night with a pup who wasn't nursing from his mother. My father told me not to interfere, that we needed to let nature take its course. But I was determined to give the little guy a chance, you know?" Her face clouded over.

Dani touched her arm. "Are you okay?"

"He didn't make it," Liz said, clearing her throat.

"I'm sorry if I've brought up bad memories."

"Please don't apologize." It was Liz's turn to touch Dani's arm.

Dani's skin was warm under her sweatshirt and jacket where Liz's fingers had touched, and an even stronger feeling of comfort ran through her body.

Liz continued. "It's because of that incident that I decided to go to veterinary school. I wanted to help animals as much as I could. So in a way, the hard lesson I learned during that night was a blessing in my life."

They entered the park. There was an enclosed area—the "Francis Bark Park." Granted, it wasn't as large as some that Dani had seen, but this was a small town. It was progress. They walked over and sat down on a bench, letting Frodo and Melanie off their leashes to frolic. "Okay, now you, Dani," Liz said, turning to her.

Dani again became lost in her eyes. *Damn it. Stop that. She's just being friendly.*

"I moved here from a small town in Indiana after graduating

from college. I received my degree in business and used it to make some money on the stock market."

"That sounds interesting."

"I was lucky."

"Now you're being modest. I get a strong sense that you're very intelligent."

Dani felt her face grow hot.

"I didn't mean to embarrass you." Liz touched Dani's arm again. Dani saw Liz's genuine concern.

"Sometimes I don't take compliments well."

"Maybe you don't get complimented enough. And if that's the case, then something's wrong."

Dani stared into her eyes. Her Scarlett O'Hara eyes. Like in the movies, it was as if time stood still. Dani no longer heard the birds chirping or the sound of Frodo and Melanie barking as they played.

"Scarlett O'Hara," Dani said in a soft voice.

"What?"

"Technically, Vivien Leigh since she brought the character to life. I mean if it weren't for her, we'd have never experienced the magic of Scarlett since it was a novel, and of course no photos were included." Dani shuddered at her words. *You're rambling like an idiot.*

Liz seemed confused.

"Your eyes, Liz. Has anyone ever told you that you have Scarlett O'Hara's eyes?"

Liz's face reddened, and she ducked her head.

Dani gently squeezed Liz's arm. "Now it's my turn to apologize for embarrassing you."

Liz met Dani's eyes again. "No one has ever told me that." She paused and took a breath. "But I have to say that's the most romantic thing anyone has ever said to me."

"Oh. I—"

"You're not going to take it back are you?"

"No, no. Absolutely not. I can't, because it's true."

Liz smiled, and it was like the sun had shot through a thick layer of clouds in a thunderstorm. The smile took Dani's breath away. She had to clench her fist to keep from pushing a lock of hair off Liz's forehead.

"I guess I should get home." Melanie sat panting in front of Liz. "I think she needs water. Unfortunately, I forgot to bring some along." She really did look disappointed.

Dani realized she, too, felt disappointed they had to end their visit, but Frodo's tongue was lolling out of his mouth. Liz was right. Both dogs needed water.

"Frodo looks a little thirsty, too." They stood up. Dani put the leash back on Frodo, and Liz did the same for Melanie.

They took their time leaving the enclosed area. Dani thought Liz seemed as reluctant as she to end their unexpected outing.

"I enjoyed this, Liz." Liz gave her that smile again. *How does she do that?* Dani wondered. *She smiles and everything seems brighter.*

"I enjoyed it, too."

Dani wasn't sure what she wanted to do, but a hug seemed like it'd be nice. Liz moved forward to Dani at the same time Dani moved to her. They hugged. It was a warm embrace. They pulled away from each other at the same time.

"We'd best get back," Dani said as she glanced down at Frodo. "Thanks again for the walk and our visit."

"Have a great Sunday, Dani."

Dani turned to leave, but Liz's voice stopped her.

"I forgot to tell you. You left before we could give you Frodo's new tags for the year."

"I don't think I can make it there this week, but—"

Liz interrupted her. "That's okay. I can bring them to you. Can I stop by your bookstore?"

Maybe Liz was aware she owned the bookstore because it was such a small town. *But maybe, just maybe, she asked around because she was interested.*

"I'd really appreciate that."

"I'll see you soon then?"

"See you soon."

They waved at each other as they headed off in opposite directions. Dani wanted to watch Liz walking away. She turned and was happy to find that Liz had also turned around. She waved again, and Liz raised her hand.

"Come on, Frodo. We need to get you some water."

It wasn't until Dani was unlocking the door that she remembered why she'd suffered through a sleepless night. She sighed. What was she going to do about C.J. James?

Chapter 8

"Did you have a good time Saturday night?" Tina asked as Dani restocked some books of a popular author. It was almost noon, and no one was in the store, which was normal for that time of day. So many good restaurants in town to choose from added to the scarcity of customers at lunch hour.

Dani grabbed another handful of books to shelve.

"Dani?"

"Hmm?"

"Saturday night? C.J. James? How'd that go?" Tina raised her eyebrows.

Dani realized lying was fruitless. Tina would see right through it.

"It was fine." Yeah, *that* sure sounded believable.

"Fine."

"Yeah, fine."

"Would we care to elaborate a little?" Tina thrust her hands on her hips. Dani had seen that stance many times. It signaled Tina would be relentless until she got answers.

Dani stood up. "What? Do you want all the details?" She hated the testiness in her voice.

"Hey, I didn't mean anything by it," Tina said, a little crestfallen.

"I'm sorry, Tina." Dani debated how much she'd tell her. She decided to be honest. "Actually, we ended up at her place—rather quickly, I might add."

Tina's eyebrows shot up again. She seemed surprised, or she was certainly giving a very good impression of a surprised best friend. At least it's not complete shock, Dani thought.

"And one thing led to another and to another. I think you get the picture."

Tina opened her mouth to say something and snapped it shut.

"It's okay, T. I can take it."

"I was going to say normally you don't act on something so fast. And then there's that one-year thing."

"Yeah, well, C.J. was very persuasive if you know what I mean."

"So, how was—"

"Kind of weird."

"Weird?"

"She made love to me, but she didn't want me to make love to her."

Tina leaned against the bookshelf with a pensive look. "I'm thinking she's moving farther and farther into the 'high maintenance' category," she said with a snort.

"I don't know what to think."

"Did she talk about seeing you again?"

"She said she'd see me soon, whatever the hell that means."

The door jingled open. Tina watched the person enter their shop. She openly admired whoever it was, and her lips formed into a soft smile of pleasure. Dani poked her head around the bookshelf.

Liz Springer.

Dani swallowed as she watched her walk toward them. She looked fantastic. She'd pulled her dark hair back from her face, which accentuated her eyes even more. She was wearing a peach camp shirt and a tan skirt. Dani's gaze traveled down to Liz's legs. Liz had slacks on at the vet's office and jeans at the park yesterday morning. Dani tried not to linger there, but damn, she had some nice, athletic legs. Dani had no trouble picturing her in a skirt that hiked up just a bit more. She physically shook her head to try to erase the image.

"Liz. It's good to see you again."

"Hi, Dani. I was hoping to catch you in here. I wasn't sure when you took your lunch." She held up Frodo's dog tags. "I promised to bring these by."

"Oh, yeah. Thanks." It made Dani happy that Liz hadn't waited long to bring the tags. She reached out to take the tags from Liz and felt that warmth again when their fingers touched. Dani glanced over at Tina who had her, "aren't you going to introduce us?" look on her face. "Liz, this is my best friend Tina Dewey. Tina, this is Dr. Liz Springer. She's the vet who saw Frodo because Dr. Patterson wasn't available."

Tina stuck out her hand.

"Hi. Dani talked about you. It's nice to put a face with the name."

Dani glared at Tina as Liz took Tina's hand. *I talked about her? Jesus, can you be any more obvious?*

"Nice to meet you, Tina."

"Dani said what a great vet you are. That you really care about what you do."

Liz seemed a little embarrassed but took the compliment well. "I do love my job." As she said this, she glanced over at Dani and smiled. Her eyes sparkled in the afternoon sun streaming through the plate-glass windows. It was like Scarlett O'Hara ascending the staircase at the Twelve Oaks plantation, glancing back at Rhett Butler at the bottom of the stairs. Dani wondered if she had the same rakish grin that Clark Gable sported in that scene.

Dani was about to say something when the bell on the door jingled again. Dani noticed Tina's reaction since Dani wasn't facing the door. The dark scowl indicated who could be entering the store.

Dani felt her stomach do a quick turn as C.J. James approached them.

"Hey, Dani," C.J. said. "Thought I'd stop by before I head over to Carl's to rehearse." She glanced at Liz, grinned, and stuck out her hand. "C.J. James."

Liz appeared uncomfortable under C.J.'s pointed stare. "Dr. Liz Springer." She took C.J.'s hand but didn't hold on long. Interesting how she introduced herself so formally, Dani thought.

C.J. kept her eyes on Liz for a moment. "Everything okay?" she asked as she turned to Dani.

"She's a vet," Dani said. "Frodo went to see her last week."

"Who's Frodo?" C.J. asked.

"My beagle."

"Oh." C.J. looked like she wasn't much of a dog person. Yet another warning sign for Dani to question her attraction to this woman. "I dropped in to say hi. Wanted to see if you were coming to any of the shows this week."

"C.J.'s the first performer in the 'Women in Music' series at Carl's," Dani told Liz.

Liz nodded but didn't look impressed. "I heard some of the

employees at the office talk about you." That was it. Nothing more, although C.J. seemed like she was at least expecting a compliment.

"I'm not sure, C.J. I'll try to make it to one of your shows," Dani said.

C.J. leaned in a little closer and rubbed her thumb slowly against Dani's arm. "I hope you do more than just try."

Shit. The touch transported Dani back to C.J.'s apartment Saturday night. She tried to shake that image from her mind. She glanced over at Liz.

Liz wasn't looking at C.J. but at Dani. Dani tried to discern what she saw in Liz's eyes. They were rounder now, which made them even more expressive. Was it disappointment? Before Dani could figure it out, C.J.'s voice cut in.

"I need to get going. Nice to meet you, Liz." Dani felt her body jerk at the familiarity in C.J.'s voice.

"Nice to meet you, Ms. James." Liz managed a tight smile as she continued to maintain her formality. "I'd better get to the office. It's very nice to meet you, Tina."

"You, too." Tina turned to Dani and gave a slight jerk of her head toward Liz.

Dani felt numb. And she felt something else... disappointment, similar to what she thought she'd seen in Liz's expression. Dani was sorry Liz was leaving the shop so quickly and that C.J. had interrupted them. More than anything, Dani was disappointed in herself. After all, C.J. had made it more than clear that they were intimate.

"I'm sorry you have to go back so soon," Dani said. "I would love to have coffee with you."

Liz gave her a small smile. "Maybe sometime." She turned to leave.

"Hey, thanks again for bringing these by." Dani held up the tags and jingled them.

The openness in Liz's eyes was no longer there. It was like the shuttering of a window by a blind.

"You're welcome. It wasn't that far for me to come over. Take care."

As Liz left the shop, Dani had an empty feeling in her gut. She rubbed her stomach to make it go away, but it didn't ease the sensation.

Tina let out a low whistle.

"What?" Dani asked.

"That's some woman." Tina's tone was serious. Too serious for Dani's fragile mood.

"Yeah, she is." Dani sat on the floor to continue her chore of stocking the shelves, but her mind was on Liz's dark hair pulled back, her expressive eyes. There was no getting around it. C.J.'s surprise visit had unnerved her. The timing couldn't have been worse.

Tina knelt down so she was at Dani's level. "What are you going to do?"

Dani kept shelving books. "What do you mean what am I going to do?"

Tina reached out and gripped Dani's shoulder, which stopped her from shelving any more books. Dani stood, and Tina joined her. "Dani, I don't know if you noticed, but Dr. Liz Springer likes you."

Dani felt her face grow hot. "I don't know about—"

"Well, I do," Tina interrupted. "I only wish that C.J. James hadn't walked in." Tina's face darkened.

"It's complicated." *God, did she actually just say that?*

Apparently, Tina thought the same thing. "Saying 'it's complicated' is a cop-out."

Dani felt herself get angry, but only because she knew Tina was right. That didn't stop her from snapping back. "Maybe I don't have everything figured out like you do. Have you ever thought of that?"

Tina's expression changed. She tried to recover, but Dani could tell she'd hurt her with her words.

"I don't think that's fair, Dani."

"I'm sorry. I have no reason to be upset with you. I'm upset and angry with myself. I shouldn't be taking it out on you."

"Apology accepted. I just wanted to make sure you noticed how much Liz is into you."

"I'm still not sure about C.J."

"I wasn't too hip on her from the very beginning." Tina smirked. "As if you couldn't tell. Let me ask you this—do you like her?"

Dani thought about it for a few seconds. She realized she hadn't even gotten a chance to figure that part out. C.J. fascinated her. Was that the same thing? Tina studied her closely.

"I think I might need some more time."

"What about the doctor?"

"I don't know." And Dani really didn't. Maybe she was afraid to think Liz was the least bit interested in her. Maybe she was afraid that it was all in her imagination, but here was Tina telling her that she could see Liz was interested. Was that just Tina pushing for someone, anyone other than C.J.?

"I can tell when you need to think about something. You get that expression like the weight of the world is on your shoulders." Tina reached out and gave Dani a hug. "Know that it isn't. You'll sort all this out."

Although Dani felt comforted by her friend's confidence in her and by the embrace, she didn't share in Tina's certainty that everything would be okay. Dani wasn't exactly batting a thousand when it came to matters of the heart. She laughed to herself. Hell, she wasn't even batting .500.

* * *

On Liz's walk back to her car, she couldn't shake the image of C.J. James making it very clear about the relationship between Dani and her. The best Liz could think to describe her feelings was—disappointed. Very disappointed. She had hoped that she and Dani might get to know one another, more than simply as a vet and client. Meeting up at the park and the time they shared there cemented that hope.

Now, it seemed to be only in her mind. She felt foolish rushing over to bring the tags to Dani.

She sighed as she slid into the driver's seat of her Outback. Sometimes, the timing in her life truly sucked.

Chapter 9

Dani stepped into Carl's on Wednesday afternoon to watch C.J. rehearse. She heard the music before she opened the door.

Carl waved at her from behind the bar. "Hey, Dani. Good to see you again."

"You, too, Carl."

"Get you anything?" He asked the question like he knew the answer would be no. Dani wasn't known to drink that much, especially at three in the afternoon.

She had asked Tina to watch the shop while she took a short break. Tina seemed to sense Dani's destination but, to her credit, didn't make a snarky comment.

"No," Dani answered. She glanced back at C.J. who hadn't looked up yet from her guitar.

"Ah. Here to see C.J.?"

"Yeah."

"Want me to get her attention?"

"That's okay. If you don't mind, I'll sit at one of the tables until she takes a break."

"Not a problem." He set a Coke in front of her. "At least drink this."

"Thanks." She approached a table in the corner. She didn't want to be conspicuous. She also didn't want to appear overly eager.

C.J. furrowed her brow while she concentrated on her music. She didn't sing as she picked her acoustic guitar. Dani had a feeling she was working out a new song. C.J. eyes were closed, and she hummed softly. A half smile crept across the corners of her mouth as if reliving a fond memory. She fiddled with the tune for a few more minutes. She glanced up when she took a drink from her bottled water. She spotted Dani and grinned.

Damn. She could melt an entire stick of butter with that smile, Dani thought.

C.J. leaned her guitar against the stand and walked over to Dani's table. She leaned over, gave Dani a peck on the cheek, and sat down.

"Hi." Dani wasn't sure exactly what she was going to say. She only knew she wanted to talk to C.J. to get some bearing on whatever it was that was going on between them. She felt like she needed to garner some control over her life that only a couple of weeks ago was so simple and uncomplicated.

C.J. took another drink from her water and peered at Dani over the bottle. Dani took a sip of her Coke. When she spoke, she kept her voice low in the muted bar. "About Saturday night—"

C.J. reached across the table and encircled Dani's hand with her long fingers.

"I have no regrets about that night. Do you?"

"I don't know what I'm feeling. The way I left. It felt cold." There. She said it.

C.J. turned Dani's hand over and softly caressed Dani's palm with her other fingers. She cleared her throat. The playfulness left her eyes. The sly grin she always seemed to sport vanished. "I'm not good at opening up, Dani. I—" She frowned. "Shit." She took in a deep breath. "I have a difficult time accepting affection." C.J. swallowed hard, like the truth was a physical object that needed to travel down a raw throat ravaged with the Strep virus.

Dani sat back in her chair. She thought she'd be confronted with the "C.J. James Live and in Concert" persona. The woman who flirted without thought. Not this woman who was baring her soul—or at least seemed to be.

"I have to be honest, C.J. It hurt the way I left your place. You were so passionate making love to me. Then, it was like you'd erected an invisible wall between us before I left."

"I know," C.J. said softly. She squeezed Dani's hand and leaned forward. "Do you think maybe you can give me another chance?"

Dani hesitated. What was keeping her from immediately answering yes? She usually trusted her instincts, but this time she was so unsure of herself. She hated it. She thought of something to say, though.

"Do you have to flirt with every woman you see?" She might as well get it all out there. "I mean, is this something in your nature?"

C.J. smiled. It wasn't one of her flashy smiles that seemed to dazzle anyone within ten feet. It was a quiet smile. "You know, you're the first woman to ever call me on that."

Dani didn't say anything.

"Seriously. Most women I've dated either haven't said anything because they were afraid I wouldn't want to be with them anymore, or they didn't care. It doesn't mean anything—"

Dani cut it her off. "It does. It's disrespectful." God, did she just say that? It sounded like she was a high school teacher scolding a student mouthing off in class. "I don't know if I used the right—"

It was C.J.'s turn to interrupt. "No. Disrespectful is definitely the right word."

Dani found she was nodding. She wondered where exactly they were going with all of this. She took a long hard look at C.J. With her blonde hair that feathered off her face, her light-blue eyes, her sensual mouth, she was incredibly cute. Right now, though, she just looked vulnerable.

"Who's the real C.J. James?"

Dani wasn't sure if she had spoken the words out loud until she saw C.J.'s reaction. C.J. had been staring down at the table, but her head jerked up at Dani's question. "I don't know," she whispered.

"Why don't we have a real date? Maybe go out to dinner? Why don't we try to get to know each other?"

"I'd like that."

"You perform here almost every night, so I'm not sure how dinner will work out."

"Sunday night would work for me. Would you like to come by my apartment to pick me up?"

"Why don't I pick you up here in front of Carl's place?" Dani wasn't ready yet to get within a foot of C.J.'s apartment.

"Is six okay with you?"

"Six is perfect." Dani rose from the table. C.J. did the same and gave Dani another kiss on the cheek. "I'll see you Sunday night, C.J."

As she walked back to the shop, Dani thought about their

conversation. She was willing to see where this would lead. Something about C.J. intrigued her. Dani hoped it was more than her looks or that she dripped sex like a swimmer dripped water onto a tiled floor.

Dani noticed a woman walking a beagle down Main Street. Nose to the ground, the beagle never raised his head as he trudged beside his owner. He pulled her along until he was able to get to a tree. Just like Frodo. She thought back to Frodo yanking her toward Liz and her dog. She laughed out loud at the image.

Liz's kind eyes appeared in Dani's mind as if it were only yesterday that Liz examined Frodo in her office. Dani's pace slowed as she realized the woman she focused on wasn't C.J. James. It was Dr. Liz Springer.

"Dani Roberts, you're one hopeless lesbian," she mumbled as she pushed open the door to her store.

* * *

Dani pulled up to the curb in front of Carl's Cavern. C.J. was leaning against the building watching the passers-by. A few of the women turned and smiled at her. C.J. gave them a cocky grin and nodded.

"Clueless," Dani said as the car came to a stop. "She's freaking clueless."

C.J. spotted Dani's car. She opened the passenger door and hopped inside.

"How you doing? You look nice."

"Thanks." Dani had tried to dress up a bit with a pair of khakis and a denim shirt. She polished it off with a leather belt, which she hardly ever wore. "I'm doing well. You look great, too."

C.J. wore black jeans and a tan cotton shirt. The weather had taken a warm turn. It was warm enough to do without jackets, but still not quite warm enough to be wearing short sleeves.

"I thought we'd go to this great steak place a few miles outside of town."

"You're the expert, Dani. I have no clue what's out beyond the great town of Francis."

"Maybe we can drive into Atlanta sometime."

"That'd be nice."

Over dinner, they talked about their childhood. Dani talked about what it was like growing up in small town Peabody, Indiana. She told the story about what a big deal it was when a McDonald's opened. They held a grand opening. The local media was there—the local media consisting of two reporters from the twice-a-week newspaper that could be found for free at the counter of the supermarket. She told C.J. about her parents who still lived there, about coming out to them when she was nineteen and beginning her sophomore year at Miami of Ohio. It surprised her how accepting they were. Her younger brother had been accepting, too.

C.J. recalled her time growing up in Cincinnati. "Actually, it's Fairfield, Ohio, which is just outside of Cincinnati." Unfortunately, C.J.'s parents weren't happy with her "choice" to be a lesbian. They refused to speak about it after C.J. came out to them and pretended they'd never had the conversation. If she brought a woman home she was dating, her parents referred to her as C.J.'s "friend."

"Was there ever anyone special that you felt was going to be more than a..." Dani let her voice trail off.

"A one-night stand?"

"Sorry. I wasn't sure how to ask the question."

C.J. reached across the table and patted her hand. "It's okay." She grew pensive, and Dani didn't think she was going to answer. After what seemed to be a full minute of silence, C.J. spoke. "Yeah," she said in a soft voice. "There was one special woman."

Dani waited.

C.J. poked at her salad with her fork. Her face became cloaked in sadness. She took a couple of deep breaths.

"Sam and I were together for two years. She—" C.J. stopped. "Ah hell." She threw her fork down and pinched her eyes with her index fingers. When she took her hand away, Dani could tell she was fighting back tears.

"Hey, I'm sorry. I shouldn't have brought this up."

C.J. blinked her eyes quickly. "You would think I'd be over this by now. It was four years ago." She took a drink of her water and smiled sadly. "She died when she was twenty-two. Twenty-two. Can you believe it?" C.J. took another drink of water.

Dani reached for C.J.'s hand and gently squeezed. "I really am sorry."

"Me, too." C.J. took another deep breath and let it out. "Ovarian cancer. But you know what was almost as painful as her death? My parents' reaction to the whole thing. They couldn't understand why I was so upset about losing a 'friend.' Can you believe it? A *friend*." This time, C.J. didn't win the battle with her tears.

Dani was unsure of what else to say. Right at that moment, the waiter brought their food. Dani didn't miss the relief that passed over C.J.'s face. She didn't seem to want to talk about it anymore as they began eating, so Dani didn't push.

"You're right, Dani." C.J. held up a piece of steak on her fork. "This is fantastic."

"Pretty awesome, huh? Normally, I douse my steak in steak sauce. But this steak? Steak sauce has never touched the steaks they serve here."

They passed on dessert when the waiter tried to tempt them with cheesecake.

Walking out to Dani's car, C.J. grabbed her hand. "I've had a really great time tonight. You were right. We need to get to know each other."

Dani drove C.J. to her apartment. C.J. seemed a little surprised when Dani got out and accompanied her up the stairs to her door. Before C.J. unlocked it, Dani leaned in and kissed C.J. softly on the lips. C.J. parted Dani's lips with her tongue, and the kiss began to intensify, but Dani reined it in.

"I enjoyed tonight, C.J. I'd like to do this again."

"On one condition."

"What's that?"

"You come to at least one show a week. I want to see you in the audience."

"That doesn't sound like a hardship at all. Deal." She thought of another question before she left. "I've been meaning to ask you this. What does 'C.J.' stand for?"

"You really don't want to know."

"Yeah, I really would."

"Carla Jolene."

Dani bit her bottom lip and tried not to laugh. She wasn't very successful.

C.J. slapped her playfully on the arm. "I told you that you wouldn't want to know. Now you get why I use C.J."

"Sorry. I had this instant vision of a big-haired country singer from the '60s."

"That's what I saw, too, and decided my career could do without the full name. Hey, not a word to anyone." She shook her finger at Dani.

Dani held up three fingers together in a Girl Scout salute. "Scout's honor." She leaned in and gave C.J. one more quick kiss. "I need to get home."

"Sure I can't tempt you into coming in?" C.J. had the same mischievous grin that Dani was sure worked on a lot of women. Hell, it had worked on her.

"No. Frodo awaits."

"I need to meet this beagle sometime."

"I'd like that. Good night, C.J." She turned to leave.

"Good night. I'll see you this week at Carl's, right?" C.J. asked as Dani headed down the stairs.

"I'll make it there one night." Dani walked down a few steps then turned back. "Oh, by the way. I flunked out of the Girl Scouts."

"You're such a bitch," C.J. said as she unlocked the door.

Dani waved before walking to her car.

Chapter 10

"Yes, we've actually had real dates." Dani picked up the cards dealt to her. It was Tuesday night and time for the biweekly poker game.

Tina shook her head in disbelief. "Man. I thought that woman was incapable of doing anything but—" She stopped when she saw Dani's face. "But singing at Carl's."

The women around the table laughed. "We're all grown-ups here, Tina, and we know what you really wanted to say," Shelly said as she rearranged the cards in her hand.

"Okay, okay. I know the woman has a reputation," Dani said. "But we really are trying to get to know each other." And they were. She and C.J. had been going out now for a few weeks. She made a habit of seeing C.J. perform every Wednesday. Carl had extended C.J.'s run at the Cavern because the artist slated to perform next in the series fell ill.

Frustrated about the reactions from her friends, Dani thought maybe she was trying to convince herself of something that was impossible.

"Hey, Dani. I didn't mean anything by it." Tina's tone was apologetic.

"We didn't either. We're glad you're dating," Shelly said.

In an obvious attempt to lighten the mood, Tina shouted, "Time to kick y'all's asses again!"

"Jesus, Tina, do we have to hear that every poker night?" Dani gave Tina a smile of thanks for changing the subject.

The evening seemed to fly by as it always did when she was with her friends. She stuck with Cokes for the night. She might be having a couple of beers at Carl's Cavern the next night and wanted to limit her alcohol intake. She noticed that Monica didn't seem to be of the same mind about alcohol consumption for the evening. She'd been downing her beers one after another.

On Monica's next trip to the kitchen to toss out her empty beer bottle, Barb pulled her aside and leaned in to say something quietly in her ear. Monica shook Barb's hand off her shoulder. "I walked over here, Barb. I don't need to be careful."

Everyone at the table exchanged worried looks. Monica had broken up with Estelle the week before. Monica told them she had been lugging an antique chair through the front door of her shop when she saw Estelle making out with a woman on the balcony of a nearby hotel. Dani shook her head in anger. She was sure Estelle had planned it so Monica would find out.

Monica kicked Estelle out the next day. Tina volunteered to go over and "throw Estelle and her shit on the street where they belong," but Dani had talked her out of saying anything to Monica.

Dani decided she'd drive Monica home. She motioned Barb over and quietly told her when Monica stumbled down the hall to the bathroom.

The women counted their chips after the last hand. Tonight, Dani came out on top. "Ha! Ha!" In a nimble move, she jumped on her chair and thrust her arms in the air. "I am the new Queen of Poker!" She pointed at Tina. "And you, madam, shall hand over your fucking trophy."

Everyone laughed except for a pouting Tina who sat in her chair with her arms folded against her chest.

They headed for the door. With the prized trophy tucked under her arm, Dani hung back as Monica made one last trip to the bathroom.

Monica teetered into the living room to join Barb, Tina, and Dani.

"Monica, Dani's going to drive you home," Barb said. Her tone left no room for argument.

"I'm fine. Fiiine." Monica narrowed her eyes in an obvious attempt to focus on Barb.

"Um, no. You're druunnk. Let Dani take you home."

"Okay. Whatever."

Dani hugged Tina and Barb. She caught up with Monica outside and led her to the car. Monica sat down and lifted the seatbelt over her shoulder. She tried to snap the buckle in place but failed miserably. "Shit," she muttered. "Shit!" She became frantic.

"Here. Let me do that." Dani reached over and buckled the seatbelt.

"Thanks," Monica said in a quiet voice. She rested her head on the seat back. They rode in silence on the trip to Monica's house. Thinking Monica might have fallen asleep, Dani glanced over at her, but she was staring out the window.

They pulled into her drive. Dani helped Monica out of the passenger side. She linked her arm with Monica's and led her to the door.

Tears filled Monica's eyes. "I can make it from here."

"Let me help you inside."

Monica didn't protest. Dani walked her to the bedroom and helped Monica out of her clothes but left on her underwear. "Do you have a nightshirt or anything?" Dani asked as she searched the dresser drawers. A quiet sob filled the room. Dani hurried over and knelt in front of Monica. "Oh, sweetie, she's really not worth it." Dani regretted the words as soon as they left her mouth.

"Don't you think I know that?" Monica cried out. "I feel like such an idiot." She buried her face in her hands.

Dani gently pulled Monica's hands away. She used her thumbs to wipe the tears streaming down Monica's cheeks and tilted her chin up so she'd meet Dani's eyes.

"You are a beautiful woman, Monica."

"Oh, God, if I hear one more person say that, I'm going to scream." Monica shook her head. "That's what's gotten me into every bad relationship. They don't see *me.*" She pounded her chest with her fist.

Dani took her hand and squeezed it. "I'm talking about your inner beauty, Monica. What's in here." She placed her hand over Monica's heart. "You're going to find the right woman who'll love you for who you are here."

Monica's lips quivered. "You think so?"

"I know so."

Monica managed a smile. "You're such a good friend. Do you know that?"

Dani rose to her feet. "And so are you. Do you think you're

okay now?"

Monica stood up and pulled Dani in for a hug. "As good as I can be," she whispered. "Go home and give Frodo a big pet from Aunt Monica."

"He'll like that." She squeezed Monica again. "You really are going to be okay."

"Yeah, I know. Eventually. Now, go." She pushed Dani toward the door.

Dani started the engine and began the drive home. As she drove, she couldn't shake the feeling that if she wasn't careful, she was heading in the same direction as Monica.

Chapter 11

Liz walked into the exam room with Rita and smiled at the young blond-haired man who sat in the chair on the other side of the exam table. She didn't spot the beagle yet, but she heard its snuffling.

"Hello. I'm Liz Springer. You're John?"

He stood to his full height, which had to be about six feet. "Yes." He nervously licked his lips.

Liz stepped around the table and knelt down to hold out her hand to the tri-colored beagle. Rita joined her. "Hey there, Moxie." Moxie sniffed her hand and gave it a tentative lick. Rita held out her hand with the same result. Liz scratched Moxie's ears. "How about we get you up on the exam table?"

Rita was about to lift Moxie onto the table when John maneuvered around her and lifted the beagle.

Liz smothered her smile. She couldn't count the number of times that a male client seemed to think that she or her female tech was helpless and incapable of lifting a dog. Rita, standing behind John, rolled her eyes at Liz.

John draped a protective arm around Moxie.

Liz opened the file and checked Moxie's pertinent information. She was being seen today because of a recent unexplained weight gain.

"So Moxie has gained..." Liz flipped the pages to check her last three visits. "Five pounds in six months." She tried to hide her surprise. "That's a significant gain, especially for the size of Moxie's breed."

John stroked Moxie's fur. "I don't understand, Dr. Springer. She's on the best dog food, the same brand she's been on since she was a puppy. I never give her any table scraps. I'm careful with her portions, never overfeeding her, yet she keeps gaining weight."

"Let's do an exam and see what we have." Liz put her stethoscope to Moxie's heart, which beat strong and steady with no sign of a murmur. She felt along the beagle's belly. No lumps, unusual growths, or distension. She peered in each of Moxie's ears with her otoscope. Everything was clear with no redness. Standing in front of Moxie, she probed both sides of her neck. No unusual swelling there, either.

John licked his lips again.

"So far, everything checks out," she said. "We can run a blood test to check for anything we need to be concerned about. One thing I'd like to rule out is hypothyroidism, which can cause weight gain and sluggishness. How has her energy been lately?"

"She's wanted to play like always. We've gone on our daily walks."

"Hmm. With the exercise and steady diet, this is a little perplexing." Liz flipped through the chart again. She thought of something. "Do you have a cat? I'm sorry I don't have that information here since this is just Moxie's chart, and Dr. Patterson is Moxie's primary vet."

"We have an eleven-year-old tabby. Max."

"And how has his weight been lately? Staying steady?"

John's brown eyes widened. "He has seemed a little thinner. Nothing we were too concerned about, obviously, or we would've brought him in."

Now we're getting somewhere. "You said 'we.' I don't mean to be personal, but I'm assuming someone lives with you who might also feed Moxie and Max?"

"My partner, Michael."

Liz closed the chart. "John, I think what we have here is a case of a very clever beagle sneaking food from Max."

"Oh, my God. I never thought of that. We put Max's bowl in another room and even set it up on his cat perch, thinking Moxie couldn't get to it."

"You'd be amazed at what lengths beagles go to in order to scarf food. I have a very strong inkling Moxie has figured out how to reach Max's food. Do you and Michael keep track of when you feed Max and Moxie?"

"Yes."

"Do either of you maybe feed her at a different time than normal?"

"Sometimes Moxie will come into the living room, sit, and stare at me. I assume Michael forgot to feed her and—" Again, John's eyes widened. "Well, the little sneak."

Liz chuckled. "Indeed, if Moxie is truly the clever thief I think she is. We'll still run that blood work, though, to be absolutely sure there's not an underlying issue."

John's whole demeanor changed, and he seemed much more relaxed.

Without being asked, Rita left the exam room to retrieve the syringe. She quickly returned and held Moxie's head while Liz drew the blood.

"So, you think my girl is going to be okay?"

"If I'm right about this, I think she's fine." Liz patted Moxie's side. "You just need to make some adjustments to where you place Max's food. And you both have to refrain from succumbing to Moxie's charms." She leaned down and scratched behind Moxie's ears. "Although I'm sure that last one might be the hardest."

John laughed. "She can be quite the drama queen when it comes to food."

After the exam, Liz sat down at her desk to enter her notes. She shook her head as she thought about the beagle's antics. Then her mind drifted to Frodo and her handsome owner. She stopped writing and stared at the wall. How long, she didn't know. She became aware of someone standing nearby. She peered up at Rita.

"Did you have a question, Rita?"

Rita glanced over her shoulder. Mary, peeking around the files, mouthed, "Go on."

"Um. Dr. Springer?"

"It's Liz, remember?"

"Right. Sorry. Liz? Um... well... um..."

"Whatever it is, it's okay to ask."

"Mary and I wanted to know if you'd like to go to Carl's Cavern tonight to see C.J. James perform."

Liz's stomach dropped as if someone had shoved her, unprepared, out of a skydiving plane.

"You look really pale. Are you okay?"

"I'm fine." Liz tried to recover her composure. Did she want to see C.J. James in action? The bigger question was did she want to see Dani and C.J. together?

"Do you think you'd like to go? Mary and I would love it if you'd join us. You'll have fun."

Liz was about to answer no, but instead said, "I'll meet you there."

Rita's young face lit up. "Great." She turned around and gave Mary a thumbs-up.

* * *

Wednesday night, with the temperatures dropping slightly, Dani decided to walk to Carl's Cavern. She dressed in a pair of faded old jeans and a Miami of Ohio sweatshirt. When she opened the door to the bar, the noise blasted her full force. Carl had the stereo turned up loud. The throbbing of the bass reverberated in the soles of Dani's sneakers as she walked across the wood plank floor.

Barb nodded at her as she approached the bar.

"What sounds good?" Barb asked.

"A Heineken."

Barb set the bottle of beer in front of Dani. Before Dani could even make a move to take money out of her billfold, Barb gave her the "don't even think about it" look. Dani held up the bottle in a salute and turned to find an empty table. She spotted one in the far corner of the bar.

As she took her seat, a petite redhead placed her hand on the back of the other chair at the table. "Do you mind if I take this?"

"Not at all." Dani glanced around the bar and noticed a lot of regulars in the audience. One brunette across the room seemed familiar, but Dani couldn't get a good look because a pole partially obstructed the view.

The music stopped abruptly, and Carl jumped up the three steps to the stage.

"Ladies! Again, I give you Ms. C.J. James." He motioned his hand toward the side of the stage where C.J. strode out. She walked over to one of her acoustic guitars and strapped it on. She softly tuned it for a brief minute and faced the crowd.

"How y'all doin' tonight?" she shouted. The place erupted in cheers. "Since I've been staying here for a few weeks, I've caught on to this 'y'all' thing." Everyone laughed. C.J. took a sip of water before she started her first song.

Dani attempted to be objective as C.J. worked through her first set, but C.J. really was that good. Dani scanned the room. Again, the dark-haired woman Dani had spotted earlier seemed familiar, but Dani still couldn't get a good view. A man dressed in khakis and a red cotton shirt seated a few tables back from the stage caught her attention. Seated alone at a small table, he listened intently. When others applauded after each song, he didn't clap.

C.J. finished her set. The houselights came up, and C.J. hopped off the stage and approached Dani's table. She carried her bottle of water with her. Dani didn't know if it was a conscious effort on C.J.'s part, but Dani noticed that C.J. wasn't drinking shots anymore.

"You sound great as usual, C.J."

"Thanks." C.J. slid a nearby chair over to their table. She was about to speak, but Dani's attention was on the man in the khakis who was heading to their table. When he reached them, he stood beside C.J.

"Ms. James, I'm David Morgenson from Different Drummer Records. We're a small label out of Nashville."

"I've heard of you."

"I'm happy to say we've heard of you, too. We had someone at your shows in Birmingham when you performed there a few months ago. We'd very much like to talk to you about joining our label." He glanced at Dani apologetically. "Is there somewhere we can talk?"

"Listen, Mr...."

"Morgenson. But you can call me David."

"David, I'm not sure if you noticed, but I'm not exactly a mainstream artist." C.J. motioned around the bar at all the women.

"We're quite aware of that, but you're in luck. We're not exactly a mainstream label. I think you can tell that by the name of our company. We like to take chances on new artists with a fresh sound. We like what we hear in you."

"I'm sorry, Dani. Do you mind if I talk with this gentleman?"

"Not at all."

C.J. stood up. "We can go backstage," she said to him as they walked away.

Damn. This could be C.J.'s big break, Dani thought. She took a swig of her beer and almost spit out the backwash at the bottom of the bottle. She started for the bar. As she did, the dark-haired woman she'd noticed earlier was also approaching the bar. Now that she was out from behind the pole, Dani could see it was Liz. Her jeans were a little tighter than the ones she had on during the walk on that Sunday at the bark park. She'd tucked in her long-sleeved, gray Cornell University T-shirt and polished it off with a thin leather belt. The shirt accentuated the soft curve of her breasts. Dani didn't realize she was staring until Barb's voice cut in.

"Yo! Space cadet. Did you want another Heineken?"

"Huh?"

"What's wrong?" Barb must have spotted Liz. She grinned. "Easy on the eyes, huh?"

"She's Frodo's vet." Which technically wasn't true, but Dani didn't want to go into details.

"So, this is the infamous Dr. Springer." Barb stared at Liz who was talking to a couple of women at the bar. "Tina was right."

"I'll take that Heineken."

Barb popped the lid and handed the bottle to Dani. She leaned closer. "What are you going to do?"

"What do you mean?"

Barb snickered. "Oh, hell, Dani, you really are dense sometimes." With that, she strode back to the other end of the bar where someone shouted for another beer.

Dani contemplated Barb's last remark when someone tapped her shoulder. She twisted around. Again, she had to catch her breath. *Liz.*

"Hi, Dani, I thought that was you but wasn't sure."

Dani felt her heartbeat throbbing in her ears. "Hi, Liz. I thought I recognized you but couldn't get a good look."

"Are you okay? You're a little flushed."

"Uh, yeah, I'm fine." She held up her bottle of Heineken. "I think it's the beer. Which is why I stop on two." God, you're such a liar, Dani thought. She tried to recover. "You decided to come out to see C.J.?"

Liz's expression changed. It was subtle, but Dani noticed her mood had shifted.

"A couple of the staff at the clinic asked if I'd like to join them." Liz took a sip of her drink. "I have to admit that she's quite good."

Dani waited for her to continue.

Liz stared down at her drink as she moved her stir stick through the ice. Her face reddened. "Are you two—"

Carl's voice cut through the din of bar noise.

"Let's give it up again for C.J.!" he shouted. With that, everyone hustled to their seats.

"I'll let you go." Liz turned to head back to her table with her friends.

"Wait." But Liz kept going. Barb watched from the end of the bar. Dani quickly walked back to her table, not wanting to get into this with Barb.

C.J. played through her second set. She even came back for an encore after a lengthy standing ovation. After she finished, the houselights came back on, and dance music blared through the loud speakers again. Eventually, C.J. walked over to sit with Dani.

"I'm sorry I can't stay long. David wants to talk to me some more about this contract thing." C.J. grinned like a little kid. "Can you believe it?"

"You're a very talented singer and songwriter. They'd be stupid not to sign you."

It was the first time she saw C.J. blush. "Thanks," she said in a soft voice.

David Morgenson approached them.

Dani nodded toward him. "I need to let you go."

"I'll see you later this week. Want to go out again on Sunday night?"

With thoughts of Liz and their interrupted conversation, Dani held back from committing. "Give me a call at the store before the weekend."

"Everything okay?"

"Yeah."

"All right. Talk to you soon." C.J. glanced back at her as she walked away with Morgenson.

Dani sat there for a few more minutes and finished her beer. After she took the last sip, she decided to head home. It was getting late.

 Chris Paynter

With her mind on everything that happened that night, she wasn't paying attention to her surroundings as she walked down Main. She heard someone's footsteps across the street. Liz, with her head down, was several yards in front of her. Dani had a running debate with herself about crossing the street and saying hello. She took the plunge.

She had to quicken her step to catch up with Liz. Liz spun around when Dani reached her.

Liz's hand flew to her chest. "Dani. You startled me."

"Sorry. I was walking home and saw you across the street. Do you mind if I join you?"

"If you'd like to," Liz said softly.

They walked in silence as they passed under each streetlight and back into shadow. Somehow, Dani didn't feel pressured to talk.

She broke the silence. "You were going to ask me something at Carl's." Enough time went by that Dani wasn't sure Liz would respond. She could tell Liz was conflicted about something.

"Are you and C.J. dating?" Liz's voice cut through the night air and straight into Dani's heart.

Dani slowed her step and stopped under the streetlight at Vine Street. Liz kept her head down as she scuffed a stone with her sneakered toe. Dani waited until Liz met her gaze.

"Yes," Dani answered in a soft, but firm voice. "But we haven't been dating that long. I don't know if it's serious, or if it even has a chance to get serious. Everything happened too fast." Dani's heart pounded with the truth of her words. She needed to slow everything down. She had to find a way.

Liz nodded but said nothing. Dani wanted to reach out and touch Liz's face. She took a step toward her, but Liz stepped back.

"I'm going to turn here to head home." Liz's face, illuminated by the streetlight, was drawn in sadness. From where they stood, Liz could keep walking with her. There were plenty of streets closer to Dani's house that Liz could cut over to her home. But Dani sensed why Liz was leaving. She didn't try to stop her.

"Okay."

Liz began walking away. Dani watched as she disappeared and reappeared from the shadows. "Turn around," Dani whispered, "please turn around."

But Liz kept walking.

Chapter 12

The next day at the store, Dani felt completely out of sorts. Last night's encounter with Liz after leaving Carl's shook her. She even had a dream about it. But in the dream, Dani called after Liz, ran to her, and embraced her. Dani woke up with a start. It was like she could still taste the kiss on her lips. It was that real.

"What is wrong with me?" Dani muttered to herself.

"Did you say something, boss?" Tina shouted from the front of the shop.

"No. Talking to myself."

Tina rose from straightening books in the corner of the store and walked over to Dani at the counter. "Barb told me Liz was at the bar last night."

"Yeah, she was."

Tina leaned her elbows on the counter and grew even more intense, if that were possible. "Barb said she agrees with me."

"About what?" Dani scrolled through an online book catalog to avoid Tina's gaze.

"She says the doc definitely seems interested in you." Tina waited for Dani's response, but Dani kept silent. "Dani?"

"I'm not sure what the hell is going on with me. I've never felt like this before. Never. I've always been sure of myself. Always had a plan. Now everything seems to be unsettled—or at least I feel that way. And as for Liz, after last night, I'm sure if she had any feelings for me, they're gone now."

Tina frowned. "What happened?"

Dani told her how she caught up with Liz on the walk home. "Liz asked me if C.J. and I were dating."

"And you answered..."

"I told her we hadn't been dating that long. Which we

haven't. It's been some weeks, but—" Dani resisted the urge to toss the computer mouse onto the counter in frustration.

"Don't go getting pissed off at me. I can see this thing with Liz going somewhere."

"Wait. Hold it right there." Dani raised her hand to ward off Tina's words. "There is no 'thing.'"

"But there could be."

"Tina, if you saw the look on her face when I told her we were dating, you'd know that's pretty much impossible now."

"There."

"There what?"

"You said 'pretty much.' That means you still have hope."

"Let me rephrase. It's impossible. It's not going to happen. There is no hope. Is that clear enough?"

Tina squeezed Dani's arm. "Hey, it's okay."

"I'm not sure that it is."

"How did you feel when you saw her reaction?"

Dani took a deep breath. "I wanted to reach out and touch her face." She raised her hand like Liz was standing in front of her. "I could see I had hurt her, and she was so sad." Dani ran her fingers through her hair as she remembered the moment. "I took a step toward her, not even thinking about what I was doing. That's when she stepped back from me and said she had to go home. She turned down another street so she didn't have to walk with me."

"Man, I'm sorry."

"If the situation were reversed, I would've done the same thing. I would've walked away and forgotten I'd ever met the other woman."

Tina appeared lost in thought.

"What? I know you, and you're thinking hard on something underneath that Braves hat of yours."

"Let me ask you this. Have you ever stopped to think about why you're having reservations about C.J. James? Why it seemed to be moving too fast for you? You've always been pretty good with your gut instinct."

There it was. Exactly what Dani had been contemplating in the weeks since she met C.J.

"I didn't mean to upset you," Tina said into the silence.

"You've not upset me. You've nailed exactly why this is such a mess. Do you think it might have something to do with I've not been with anyone since Katie? And I jumped on the first woman who comes along who has shown interest?"

"Define 'jumped on.'"

Dani smacked Tina's shoulder. "Very funny."

The ringing phone interrupted their conversation.

"Dani's Den of Books," Dani answered.

"Guess who you're talking to?" an excited C.J. said on the other end.

"The hot new lesbian artist who's been breaking hearts at Carl's Cavern for the past five weeks?"

Tina opened her mouth and made a gagging motion with her index finger. Dani waved her off.

C.J. laughed. "No. Well, yes." She laughed again. "You're too much, Dani." She cleared her throat. "You're talking to the newly signed out-lesbian artist to Different Drummer Records."

"That's great, C.J. I'm so happy for you."

"They want me to come up to Nashville next week to play my songs for them in person so they can decide which ones will go on the first album. Hey, do you still want to get together for our Sunday night dinner?"

"Sure. We can celebrate. I'll pick you up at six at your apartment."

"See you then."

Before Dani hung up, she said, "Hey, C.J.?"

"Yeah?"

"Congratulations again."

"Thanks."

Dani hung up. She clicked the mouse to open up the book catalogue page when her mind drifted back to her conservation with Tina about Liz.

"There's nothing there now, Dani," she whispered.

* * *

Dani sat across from C.J. at the restaurant and listened to her talking animatedly about her record deal.

"I still can't believe they don't care that I'm gay. I mean granted, not all my songs are about being gay, but I sure as shit don't hide the fact when I sing about love." C.J. took a breath to sip from her Coke. "Damn, Dani, I'm monopolizing the conversation. I haven't even asked how you're doing or how things are at the store."

"Things are fine, and please don't apologize. You should be excited about this. It's a fantastic opportunity. I can see it opening up a whole new audience for you."

"Maybe you're right. Although I can't imagine a seventy-five-year-old straight woman sitting in her living room listening to me sing about a past female lover."

Dani laughed at the image. "No. I think you're right on that one."

They left the restaurant. On their drive back, C.J. asked, "Can you come inside for just a few minutes? I have something I want you to hear."

"All right."

Dani followed behind C.J. as they walked up the stairs to her apartment.

C.J. flipped on the light. "Feel free to sit wherever you want." She went to the back of the apartment to what Dani assumed was her bedroom.

Dani glanced around the living room. She hadn't been able to see much in the dark from her first "visit" here. It wasn't that big of a room. The two chairs and the couch definitely said "furnished apartment." They were clean, but worn. Dani's gaze traveled over to the couch. She definitely didn't want to sit there, so she plopped down into one of the overstuffed chairs.

C.J. emerged from the bedroom carrying her twelve-string acoustic guitar. She sat down in the chair across from Dani. "I'm not going to bite," she said as she placed picks on her fingers.

Dani laughed—a little too hard.

C.J. strummed the guitar a few times. "I've been working on a new song. I'm not quite done, but I wanted you to hear what I have so far."

"Okay." Dani settled back into her chair.

C.J. softly picked her guitar and sang the first few lines. It was a beautiful love song:

Your eyes to me were like a pool of light,
They shimmered and took me to another world.
Where I knew everything would be all right,
'Cause you opened my heart to let my love unfurl.

Dani was caught up in the lyrics and in the feeling C.J. put into the song.

When C.J. finished, she paused for a few seconds with her head down before she met Dani's gaze. "That's all I have so far."

"It's beautiful. You need to finish it, and I hope you play that for them in Nashville. What's the name of it?"

"It's called 'Dani's Eyes.'"

Dani didn't know what to say. A part of her was flattered, while the cautious part of her wondered if it could've easily been titled "Jenny's Eyes" or "Julie's Eyes" for the other women C.J. had slept with.

"So you like it?" C.J. asked.

"I do. I'm just a little speechless right now."

C.J. leaned the guitar against the side of the chair, stood, and walked over to Dani. She held out her hand to Dani and lifted her to her feet.

"When I'm done, I want to release it to the universe if you'll let me." C.J. squeezed Dani's hand. Before Dani could say anything, C.J. pulled her tight against her body and kissed her passionately.

Dani felt her head spinning. The song played in an endless loop in her mind as C.J. led her into her bedroom. C.J. pulled Dani's shirt above her head and, with an upraised eyebrow, asked permission to unsnap her bra. In no time, Dani stood in front of C.J. completely nude. Without asking, for fear of rejection, Dani pulled C.J.'s T-shirt off. C.J. wore no bra. She kept Dani's gaze as she tugged off her jeans and underwear. Dani stepped back to look at C.J. The room was dark, but enough light allowed Dani to see every curve of C.J.'s body.

Dani ran her fingertips lightly across C.J.'s chest. She started to go lower, but C.J. grabbed her hand and pushed Dani back onto the bed. C.J. pressed her mouth into Dani's neck and worked her way lower and lower. Dani had wanted to make love to C.J., but once she felt C.J.'s mouth on her, all thought left her mind. She allowed herself to just... feel. C.J. worked her lips and tongue until Dani was about to beg. Then, C.J. sucked her clit, and Dani soared to a climax. C.J. pressed her tongue hard into Dani's wet folds, and Dani cried out.

C.J. kissed her way back up to Dani's breasts then lay on her back beside her. Dani was breathing too hard to utter any words. C.J. leaned up to draw the comforter over their bodies and pulled Dani close.

Dani reached up and ran her fingers through C.J.'s blonde hair that flowed through her fingers like water. Still aroused, she dropped her hand under the comforter to brush lightly against C.J.'s breast. She looked down at Dani and smiled.

"Hey," C.J. said.

"Hey." Dani flicked her thumb back and forth against C.J.'s nipple.

"It's okay, Dani, you don't have to—"

Dani pressed her fingers against C.J.'s lips. "Shh." She eased her hand below the comforter again and captured C.J.'s breast.

"Dani—"

Dani softly kissed away her protests. The kiss intensified as Dani pulled aside the comforter and trailed kisses to C.J.'s neck and down to her breast. She captured C.J.'s nipple with her mouth. C.J. arched her back in response.

Dani moved so she could position herself on top of C.J. and felt C.J.'s nipples harden against hers. With the heat radiating between C.J.'s legs, Dani pushed C.J.'s legs apart with her knee. She lightly caressed C.J.'s body with her fingertips as her hand dipped even lower. Dani pushed her palm into her wetness and thrust her fingers inside. C.J. raised her hips to arch even more against Dani's hand.

Dani wanted to hear C.J. cry out with pleasure just as Dani had. She lowered her mouth to C.J.'s and kissed her hard. She kissed C.J.'s chest until she reached her breasts and took turns sucking on each nipple while still pushing deep inside of her. C.J. let out a low moan. Dani smiled against her breast as she continued to move her hand, stroked C.J.'s wet folds, and delved as deep as she could inside. Feeling the beginning throbbing of C.J.'s release, Dani pushed hard while she thumbed C.J.'s clit.

"Oh, God!" C.J. tensed as she climaxed.

Dani kissed her way back up to C.J.'s mouth. She lay next to

C.J., who had one arm draped across her eyes. The other hand clutched the comforter wadded up between them. Dani placed a kiss on C.J.'s, cheek, surprised when her lips touched wetness. Dani reached up and gently pulled C.J.'s arm away from her face.

"Hey, are you okay?" Dani whispered.

C.J. drew in a breath. "Yeah." She wiped her eyes. "It's been so long since anyone has made love to me like that."

Dani caressed C.J.'s face. "You deserve to feel like this again, C.J."

The light filtering in from the streetlight outside the apartment captured the sudden distance in C.J.'s eyes. One minute, C.J.'s blue eyes were clear and the next, as Dani had uttered her words, they were like a dark cloud drifting across the sun.

"Hey." She brushed her fingers through C.J.'s hair again. "Hey, where are you?"

C.J. gave her a weak smile. "I'm here."

"No. You're somewhere far away."

C.J. sat up, and Dani joined her. C.J. leaned over and gave Dani a quick kiss on the cheek. "Really. I'm fine." A shiver ran through Dani's body. "Cold?" C.J. asked, just like the very first time she'd made love to Dani. She pulled the crumpled comforter from between them and threw it over their bodies.

Yes, Dani felt a chill, but it wasn't from the room being cool. She laid her head on C.J.'s shoulder and neither spoke for several minutes. C.J.'s fingers lightly brushed Dani's arm, but it didn't feel like an affectionate thing—more of an absentminded gesture.

Silence enveloped the room. It pressed down on Dani, so much so that she lifted her hand to her chest as she tried to catch her breath.

"You all right?" C.J. asked.

Dani pulled out from under C.J.'s arm. She felt the need to leave, just as she had before.

"You're going?"

Dani nodded. She got up and dressed in almost the same hurry as she had the last time. She turned to C.J., and she knew she needed to say something.

"You're going to have to let me in sometime, C.J.," she said softly.

C.J. didn't respond. Dani was to the front door when she heard

C.J.'s footsteps behind her. C.J. stood in the doorway of the bedroom, wrapped in the comforter. Dani had no more words. She opened the door and left.

Chapter 13

Frodo yanked hard on his leash. He spotted a squirrel that raced ahead of them and scampered up a tree. Frodo stood at the bottom, his tail pointed straight up in the air.

"Trust me, Frodo, he's not coming back down." The squirrel chattered at them, scolding Frodo. *If this were a Looney Tunes' cartoon, an acorn would fly out of the tree and hit Frodo square on the head.* She laughed to herself as the image came to mind.

At least I'm laughing about something, she thought, when Frodo gave up his quest. It was early Sunday morning and two weeks since she'd left C.J.'s apartment. C.J. had traveled last week to Nashville to play her songs for the executives from Different Drummer. The Atlanta gay newspaper heralded this week as the end of her run at Carl's Cavern. The announcement also mentioned C.J.'s signing with Different Drummer and that she would head out of Francis to record her first album in Nashville.

They continued their walk down the street. The days grew hotter and hotter with each passing day in May. Patty, the teenager Dani hired for the summer months to walk Frodo during the day while Dani was at the bookstore, would start working after the last week of school.

They made their way over to the bark park so Frodo could roam free awhile. As they approached the park, Dani's pace slowed. She spotted the blonde cocker spaniel first. Liz, dressed in shorts and a tank top, sat nearby on a bench as she read a book.

Liz looked up from her book. Dani didn't know what to do. It would be rude to walk away, but at the same time, she wasn't sure if Liz would want to talk to her.

Relief flooded Dani when Liz waved at her and smiled. Dani didn't even realize she had been holding her breath until she exhaled after Liz's gesture. Frodo was still investigating the ground where they stood, but then he spotted Liz and Melanie. In no time, he was in his sled dog mode, yanking Dani toward the enclosed area.

Dani opened the gate and closed it. She reached down and unhooked Frodo from his leash. He made a beeline for Melanie, greeted her with a perfunctory sniff, and sprinted over to Liz. Before Dani could make it over there, he jumped up on the bench and licked Liz's face several times.

"I'm so sorry, Liz. He sometimes doesn't have manners."

Liz giggled as Frodo licked her face again. "Please, Dani. He's such a sweet dog."

Dani stood there awkwardly. She was afraid to push Frodo down because she didn't know if Liz would want Dani sitting next to her on the bench. Instead, Liz pushed Frodo to the ground. She gave him another scratch behind the ears. He flew off in the other direction after Melanie.

Liz patted the bench. "Please sit down."

Dani joined her on the bench. She ran her hands over her baggy denim shorts.

Liz set her book aside. "How have you been?"

Dani looked away. Anywhere but at those eyes, she thought. "I've been okay. How are things for you?" She kept her attention on the dogs.

"Good. Things have been good. I saw where C.J. is finishing up this week at Carl's and headed for Nashville."

Dani nodded.

"How are things between the two of you?"

"I'm not sure. We haven't talked in a couple of weeks."

"Oh, Dani, I'm sorry to hear that. Are you okay?" Liz touched her arm.

As always, a feeling of warmth came over Dani. She stared down at her sneakers, but the compassion in Liz's voice made her turn back to Liz.

"I think so," Dani said. "To be honest, I'm not sure." She paused, gathering her thoughts. "I just feel mixed up. Have you ever felt like that? Where everything seems to be puttering along nicely in your life, then something comes along to send it all off kilter?"

Liz stiffened beside her. Her expression changed, and a sad

smile crept across her lips.

Wondering if Liz might be thinking about her, Dani felt her face flush. "I'm sorry. I didn't mean—"

"It's okay, Dani. Believe it or not, I know what you're feeling." She stared at Melanie and Frodo as they frolicked in front of them.

"Liz, I—"

Liz squeezed her arm to interrupt her. "Why don't we just leave it there?" At that moment, Melanie ran over to sit in front of Liz. Liz reached down and petted Melanie. "We'd better go," she said in a soft voice. She stood and hooked Melanie's leash back on her collar.

"I didn't mean to upset you." Dani pushed herself off the bench to stand in front of her.

"You didn't. I only wish the best for you, Dani." Liz walked away in a hurry—almost running.

Frodo sat down beside Dani. He looked up at her then at Liz and Melanie who were almost at the corner. It was like he was telling her, "Go after her, Mommy. What's wrong with you?"

Dani shook her head. "No, buddy. I think I've done enough damage."

As they began their walk back home, she vaguely wondered if there would ever be a time when Liz Springer would be walking toward her and not away.

* * *

Dani taped the small poster that announced a future author reading and signing. The woman was one of Dani's favorite lesfic romance authors, and Dani looked forward to her visit. She gazed out of the window of the front door for several minutes until Tina interrupted her daydreaming.

"See anything new out there in Francis?"

Dani glanced over her shoulder at Tina who was at the counter straightening up postcard announcements.

"Nope. Still looks the same."

"Glad we're in here, though. The days are starting to get hotter." Tina stacked the last of the announcements of upcoming events and joined her at the door. She pushed the bill of her cap up, crossed her arms, and rocked back on her heels. "So."

Dani waited for more, but Tina seemed ready to outlast her. "So."

"You going to make me ask? You haven't talked about the woman for the past couple of weeks."

Dani sighed. "That's because I haven't heard from her for the past couple of weeks."

"What's up with that?"

Dani walked back to the counter and sat on one of the stools. She fiddled with a postcard and tried to convince herself it was the most fascinating information in the history of mankind.

Tina snatched it from her hands and slapped it back on top of the stack. "Dani?"

Dani took another breath before telling Tina about the last night she'd spent with C.J. James, including the cold brushoff before Dani left.

"Damn. What is it with her?"

"I never told you this because I thought it was C.J.'s business, but C.J. lost a lover to cancer four years ago. She was only twenty-two."

Tina let out a low whistle. "That had to be rough, especially with her partner being that young. Well, that explains some things."

They remained quiet for a while.

"I think you're going to have to talk to her," Tina said.

"What?" Dani couldn't believe that Tina, of all people, was suggesting she talk to C.J.

"You need to find out where your true feelings lie, and the only way you can do that is to talk to C.J. To get an understanding of where she's coming from. You can't just let her leave for Nashville without seeing you again."

"She's had plenty of opportunity to come in here or to call me."

"True. But maybe she's a little embarrassed."

Dani gave her a skeptical look.

Tina threw her hands up. "Hell, I don't know. I'm grasping at straws. I'd think you'd follow my advice considering how I feel about her. It takes a lot for me to say this shit."

Dani chuckled despite the seriousness of the conversation. "I love your way with words."

"No one ever accused me of being eloquent. But no one has ever accused me of being dishonest, either."

Dani thought back to that night and what preceded the lovemaking. "There's something I didn't tell you."

"Yeah?"

"She wrote a song for me."

"Wow. Even I have to say that's pretty romantic. I'll bite. What's the name of the song?"

"'Dani's Eyes.'"

"Definitely romantic." Tina made a show of leaning over the counter and staring hard at Dani. "I guess they're worthy of a song."

Dani smacked her arm. "Stop."

"All right. Yet another reason to swallow your pride and head on over to Carl's this week before she closes out Saturday night. Look at it this way. It can't hurt."

"I guess not." The front door's bell jingled as a customer walked in. That was their cue to stop the personal talk. They greeted the woman with hellos. As she watched the woman head over to the best-selling lesbian romances, Dani made a decision. She'd go see C.J. Wednesday.

* * *

Dani pushed through the door to Carl's Wednesday afternoon when she knew C.J. would be rehearsing.

"Hey, stranger," Carl said when he saw her enter. He was moving tables back into place where customers had pushed them together the night before.

"Hey, Carl."

"Get you anything?"

"Nah. I'm good. Is—"

"Yeah, C.J.'s here. I think she's in the back. She should be out shortly."

"Do you mind if I take a seat?"

"Of course not." He went back to rearranging the tables.

A few minutes later, C.J., wearing a worn, gray Cincinnati Reds T-shirt and a pair of baggy, red shorts, walked onto stage. She grabbed her guitar and started strumming. She finally saw Dani. Her face registered surprise, which Dani thought she quickly tried to cover. "Hey, Dani." She set the guitar aside and jumped down from the stage to sit with her.

They stared at each other, not speaking for a while.

C.J. said, "I figured I might be the last person you'd want to see, which is why I've not called the past couple of weeks." She ran her fingers through her hair, and each strand magically fell back into place. "I don't know what to do when someone gets close to me and cracks my shell, you know?"

Dani let her continue.

"Which you've done a splendid job of by the way."

"C.J., you only get so many free passes on this. Using the 'I don't know what to do when someone gets close' excuse only goes so far. It's not fair."

"I never meant to hurt you."

"Well, you did." Dani was surprised at her own honesty, but it felt good to speak her mind.

"I'll try, Dani. Just give me a chance, okay?"

Dani felt the same hesitation grip her body as it had before. C.J. interrupted her thoughts.

"I'm leaving for Nashville Saturday after the show. Come with me."

Dani sat back in her chair. She wasn't expecting this. "C.J., I—"

"Please hear me out. I need to get up there and find a place to stay. It looks like I'll be there for a year or so. The good thing is, I have these songs ready to go. They've already said they're going to release one cut to the alternative rock stations just to get some interest going. You know, one of those, 'here's blah, blah, blah from C.J. James's debut album that will be in the stores on—'" C.J. held up her hands dramatically and made quotation marks in the air with her fingers. "Insert the date."

Dani laughed nervously. "Yeah, I know what you mean." She paused. "But you'll have your hands full cutting that album. They'll have you performing around Nashville, too. I just know it."

"That doesn't mean that I don't want you there with me."

Dani hesitated as she thought of another excuse. "Besides that, the summer is our busiest time of the year. I can't go off and leave Tina with the store all by herself."

It was C.J.'s turn to lean back in her chair. "Okay, okay. I get the picture." She sat forward again suddenly. "At least come up for a weekend. You can do that, can't you?"

Dani thought about it. She tried to remember what she had going on in the coming weeks.

"I may be able to come in July. Let me check the calendar at the office."

"July?" C.J. asked, clearly disappointed.

"I'm sorry. That's the best I can do. I have a business to run."

"Okay. As long as I get to have time with you, that's cool with me." C.J. rapped her knuckles on the table. "Well, I need to rehearse for tonight. You're welcome to stay and listen."

Dani stood up. "I should get back to the store. Tina needs a break."

C.J. came around the table to give Dani a hug. It was the warmest embrace she'd ever given Dani.

"See you tonight? I mean, you'll be here tonight, right?" C.J. looked like she was ready to pounce on Dani if she said no.

"We have extended hours tonight and tomorrow night at the store, but I'll be here Friday and Saturday."

C.J. smiled. "Great. That sounds great." She hugged Dani again before Dani left the bar.

Chapter 14

Liz plopped down at the picnic table across from her sister Laurie. They were enjoying a family barbeque. The men congregated around the grill like some sort of throwback to the days of the cavemen. Her nieces and nephews—all five of them—ran around the spacious backyard in a weird alternative baseball game. Liz was still trying to figure it out when Lacey sat down next to her.

Liz motioned at the kids. "What are they doing?"

"Oh that? It's a game my Tucker made up," Laurie said. "It's called 'ballbase.'"

"Ballbase?"

"Yeah. Watch them. They hit the whiffle ball and run in the opposite direction. Third base is now first and first is third."

So far, in the few minutes Liz had watched the kids, only the three boys were the ones pitching and hitting. The two girls were relegated to the field.

"Why are Tucker, Tanner, and Eric the only ones allowed to hit and pitch?"

"Why do you think?" Laurie said. When Liz didn't answer fast enough, Lacey cut in.

"Because they're boys, silly."

"Please tell me you don't agree with that. I've seen plenty of girls hit the snot out of the ball when I played softball in high school."

Lacey crunched down on a potato chip. "Nah. I don't agree with it. This is called keeping the peace."

"And you're okay with your two girls being shoved out into the outfield." Liz glanced over at them. Lacey's youngest, six-year-old Linda, tugged her cap down lower over her eyes and stuck her tongue out as the ball was hit to her. She was about to catch it when Tucker ran over from the "pitcher's mound" and cut in front of her to catch

                    Chris Paynter

the ball. "Look at that. They won't even let them catch the ball." She pointed emphatically at the kids. "That is why I never play co-ed softball. Guys are impossible to play with. They let their egos lead them around."

Laurie shrugged. "At least it's better than something else leading them around."

Lacey snorted out her drink of Pepsi. "So, so true. As is unfortunately the case the older they get."

"God, I'm so glad I'm a lesbian," Liz said.

Laurie, who, along with Lacey, favored their father with her blonde hair and blue eyes, got a dreamy look on her face. "I might even take a trip to the dark side for that singer at Carl's."

Liz sputtered on her iced tea. Lacey patted her back. "You okay there, baby sis?"

Liz dabbed at her mouth with her napkin. She glared at Laurie. "Don't go saying stuff like that when my mouth is full of liquid."

"Have you seen her? I know you don't go out much, but daaamn." Laurie fanned her face. "I went with my best friend one night to see what all the fuss was about." She leaned in closer and said in a hushed tone, "I think all the women in there were creaming in their jeans."

Lacey hooted and pointed at Liz. "Oh, my God. I wish you could see your face."

Liz's cheeks heated up even more. Not only did she not want to have this conversation about C.J. James, she especially didn't want to have it with her two straight sisters.

"I went once," she muttered.

"And?" Laurie asked. "Damn, Liz. You had to think she was hot."

"Yes, she's attractive, but she also reminds me of my ex. If you remember, that's not a good thing." Liz thought of Dani Roberts. "Besides..."

Her sisters waited for her to continue. Lacey smacked her arm. "Besides what?"

"She's seeing a client of mine." Liz pushed the condensation off her glass of iced tea. "I can't help but think Dani might get her heart broken."

"Dani?" Lacey asked.

"My client. Dani Roberts. She owns the lesbian-feminist bookstore in town."

"Oh, yeah. I've actually gone in there to check it out before," Lacey said. "She has a nice selection of kids' books, too. There's a whole separate children's section. I think it's cool she doesn't just cater to the LG... LGB..."

Liz came to her rescue. "LGBTQ."

"Good Lord, I don't know how y'all remember that."

"Why are you so worried about this Dani? Isn't she a big girl?" Laurie said. She grinned. "Besides, like I said, I can see the attraction to taking a ride on the C.J. James train."

Liz's mouth dropped open. "Have you been turned into one of those pod people?" She made a show at staring up at the sky. "I don't see the mother ship, but it can always be hovering nearby."

"Pod people?"

"You know? From *Invasion of the Body Snatchers*? You're an alien, aren't you? Who's replaced my real sister?"

"Very funny. What can I say? I've been streaming *The L Word*. It's rather fascinating. Besides, it looks like y'all have way better sex than we do."

Lacey burst out laughing. "Amen, sister!" She high-fived Laurie over the table.

After their cackling subsided to a few snickers, Laurie said, "If I didn't know any better, I'd say you like Dani."

"What?" Liz stiffened. "What makes you say that?"

Lacey pointed at her. "For one, you've got that far-away look in your eyes like when you were mooning over Molly Ann Franklin in high school. You followed her around like a lost puppy for almost a year."

Liz stabbed at her ice with her straw. "So? That doesn't mean anything."

Liz didn't miss the exchanged glance Laurie and Lacey shared. "Hey, it's okay, Liz," Laurie said as she squeezed Liz's arm. "Don't you think it's time you at least got out there again?"

"If by 'out there,' you mean dating, I'll get out there when I damn well please." She was still stabbing at her ice when a silence settled over the table. Her sisters wouldn't meet her eyes. "What?" A sudden dread hit her stomach. "Oh, no. Please don't tell me you're trying to set me up with someone."

"Welll..." Lacey tipped her head back and forth. "It's not us."

"Then who?" Liz snapped. Their mother's voice cut into their conversation.

"You girls. Always hiding away, gossiping." Ginny, their mother, was heading toward their table, but she wasn't alone. A tall woman with short blonde hair accompanied her. If the muscles in her legs were any indication, she looked like an athlete, maybe a runner.

As soon as they reached the picnic table, Lacey and Laurie popped up like bobbers in a lake after a bite from a big bass.

"We're going over to talk to the men," Lacey said.

"Yeah, I think they need some help on those burgers." As they walked away, now behind Ginny and the woman, Laurie pointed at the woman and gave a thumbs-up. Liz glared at her.

"Liz, honey, this is Michelle Richards. She just moved into the Coopers' old place down the street. She's from Atlanta and hasn't made a lot of friends yet."

So, you thought you'd introduce her to your lesbian daughter to welcome her into the gayborhood. Liz loved her mother, but sometimes... She realized she hadn't said anything. She rose halfway off the bench and held out her hand.

"Hi, it's nice to meet you, Michelle."

With that, Ginny made her move. "I'll let you girls get acquainted." As she left, she, too, offered encouragement by way of an inclination of her head toward Michelle and a wink.

I'm going to kill her. After I kill her, I'm going to kill my sisters. It'll just leave me and Dad, but hey, we can make do. I'll even help raise the kids. Michelle's voice cut in to her murderous thoughts.

"Something tells me you had no clue I'd be here," Michelle said with a sheepish grin as she sat across from Liz.

Liz was about to lie but decided for honesty. "No clue."

"Look, if it makes you uncomfortable, I can mosey back to my house. I have a frozen dinner I can pop into the microwave." Michelle's blue eyes twinkled in the sunlight. "But I have to say, those burgers sure do smell wonderful."

Liz couldn't help it. She laughed. "I'd hate to have you suffer at home with, what? A Marie Callender's lasagna?"

Michelle feigned surprise with her hand clasped to her chest.

"How did you know? Do I look like a Marie Callender kind of girl to you?"

At least Michelle had a sense of humor. She was also easy on the eyes. Oh, what the hell, Liz thought. It's not going to hurt to at least talk to her.

Which is what they did for the next half hour until the burgers and hotdogs were ready. As Lacey, Laurie, and their husbands settled at the other picnic table, her parents, Ginny and Bruce, sat down with Liz and Michelle. The kids had their own card table set up close to their parents' picnic table. Liz let her mother draw out more information about Michelle, a pediatrician at the local hospital. Liz kept mostly quiet and allowed her mother to dominate the conversation. After eating, Michelle stood up to help clear the table.

Ginny stopped her with a hand to her shoulder. "Oh, no. You and Liz visit. I've got this."

Ginny and Bruce left, and Michelle waggled her eyebrows at Liz. "Not real subtle, huh?"

"Not too much, no."

Michelle glanced at her watch. "Damn. I hate to have to eat and run, but I need to take care of Brutus."

"Brutus?"

"My Great Dane."

Okay. A dog person. That's another plus, Liz thought.

"Listen," Michelle said, "I was thinking, well, if you want, I mean—"

"It's okay. You can ask."

"There's a singer at Carl's. Her last night is tonight before she heads out of town. I've heard good things about her and wondered if you'd like to go." Michelle stopped. "Or maybe not."

Liz tried to wipe away what she was sure was a discouraging look from her face. "I'm sorry. You're right. She's quite good."

"But..."

Liz made a quick decision to shove aside her discomfort at seeing C.J., and more than likely Dani, tonight at Carl's. "I'd love to go." Liz couldn't believe she was able to utter those words with any conviction, but Michelle seemed to believe her.

"Great. I don't know where you live, but I'd be happy to pick you up if you want to give me your address."

"Why don't we just meet up there? It'd be easier that way. I live within walking distance of the club."

"All right. Six okay? I think she starts at seven-thirty. We might at least beat some of the crowd."

Liz swallowed the last of her doubt and said, "See you there at six."

* * *

Dani pulled a short-sleeved, Cincinnati Reds T-shirt over her head and yanked on a pair of jeans. She sat down and slipped on her old sneakers. After she tied the last knot, she stood and checked herself in the mirror. She ran her fingers through her hair. The little bit of gray that showed through blended in nicely with the darker brown.

At the door with Frodo hot on her heals, she bent down and stroked behind his ears. "Mommy will be home in a few hours." His ears flattened to his head and his tail drooped. "Please don't give me that, 'how could you be so horrible?' look. I won't be out all night. Take a long nap, and I'll be home."

Dani stood at her car and debated about driving. She craned her neck to look up at the night sky, and the view took her breath away. "Okay, that makes up my mind for me."

As she walked, she gazed skyward as much as possible, picking out the constellations her dad had taught her as a kid back home in Peabody. They always had a spectacular view of the starlit sky. For hours one night, they sat in their backyard on a blanket with Dani's brother, counting falling stars. Dani smiled at the memory. Sometimes, small towns really beat the big city life.

As expected, the place was packed when she entered Carl's Cavern—so much so that Dani didn't think she'd find a table. Barb motioned her over to the bar.

"Hey, Dani. C.J. said to let you know she reserved a table for you up front."

"Cool. I thought I was going to be stuck standing in the back." There was a line of women against the back wall. Dani knew the place had to be at capacity or close to it.

Barb plopped a Heineken in front of her without asking. "Here.

On me as always."

"Thanks, Barb."

Dani made her way around the tables and spotted the empty one next to the stage. It had a card on it that said "Reserved." One chair remained. Dani took her seat and ignored the stares of the women around her.

She sipped her beer slowly as always but found she was scanning the room. Suddenly, it hit her—she was searching for Liz. Dani tried to stop herself, but still managed to peek behind the pole where Liz sat with her colleagues that one night. The table was full of other women who appeared to be "two sheets to the wind," as her father would say.

Carl breezed by Dani and jumped up on the stage.

"Ladies! Tonight Ms. C.J. James is giving her last performance in Francis before heading to Music City."

The whole room groaned. A few lusty "boos" rang out, then laughter.

"I know, I know. I'm disappointed, too, but this is a fantastic opportunity for C.J. She signed with Different Drummer Records and will cut her debut album with them later this year."

The place erupted in cheers.

"So now, without further ado." He smiled. "I've always wanted to say that, by the way." Everyone laughed. He motioned dramatically to the side of the stage. "I give you Cincinnati's own and now Francis, Georgia's, adopted daughter, C.J. James."

C.J. entered to a standing ovation. Dani rose to her feet with everyone in the bar. C.J. looked genuinely touched. She bowed low and raised her hands to quiet the place, but the ovation continued. She walked to the mic.

"Please, please. You're too kind. Thank you so much." She again motioned for everyone to sit down. "Thank you." Everyone settled into their seats. C.J. reached for her twelve-string acoustic and placed the pill bottle on her finger. She plugged in the guitar. When she turned around, she paused and looked pointedly at Dani. She nodded ever-so-slightly and gave Dani a smile.

Dani returned the smile with a nod and a tip of her bottle of beer. If women hadn't been staring at her before, they sure as hell were now.

"How 'bout some blues?" C.J. shouted.

Applause and whistles rang out in the room.

C.J. played with a gusto Dani hadn't seen before now. She ripped through some other fast tunes then settled down to slower acoustic playing. One song was entirely musical. It was beautiful.

Eventually it was time for a break. The houselights went up, and C.J. left the stage. Dani decided to get another beer and made it back to the bar.

"She sounds fantastic tonight, doesn't she?" Barb asked as she set another Heineken in front of Dani.

"She sure does."

Barb leaned over. "So how are you two?"

"I think we're okay. C.J. asked me to join her in Nashville. I told her I'd try to come up and visit on a weekend later this summer."

"What's wrong? You don't seem too excited about the prospect. She invited you, Dani. That says something." Someone shouted for Barb from the other end of the bar. As Barb walked away, she motioned toward Dani's table. "I think you can go back there now."

Dani turned and saw C.J. had pulled up a chair. Women held out CDs for autographs. Dani grabbed her beer and maneuvered her way through the crowd. She got stuck behind a group of women who didn't seem in a hurry to break up their conversation. Dani was about to ask them to let her through when she spotted Liz seated at a table with a tall blonde. Liz laughed at something the blonde said, but then she locked eyes with Dani. The blonde must have noticed because she turned around.

Fuck.

Liz gave Dani a small wave and a smile. "Hi, Dani."

Dani's feet felt like lead as she stepped up to their table. "Hi, Liz."

The other woman stuck out her hand. "Michelle Richards."

Dani took it and tried not to wince at the bone-crunching grip. "Dani Roberts."

"Oh, hey. You own that bookstore, don't you?"

"Yes."

"Love that place. It reminds me of Charis in Atlanta."

"Thank you. That's quite a compliment." Dani felt Liz's gaze and glanced over. "Enjoying the show?"

"I don't know about Liz, but I think she's freaking awesome. I can see why she got signed to a Nashville contract."

Dani waited for Liz's response.

"She's a great musician and singer. I'm sure she'll be a big success."

Dani noticed the women had scattered so she could get to her seat. "I'd better go." She motioned toward the table.

Liz focused on C.J. who was still signing autographs. "Yeah, you'd better."

Michelle looked back and forth between them and raised her eyebrows at Liz.

"Nice meeting you, Michelle. Liz, great seeing you as always."

Liz gave her a tight smile. Dani made an abrupt getaway, trying to shake off the image of Liz with another woman. Which she realized was a totally immature reaction considering she was about to sit down with C.J.

"I need to take a break, if you don't mind," C.J. said to the women as Dani got within earshot. "I'll be available after the show." She handed a signed copy of the CD that Dani first stocked at her shop to the last woman. The woman stared at C.J. with huge puppy dog eyes. She lingered for a few seconds more before walking away with her friends.

"I see you still have it," Dani said, taking her seat.

"Stop it." C.J. chuckled.

"How are you feeling? Excited about leaving for Nashville?"

"Excited and scared at the same time." C.J. took a drink of her bottled water. "It's a big step for me."

"It is, but you're ready whether you realize it or not. You sound fucking awesome tonight, C.J."

"Thanks."

They talked about C.J.'s plans when she got to Nashville, about her good relationship with David Morgenson. "He's really a great guy. He's been very fair about the contract thing, too."

Before they knew it, the houselights blinked on and off.

"That's my cue." C.J. stood, but before she walked away, she leaned over and brushed Dani's lips with hers. "It really meant a lot to me to have you here tonight," she whispered. She kissed Dani again and hopped back on stage.

Dani felt her face redden with the hundreds of eyes focused on her. She kept her head down, staring at her beer. Carl's voice brought Dani out of her reverie.

"All right. One last time, ladies. Give it up for C.J. James!"

Again, the place erupted with thunderous applause.

"Thanks, everybody. It's been such a privilege to play here the past seven weeks. And I want to especially thank Mr. Carl Griffith for everything he's done for me here. I wouldn't be heading to Nashville if it weren't for his generosity in allowing me to extend my stay. Another artist had to cancel, but I know there were plenty of other capable artists that he could've called to fill the weeks. The fact that he wanted me to stay longer will never, ever be forgotten." She held up her bottled water. "Carl, I know this isn't a shot of whiskey, but it means just as much to me as an alcohol salute. Thank you, thank you, thank you." She bowed to Carl who stood in the back of the bar. He returned the gesture.

C.J. sat down on her stool and began her second set. Dani let the music flow over her. She breathed in the sound like it was one of the aromatic lilac bushes along her walks with Frodo. It was soothing. It was liquid.

Eventually, C.J. wound down to her last song of the night. She paused before looking directly at Dani. "I want to share with you a special song for a very special lady. It's called 'Dani's Eyes.'"

She wrote her a frigging song, Liz thought. A *song*. How the hell can you compete with that? Liz took a long drink from her vodka tonic.

Michelle, who had moved her chair to sit next to Liz, leaned in to her ear. "You feeling all right? You're a little pale."

"Fine. I'm fine." Liz finished off her drink in one big gulp. *Just peachy.*

She finished the song, Dani thought as her face instantly flushed. Like the first time Dani had heard it, she didn't know quite how to react. Maybe some of it was because she didn't think she was worthy of a song. Or maybe some of it was because she didn't think her relationship with C.J. was worthy of a song. She tried to shake off those thoughts.

The first chords gently wafted over the hushed room as C.J. sang the lyrics, almost like a whisper. She closed her eyes when she began, and when she opened them, she only looked down at her guitar as her fingers caressed the strings like a lover. She sang the last lines:

We touched and I felt something deep inside.
What I'd lost had been found in Dani's eyes.
Yes, what I'd lost had been found in Dani's eyes.

When she finished, at first no one clapped. Dani ventured a glance at the women around her. Some were wiping away tears. Others simply sat there with awestruck expressions. Then, the first person began applauding in the back of the room. One by one, everyone joined in and rose to their feet. The sound was deafening.

C.J. smiled and stood. She stepped away from her stool and bowed. The applause continued and a chant began, "C.J.! C.J.! C.J.!"

C.J. leaned into the microphone. "Thank you, everyone. Thank you so, so much. God bless you." She waved to the crowd, brought her hand to her lips, and blew Dani a kiss before walking off the stage.

Everyone continued to clap. C.J. stepped out on the stage again, gave a big wave, and walked backstage. The houselights came up. Some shuffled toward the door, others seemed like they were hanging around until later.

Dani took her last sip of beer as she tried to recover from hearing that song. She felt a hand on her shoulder and turned to see Carl.

"C.J. asked you to come backstage."

She tapped on the door and entered the backstage room. "Hey, C.J., it's me."

"Come on in, Dani."

Dani walked in as C.J. pulled on a fresh T-shirt. She ran her fingers through her blonde hair. Dani still didn't know why she made the effort. Her hair was never out of place.

"Great show."

C.J. gave her a hug. "I'm so glad you could make it tonight. You'll never know how much this means to me." She pulled back. "I wanted you to hear your song again, finished. I wanted everyone to hear your song."

"I didn't know what to do. I felt like everyone had shifted their attention over to my table."

"As they should." C.J. brushed back Dani's hair. "I'd love to have spent another night with you before I leave, but I have to pack up all my gear since I'm driving up tonight."

"Please tell me you're stopping along the way. It's ten now, and that's over a four-hour drive."

"Don't worry. I plan to crash in Chattanooga and head up early tomorrow. They want me there in the early afternoon. I figured it'd be better from Chattanooga. I'll at least be a little fresher." C.J. stepped forward and brushed her lips against Dani's. "I've enjoyed the time I've spent with you here. I'm sorry again about fucking up these past couple of weeks."

"You didn't—"

C.J. stopped her with a touch of her finger to Dani's lips. "We both know I did. I'd like to make it up to you in Nashville. You'll still come up, yes?"

"I'm not sure what weekend yet, but I'll definitely make it up to see you."

C.J. gave Dani another kiss. This one was much longer and a lot more passionate. She pulled out of the kiss and nipped at Dani's lower lip. "Take care. I'll see you soon."

"See you soon." Dani paused at the door and turned back one last time before taking her leave.

On her way out of the bar, Dani used every ounce of her willpower not to check out Liz and Michelle's table. She instead tried to focus on the fact she'd be visiting C.J. soon in Nashville.

"And that's a good thing," she said under her breath as she waved at Barb.

Chapter 15

"Yo! Darrryl! You're killin' my fantasy team, dude!" Barb bellowed from the stands at Turner Field. She was harassing Bip Monroe, the star third baseman for the Atlanta Braves, who swung a bat in the on-deck circle. Dani scrunched down into her seat a little more as Monroe looked their way. What was truly amazing was that a half smile crossed his lips. Bip Monroe never smiled.

"Darling, don't you think you need to let up a little?" Tina said. They were seated in the fourth row up from the Braves dugout. Barb wasn't hard to miss, either, in her red Braves T-shirt with the sleeves rolled up high on her arms and a blue Braves hat perched on her head. The T-shirt had Bip's name and number on the back.

"Oh, please. Daryl's cool with it. Aren't you Darryl?"

Dani moved down even more in her seat. If she crouched any farther, she'd end up on the hard concrete in front of her. When she attended her first game with Barb and Tina, she couldn't figure out who Barb was screaming at when she yelled out "Darryl!" Then she realized Bip Monroe's full name was Darryl Duane Monroe, Jr. After finding that out, Dani could understand why he went by the nickname.

Bip glanced their way. He returned to his task of applying more pine tar to his bat handle.

"Barb, you're too much," Tina muttered and took a drink of her beer.

Barb and Tina had decided that Dani needed to get "out." Barb purchased the tickets from a friend who couldn't make the game. The Braves were playing the Reds that night. Barb prodded Dani even more and told her at least the Braves were playing Dani's favorite team. Dani wore her Reds hat to give Barb a hard time.

"Tina, he's been on the disabled list twice already this season. I mean the man can hit, but only when he actually plays." Barb took a sip of her Coke.

"And yet you wear his T-shirt."

"So? I can still give him a hard time. Ain't that right, Darryl?" Barb shouted at him before he headed to the plate. He promptly hit a three-run home run. When he walked toward the dugout, Barb got off another parting shot. "See! I knew you had it in you, Bip!"

He chuckled as he headed down the dugout steps and received high fives from his teammates. *Only Barb can get away with this,* Dani thought. *If it'd been me, security would've hauled my ass out of here by now.*

"You're waiting until later next month to go up to Nashville?" Tina asked as she watched the play on the field.

Dani thought about her answer. Tina clapped when the Braves catcher smacked a single between the second baseman and shortstop to prolong the inning.

"I didn't want to tell you, because I figured what your reaction would be. Brenda McFarland called me. Remember her? My friend from New York?"

"The one who sold you the Gutenberg Bible?"

Dani laughed. "Yeah, she's the one." Dani cracked a peanut from its shell and munched on it. "There's a three-day conference in Nashville next weekend for feminist and lesbian bookstore owners, plus readers. She asked if I was going."

"Hello, Dani. How much more encouragement do you need to take the trip up north?"

"Don't worry. I'm calling her back tomorrow to let her know I'm interested. I need to make sure I can still register for the conference."

"They sell same-day registration to those things all the time, remember?" Tina nudged Barb who was busy eyeing a very toned and tanned blonde two rows down. "Did you hear that, honey?" Then she saw what had Barb's attention. Tina nudged her harder. "Do you think you could be any more obvious?"

Barb turned to her. "What?"

"You're freaking hopeless."

Barb gave Tina a wicked grin. "But I'm in love with you, my sweet."

"You're forgiven." Tina stuck her thumb in Dani's direction.

"Did you hear what she said?"

"No. I was, uh, preoccupied."

"She's going to Nashville next weekend."

"It's about time you took the plunge, Dani. How long has it been since you saw C.J.? Two weeks?"

"About that, yeah."

The Reds leadoff hitter lined a double to right center in the top of the inning. Dani cheered and ignored Barb's glare.

Tina changed the subject. "Did you know Monica started dating again?"

"No." Now that Dani thought about it, Monica hadn't been to the last poker night.

"Seems to be a super nice lady. She's very affectionate to Monica and treats her with respect. So far, she has the Tina Dewey Stamp of Approval. Now, if she starts screwing up, I won't be responsible for my actions."

"Don't worry," Dani said. "I'll join you in taking her to the woodshed if necessary."

Tina had just taken a drink of Coke and almost spit it out when she started laughing. "Good to know you're with me on this one, boss."

The game ended with the Braves on top 5-2. The women made the long trek to one of the far paying lots where Barb had parked her Explorer. Dani was reaching for the back-door handle when she heard Barb shout behind her.

"Aha! What do I do when I see one of these, hon?" Barb pointed at a bumper sticker on the Prius parked next to the Explorer.

Curious, Dani joined Barb and Tina as they stared down at the bumper sticker. Dani had seen these bumper stickers before, and they always set her teeth on edge. It consisted of a silhouette of a "boy" stick figure, a plus sign, and a "girl" stick figure, complete with a dress, followed by an equals sign, and the word "Marriage."

Tina rolled her eyes. "Oh, Lord."

Barb marched past Dani to the passenger side of the Explorer, keyed open the door, reached in, and pulled out a black Sharpie from the glove compartment. She promptly stomped back to the bumper of the Prius.

Tina peered around, nervously. "Hurry up if you're going to do it. I don't want some far-right nut job confronting us."

Dani laughed when she saw what Barb was doing. She'd quickly drawn a dress on the male stick figure.

Barb capped the Sharpie with a flourish. "There. Isn't that better?"

Tina grabbed her arm and pulled her toward their Explorer. "You made your point. A good one, I might add, but let's go."

They all piled in and quickly pulled out of their parking space.

"Barb, you are officially my hero," Dani said as she craned her neck to see if the Prius's owners had arrived.

"Aw, Dani. You say the nicest things."

On the drive home, Dani thought of her last conversation with C.J. the week before. C.J. told Dani that the record company booked her at Mickey's Place. The clan had made a few trips to Nashville, and they frequently hit Mickey's while they were in town. It was a lesbian nightclub but was also straight-friendly. Mickey, an older lesbian who had owned the place for over twenty years, was very influential in the Nashville music scene. A lot of lesbian artists, as well as straight female artists, got their big breaks there.

Dani hadn't heard from C.J. since last Wednesday, but she was sure C.J. was busy getting to learn the area and working on her recordings. She knew where C.J. was staying, but she wanted to surprise her at the nightclub first.

Dani leaned her head back on the seat. Although Barb had the air on full blast in the Explorer, she had cracked the moon roof open. They were on a state road now, and the lights from the city had long faded behind them. She took in the Georgia sky through the opening. If she could write a song, it would be about the stars of Georgia. She drifted off with one of C.J.'s tunes playing through her mind.

* * *

"You guys are sure you don't mind babysitting him?"

It was early Friday morning. Barb and Tina were over at her house watching Dani descend the stairs with her suitcase in tow. They had readily agreed to take Frodo home with them for the weekend and stopped by to pick him up.

"Would you please stop asking us that?" Barb said. "Does it look like we have a problem here?"

Dani set her suitcase down in the living room. Barb and Tina were perched on the couch with Frodo between them. They were petting him, and he looked like he was in heaven. He hadn't even come over to sniff the suitcase and didn't seem depressed about her leaving.

"Okay, I get your point."

Barb and Tina stood up and gave Dani a hug. They started out the door with Frodo.

"Hey, little man, don't you want to say goodbye to Mommy?" Dani asked.

Frodo stopped and turned. She could almost see him sigh before he sat down for Dani to pet him.

"I'm *so* sorry," Dani said with a laugh. "I swear when you stay with Barb and Tina, it's like I don't even exist." She leaned down to pet him, and he licked her hand. His eyes said, "Don't worry, Mom. These guys have it covered."

Barb lifted Frodo into the back of the Explorer. They hopped into the driver and passenger seats. Barb started the engine, and Tina powered down her window.

"You have a good time, Dani. Let us know when you get there."

"You'll be okay with the store over the weekend?"

"For the umpteenth time, yes," Tina said, this time with a little irritation.

"Sorry. I think I'm nervous."

"Nah. Never would've guessed."

"In answer to your question, of course I'll call when I get there. Take care of my little guy."

Tina waved as they pulled out of the driveway.

Dani double-checked her bag. She scrolled through her cell phone contacts to make sure she had Brenda's number and the hotel where they'd be staying. She was to call Brenda when she got close to Nashville. She had already entered the hotel address into her car's GPS system. Brenda still insisted she call as she got closer, because, as Brenda said, "Sometimes those GPS directions suck."

Dani grabbed a bottle of water from the refrigerator and headed out to her car. She opened the hatchback to the MINI Cooper and set her bag inside. As she backed out of the driveway, she smiled. She wasn't overly impulsive. Her last impulsive act was to close the shop on a Friday and drive with Barb and Tina to Macon for a blues concert. That was a year ago.

"Hope you're ready for me, C.J.," she said as she merged onto the Interstate.

Chapter 16

Traffic was always crazy around Nashville. During rush hour, it was especially horrendous. Dani had left at the right time from Francis, though. After her four-and-a-half-hour drive, she hit the outskirts of Nashville at ten Central Standard Time. Sometimes she loved Daylight Savings Time—especially when she gained an hour.

Traffic slowed enough in front of her that she could reach Brenda on the car's Bluetooth device.

"Made good time, huh?" Brenda asked in her strong New York accent.

"I'm just now entering Nashville." Dani told her where her GPS was directing her to make sure it jibed with Brenda's directions.

"What do you know? The GPS doesn't have you driving in circles. I'll be down in the lobby after you get your car valeted."

"See you in about thirty minutes." Dani ended the call and concentrated on the Exit signs.

After a semi almost ran her off the road, she swung off the Interstate and maneuvered the turns in the city to the Nashville Marriott at Vanderbilt University. She pulled up in the roundabout, and the heat slapped her in the face when she stepped out of the car. The valet hustled over to take her keys. Dani walked to the back of the car to grab her suitcase. She had a brief tussle over the bag with a bellhop. He relented when she practically shouted, "Thanks, but I've got it."

As she walked into the hotel, she heard someone holler from the other side of the opulent, marble-floored lobby.

"Roberts!"

Dressed in cargo shorts and a polo shirt, Brenda hurried to meet her. Five-two, if even that, she was in her early fifties with short gray hair. She gave Dani a tight hug.

"You look fantastic as always," Dani said as she held Brenda at arm's length.

"Why don't you get checked in, and I'll take you to brunch."

"Food sounds like the ticket." Dani picked up her suitcase and started for the front desk. After she obtained her key card and took her bag upstairs, she joined Brenda again in the lobby.

"There's a great place within walking distance that serves fantastic omelets," Brenda said as they left the hotel. "And it's not so far that we'll be puddles of goo before we get there."

"Good. Damn, I thought Atlanta was bad in June." She had to pick up her pace to keep up with her diminutive friend.

A wave of cool air rushed to greet them when they entered the restaurant.

"God, that's almost orgasmic," Brenda said under her breath.

After the hostess seated them and they had placed their orders, Brenda peppered Dani with questions. She asked about business at the store, about Dani's ex, and if Dani was dating anyone new. On the last question, Dani hesitated.

"Dish. You can't squirm your way out of this one."

Dani filled Brenda in on her relationship with C.J. and told her C.J. was recording in Nashville. "She's also performing at Mickey's Place tonight."

Brenda sat back in her bench. "Oh, I see. You're not simply here for the conference or to meet up with your old friend, Brenda. It's to vo-dee-o-dodo with your new girlfriend."

"Please don't give me a hard time. C.J. wanted me here with her sooner. I told her I didn't think I could visit until later this summer, but I managed to get away early. The conference is important and seeing you is important to me, too. I hope you know that."

"Oh, please. I was teasing." Brenda thanked the server after she brought their coffee. "What can you tell me about this Ms. James?"

Dani recounted how she first heard of C.J., ordered her CDs, and after a lunch outing, had started dating her.

"She's going places, Brenda. I think she'll make it regionally, but she just might make it nationally. The music business is a funny thing, though." Dani took a sip of coffee and changed the subject. "What time is the first meeting today?"

"Clever, Ms. Roberts, clever. We'll return to this topic again, I hope you know." Brenda pulled out paperwork from one of the side pockets of her cargo shorts. "Our first meeting isn't until one o'clock back at Room 3 at the hotel. We have plenty of time to catch up on everything."

Over their omelets, Brenda talked about Brooklyn and competing with other bookstores in her area. "It's not like Francis, Dani. It can get a bit ruthless, you know? More and more of the brick and mortar stores are closing in the city. Then there's Amazon. Good God. How do we compete with that, plus the other online ebook stores?"

"What about including a children's section in your store? That's worked for me. Or maybe add a small area for coffee and pastries. Please don't give up the business."

"I'm fine for now. I have enough traffic coming in daily. I'll give your other ideas consideration, though."

"We've been pretty lucky. There's another bookstore in town, but they sell mostly old books. Great guys, though." She thought about Phil and Ben and their ten-year-old golden retriever that greeted everyone who entered their store.

They finished their omelets, paid their bill, and walked back to the hotel.

"I'm going to take a shower and change," Dani said when they entered the lobby.

"I'll see you back here, and we'll head to the first panel discussion."

After meeting up again, they left for Room 3. God, it was nice seeing all of these women, Dani thought. Every size, shape, and color. It was empowering to know that each of these women either owned their own bookstore, no matter how big or how small, or were lesfic readers.

Brenda and Dani registered, entered the room, and took their seats. The first panel discussion was about the difficulties in maintaining a lesbian and feminist bookstore with the main brick and mortar stores closing. It was such a small niche in the book world anyway.

The rest of the afternoon proved to be just as interesting. It wound down around five-thirty. Dani and Brenda talked with a couple of the women as they left the building. They made quick introductions.

"Hey, some of us are heading over to Mickey's Place tonight to hear this new musician," the woman named Nikki said. "What was her name, Donna?" She turned to the woman who was her partner.

"C.J. James, I think," Donna answered.

Dani thought Brenda was about to say something about her relationship with C.J., so she nudged her. Brenda glanced at her and nodded slightly. Dani was glad she caught on that she didn't want the women to know that she and C.J. were dating.

"That sounds great," Brenda said. "What time are you going to be there?"

"I think she starts at eight," Donna said. "We thought we'd meet up at seven."

Brenda and Dani agreed. When they walked away, Brenda asked Dani if she would mind sharing the evening with others instead of being at the nightclub on her own.

"Nah. It's a surprise that I'm here this early anyway. I'll see C.J. after the show."

Brenda gave Dani a wicked grin. "Yeah, I just bet you will."

Dani playfully shoved Brenda as they stepped into the elevator.

Chapter 17

Dani decided to dress up a bit for the show. She pulled a pair of black slacks off the hanger, laid them on the bed, and flipped through her dress shirts. Indecisive at home, she brought three with her. *You'd think this was a first date,* she thought. She settled on a white cotton shirt with black pinstripes. She threaded a thin, black belt through her pants loops and finished the outfit with her black half-boots.

After running gel through her hair, she left the hotel room for the elevator to meet Brenda in the lobby. Brenda, who stood by the entrance, had also dressed up in slacks and a cotton shirt.

"Hey, girl, you look spiffy," Dani said as she approached.

When Brenda turned, the expression on her face let Dani know she'd accomplished what she'd set out for in her appearance.

"Damn, woman, you look hot."

An elderly couple was walking nearby. Their jaws dropped when they overheard Brenda's exclamation. Brenda and Dani saw their reactions at the same time and burst out laughing.

"Guess they don't see too many lesbians where they come from," Brenda mumbled as they headed outside.

It didn't take long to hail a taxi. Mickey's Place was about a fifteen-minute drive. Well, the way the cabbie was zooming in and out of traffic, maybe five. On the way there, Brenda asked Dani to fill her in on C.J.'s music.

Women were lined up outside the club when the taxi stopped under the awning. Dani and Brenda walked to the back of the line until they heard Donna and Nikki shout at them. They motioned for Dani and Brenda to join them farther up in the line. Normally, Dani hated to cut in front of people. She always knew how she felt when a group of friends "held places" in line for their other friends. Tonight, however, she was thankful. She wanted to be able to grab a table in the club.

The doors opened. Dani and Brenda handed over the admission fee. It didn't take long at all for the tables toward the front to fill up, but they were able to get one in the middle of the club. When they sat down, Donna introduced everyone else. As always during mass introductions, the names went in one ear and out the other for Dani.

She ordered a beer, and Brenda ordered a Scotch and water. The hour seemed to drag, but eventually the houselights went down. The place erupted in cheers.

Mickey Cunningham made her way to the microphone in the center of the stage. Short and stocky with salt-and-pepper hair, she was dressed in a black suit with a white shirt and black string tie. And cowboy boots. It was Nashville, after all.

"Hey, everyone!" she boomed. She didn't really need the microphone. "If you haven't seen tonight's artist perform yet, you're in for a real treat. She hails from Cincinnati, O-hi-o, but we won't hold that against her." Laughter rang out in the club. "She recently signed with Different Drummer Records based right here in Music City. I'm excited she's with us. I know you will be, too, once you hear her fantastic voice and wicked gee-tar playin'. Ladies," she said as she put her hand over her eyes to peer out in the crowd, "and a few gentlemen." Everyone laughed again. "Please give a warm welcome to C.J. James." She swept her hand with a flourish to the side of the stage.

C.J. walked out with a big grin that showed off her dimples. She was dressed in skin-tight, black leather pants and a royal-blue shirt that shimmered in the spotlight, unbuttoned to show a lot of cleavage. The shirt brought out the blue in her eyes even more. She ran her fingers through her hair in what Dani now recognized was a nervous gesture. The hair again lay down as perfectly as if a hairdresser did a comb-through.

God, she looks great. Dani was mesmerized as if seeing her for the first time. She heard someone talking at their table but wasn't sure who was speaking until Brenda tapped her knee.

"You sure know how to pick 'em." Brenda's dark eyes twinkled in the light from the candle sitting in the middle of the table.

Three band members dressed in various degrees of disheveled clothing walked onto the stage behind C.J. Dani hadn't noticed until now that there were a set of drums, a bass, and a set of other electric guitars lined up on stage. C.J.'s acoustic guitars were also there.

To Dani's surprise, C.J. grabbed one of the electric guitars. She picked up her green glass pill bottle off the stool set up in the back of the stage.

"How y'all doin' tonight?" she shouted. "I learned to say 'y'all' down in a little town just outside of Atlanta that I'm sure a few of you ladies know about."

Someone shouted out, "Francis!"

"See? I knew I wouldn't be disappointed." C.J. adjusted the guitar strap. "If anyone saw me perform down there, you can see that I've gained a few musicians since then." She motioned to the guys behind her. "I never had the opportunity to play the way I'm going to play for you tonight. Not until I met up with these boys. But let's get started with some blues."

The place erupted in cheers. A few of the women stood up and whistled. C.J. placed the pill bottle on her left middle finger. She turned to the band. "One, two. A one, two, three and..." With that, she ripped into a hard and mean introduction to one of her songs, letting her finger with the pill bottle slide sensually across the neck of the guitar. It sounded completely different without the acoustic guitar and with the band. But damn, it was hot. No, it was better than hot. It was perfect.

The crowd roared their approval. C.J. grinned and continued to play. When she started singing, Dani again was lost.

Dani glanced at the women at their table. They were all clapping in time with the beat. C.J. played a few more hard blues tunes then switched over to her twelve-string acoustic guitar. The guys in the band strolled off the stage as C.J. pulled up the stool and sat down. She adjusted the mic to mouth level.

"Let's slow it down a little, shall we?" she said in her, low throaty voice. She started in on the song. A woman screamed in the back. "You like this, huh?" C.J. flashed her trademark smile and deep dimples. With the music drifting over the speakers to the far reaches of the club, Dani could almost feel the crowd release a collective sigh.

C.J. ran through five acoustic songs. The band eventually made it back on stage, and C.J. grabbed the electric guitar again.

"I'm going to do something different for you tonight, if you don't mind. I'd like to do a couple of cover songs of one of my idols. How does some Bonnie Raitt sound?" Everyone clapped in approval. She sang "Something to Talk About" and "Thing Called Love." After that, she immediately went into another of her own blues compositions. You could definitely hear Raitt's influence in C.J.'s music. While she played some of the solo sections of the songs with the spotlight focused solely on her, Dani watched the women at the front tables. Their enraptured expressions said everything.

When C.J. finished her last song and walked off the stage, the crowd rose to their feet in one motion. They clapped in unison until she came back out. She picked up her twelve-string acoustic and settled onto her stool.

"Thank you so much. Every crowd has been fantastic to me since I started playing here at Mickey's. Y'all are the best." Cheers greeted this last statement. She strummed the guitar a few times. "I want to finish tonight's show with a recent composition of mine. It'll be the first release from my debut album with Different Drummer. You should be hearing it soon on your alternative rock stations." C.J. grinned. "I like saying that—'alternative rock.' This is a special song to me. I hope you like it, too." She played the opening chords of the song. "It's called 'Dani's Eyes.'"

Dani felt Brenda's gaze, but she didn't shift her attention from the stage. She tried not to show emotion, not wanting any of the others to make the connection between her and the song.

When C.J. sang the last two lines, "What I'd lost had been found in Dani's eyes. Yes, what I'd lost had been found in Dani's eyes," the same thing happened here that happened at Carl's Cavern. The crowd sat in stunned silence. Then one by one, everyone rose to their feet, cheering and clapping. The sound was even more deafening here because of the size of the audience.

C.J. stood and gave a bow. "You've been great. Thank you so much. Thank you." She walked off and came back out for one last bow when Mickey called her onto the stage. Then she was gone.

Most started for the exits, but she noticed some of the women stayed close to the stage as if anticipating C.J. reappearing after freshening up.

"You're going backstage, right?" Brenda asked. It was more of a statement, though.

"I was going to try, but—"

"Try hell! We'll get you back there."

Brenda headed in the direction of the backstage area. A group of about ten women still lingered, excitedly talking about C.J. James in loud whispers. Two beefy bouncers guarded the hallway that must lead to the backstage area.

"Brenda, I don't—"

Brenda grabbed her arm and pulled her off to the side. "Look, I'm going to cause a scene." She kept her attention on the bouncers.

Dani almost started laughing.

"Stop it," Brenda hissed. "I'm serious. That's the only way you're going to get near her dressing room. Do you honestly think if you say, 'C.J.'s my girlfriend,' they'll believe you?"

"Okay," Dani reluctantly agreed. "But don't get yourself arrested, okay?"

Brenda patted her on the arm with a "watch this" look on her face. She staggered up to the front of the group of women. She then did a believable impression of a falling down drunk determined to see the "star."

When the bouncers converged on Brenda, Dani slipped past the group of women who also had turned their attention to Brenda. Dani wasn't exactly sure where to go as she walked down the dark hallway. She spotted a large star on a door. Can it be that simple? She tapped on the door. She heard some muffled voices on the other side. Eventually, she heard C.J. say, "Yeah?"

Dani put her hand on the doorknob and slowly opened the door. She poked her head inside... and immediately felt sick to her stomach.

C.J. fumbled with the buttons of her shirt with one hand while trying to pull her leather pants up with the other. Sitting on the dressing room table was a curvy blonde who either had a fake ID to get into the place or had just turned twenty-one. Dani was opting for the fake ID. She had a hard time focusing on her face, though, because she was bare breasted and only wearing a thong. Dani's brain was trying to figure out why she even bothered to wear the damn thing.

"Dani. You're here." C.J.'s voice brought Dani out of her fog. She turned back to C.J. who by now had gotten her clothes in order. The blonde jumped off the table and haphazardly dressed. She didn't even bother to put on her bra but pulled her shirt back on and quickly donned her jeans.

"Don't leave on my account," Dani said. The blonde brushed past her as she stood in the doorway.

"Dani, look—"

Dani cut her off. "I swear to God, C.J., if you're about to say, 'Look, I can explain,' just don't." Dani held up her hand like she was fending off a blow.

"I didn't know you'd be here this soon. You didn't call to tell me you were coming in."

Dani tried to let that logic settle in her brain. "So, what you're saying is, you needed advanced warning in case I caught you in the act?" Dani was so angry she felt tears prick the back of her eyes. Fuck. She wasn't going to cry. Not here. Not in front of C.J. James.

"Dani, I—"

Dani didn't want to hear anymore. She wanted to be anywhere but where she was standing at that moment in time. She made a move to leave. C.J. grabbed her arm.

Dani turned back to her and saw C.J.'s tears. It's a little late for that, Dani thought. Small, bright lights danced in front of her eyes. She felt like she was going to faint. She could only think to say, "And you sang that song. I can't believe you sang that song. God, C.J., all along, I wondered why I couldn't give in and trust you. Well, this is why." She yanked away from C.J.'s grasp. Before she left, she had one thing more to say. "Do me a favor and change the name of the song. I don't want my name associated with it." She stumbled down the hall.

"Dani, wait."

C.J.'s footsteps fell closely behind her. Dani quickened her pace.

When she made it back out to the bouncers and the group of women, Dani saw that one of the bouncers had Brenda by the arm and was leading her toward the exit. Dani pushed her way through the women and past the other bouncer who looked surprised when he saw Dani emerge from backstage.

C.J. still yelled for her but the screams of the women gathered there drowned her out.

"Oh, C.J., I love your music! Can you please autograph my T-shirt?" one woman shouted.

Dani kept walking. She didn't know how she was putting one foot in front of the other, but she was. Eventually, she caught up with Brenda outside the club. Brenda had just hailed a cab. When she opened the door to get inside, she looked shocked to find Dani right behind her.

Dani leaned back on the seat and closed her eyes as her head pounded like a kettle drum.

"Oh, honey, what happened?" Brenda asked.

Dani shook her head. She couldn't even look at Brenda. If she did, she'd lose it.

Brenda told the taxi driver, "If you get us there in ten minutes, you'll get an extra twenty." With that, the driver punched the cab into a breakneck speed. Horns blared around them, followed by the sound of squealing tires.

When they pulled up to the Marriott, Brenda handed over the money. She caught up to Dani who was stalking through the lobby to the elevator. Brenda linked her arm with Dani's. "You're not going to be alone tonight. You're coming to my room." Brenda saw the expression on Dani's face. "Not for *that*." Brenda punched the number to her floor once they entered the elevator. "I've got a bottle of Chivas Regal. We're going to drink that baby until it's gone."

Dani didn't even have the strength to argue that it was too expensive to drown her sorrows in—she didn't have the strength for anything.

They reached Brenda's room. She slid her key card into the slot, opened the door, and flipped on the lights. She motioned Dani to one of the chairs by the bed. "You sit there. I'll run and get some ice."

Brenda wasn't gone for a full minute before she was dropping ice cubes into two glasses. She opened the bottle of Scotch and poured until it reached the lip of each glass. Brenda handed one to Dani.

"Drink. I don't want any argument."

Dani downed the glass in three big gulps. Even though the Scotch was incredibly smooth and unlike anything Dani ever tasted, it still burned her throat. Brenda poured her another. Dani downed it again. When Brenda poured her the next drink, Dani didn't down it, but stared at the ice floating in the crystal. She couldn't get the image of the blonde out of her head no matter how hard she tried. And the look on C.J.'s face...

"What happened?" Brenda sat down on the end of the bed in front of Dani's chair. She watched Dani closely over the rim of the glass.

Dani sighed deeply. She took another drink. "Let's just say that I sure as hell surprised her." She gave a hollow laugh.

"Oh, honey." Brenda reached out and patted her on the knee. "I'm so sorry."

"I'm sorry I was such a pushover. I fell for her act. I feel so fucking foolish." She took another big gulp of the Scotch and shook her head. "Maybe it says something that I'm not a blubbering mess. I'm just so angry. I actually thought I was going to faint in that dressing room."

Brenda let her vent. Dani rose up and sat down on the bed with her back against the headboard. Brenda joined her.

"The really sad thing, Brenda, is I held back and held back, afraid something like this would happen. Something told me to do that. My instincts were that she was dangerous. That she was incapable of monogamy. Hell, I saw how other women were around her. But then we shared these intimate moments, and I allowed myself to think that maybe I could trust her."

Brenda motioned where Dani had left her glass on the table. "You done?"

"Yeah."

Brenda dropped more ice in her glass, poured a splash of Scotch, and rejoined Dani on the bed. "I won't say, 'she's not worth it' because I've had friends say that to me before, and I've always wanted to slap the shit out of them."

Dani smiled through her sadness. She remembered saying that exact thing to Monica and recalled Monica's reaction to her words.

"But what I will say is you're a wonderful woman, Dani Roberts. You will love someone, and they will love you. And all this other bullshit?" Brenda threw her hand up in the air in dismissal. "All this other bullshit won't matter."

Suddenly, Liz's beautiful face and haunting eyes appeared in Dani's mind like a still shot from a movie. "There's a woman back home."

"Dani, you can't leave an opening line like that hanging. Tell me."

"Her name is Liz Springer. She's a vet. I first met her when Frodo's regular vet couldn't see him. I've run into her a couple of other times. We've talked." She shook her head. "Never mind. I think I totally fucked that one up. I could blame it on C.J. James, but it's all on me. I'm the one who tried to trap lightning in a bottle. We saw how that turned out."

"Forget about that. I'm a hopeless romantic. Tell me more."

So, Dani did just that. She told Brenda how she felt when she was around Liz, how the feeling of comfort would wash over her, how she felt a warmth whenever they'd touch, innocent or not.

"And?"

"And what?"

"I swear to God you need to have someone smack you upside the head."

Dani snorted. "Trust me. My best friend, Tina, would gladly volunteer for that job. She never liked C.J. James, and she's pushed me to go after Liz. But I was blinded by C.J.'s charisma. That's on me."

"Is that what they're calling it these days? I'm a little more blunt. It's called sex appeal. That woman's definitely got it. Unfortunately, she doesn't know when to turn it off." Brenda stood up, retrieved Dani's glass, and filled it with more Scotch, obviously ignoring Dani's earlier comment that she was done. She handed the glass to Dani. "Now drink the rest of this shit. I don't want to waste it."

Dani took a long sip. "Let me say that this definitely fogs the brain enough to dull the ache a little."

"It does, doesn't it? Trust me, Chivas and I have partied many a night, and he's always respected me in the morning."

Dani couldn't help but laugh. "You such a good friend, Brenda."

"You're only saying that because I sold you that book for way less than it was worth."

"That's it, huh?"

"That's it."

They sat and drank until the Scotch was gone. Brenda gave Dani more encouragement to go after Liz when she got back home, even providing pointers on how to break the ice. She talked about old lovers she had shared her bed with over the years. Dani listened until her head felt heavy. The room was finally quiet. Dani swung her legs over the bed. Everything started spinning in front of her. She lay back on the pillow and rubbed her forehead with her fingers.

"Dani, why don't you stay here tonight instead of trying to make it back to your room?"

Dani attempted to get a reading of the digital clock: 2:00 a.m. She didn't put up any resistance as Brenda helped her out of her clothes, gently laid her back down, and pulled the covers over her.

"You sleep," Brenda whispered and switched off the lamp beside the bed.

Dani heard Brenda get settled in the other queen bed. Then she drifted off into a dreamless sleep.

Chapter 18

As they battled through their respective hangovers, Brenda talked Dani into staying at least for the morning sessions of the conference on Saturday. "I want you to clear your mind some before taking the drive to Francis. Focusing on something other than C.J. James might help."

At the noon break for lunch, Dani headed to the lobby with Brenda. "Guess I'll be on my way," Dani said.

"Are you sure? I'm worried about you."

Dani pulled Brenda in for a hug. "I'll be fine. I want to get back home." She gave her a tight squeeze. "I'll never be able to repay you for last night," she whispered into Brenda's ear.

"If I had a dollar for every time a woman told me that in the morning, I'd be one rich lady."

Dani laughed. "You're so good for me. Please tell me you'll come to Georgia in the fall when the summer heat breaks."

"Only if you promise to come to New York in the winter when the Rockefeller Center tree is lit up."

"Deal." Dani hugged her again.

"Take care, Dani."

"Thanks, Brenda. You, too." Dani left for her room to pack her suitcase and make the trip home to Francis.

* * *

Dani leaned her elbow against the car door as she kept her other hand on the wheel. She rubbed her temple, trying to erase the image of C.J. and the blonde in the dressing room. She sat up straighter and put both hands on the steering wheel as she shook off the memory. These stretches through the mountains of Tennessee were hard enough as it was, let alone if she allowed distractions.

She pushed the button to turn on the radio. With her thumb on the steering wheel's controls, she steadily flipped through the stations. Nothing sounded good. She was sure that nothing would for a very long time. A sad song about lost love flowed through her stereo speakers. She was about to change the station yet again, but something made her stop. She listened to the melody and became caught up in the words.

Dani's thoughts drifted to Liz as the words penetrated her heart. The chorus to the song repeated in her mind long after it was over. She recalled the times Liz had walked away from her... always away. Something had pulled her to Liz like a sun-scorched blade of glass to the first drop of rain. Something telling her that this was the woman she needed to get to know.

Lost in her thoughts, time passed swiftly and soon she saw the Atlanta signs and, a little farther, the Exit sign to Francis. As she pulled onto the ramp, strong wind buffeted the car. The sky darkened, and rain pelted her windshield. She flipped on the wipers, first on regular speed, then switched them over to full speed as rain poured down in torrents. She turned on her lights, hunched over the steering wheel, and peered into the blackness. Driving past the vet's office, she noticed a car still parked in the lot. She wondered if it was Liz's and had a sudden urge to pull into the lot to see if she was there. She admonished herself. *Jesus, Dani. I'm sure you're still the last person she wants to see these days.*

Lightning flashed overhead, blinding Dani. In a terrifying instant, she spotted a set of headlights coming her way. This was a two-lane highway. Sure as hell those lights were aiming straight for her. Oh, God, a car was in her lane, trying to pass a semi. Dani swerved hard to the right to avoid a head-on collision.

The tires lost their grip and slid off the road. She tried to stay on the shoulder as the on-coming car swept past her, but it was too steep. Her car careened down the embankment and barreled straight for a large tree. Dani yanked the wheel, but the passenger side slammed into the tree with a bone-jarring jolt. The air bag exploded in her face, and a sharp pain shot through her left wrist. Then everything went black.

Dani moaned as she struggled to regain consciousness. Her wrist throbbed. Her face was sore, but the airbag had saved her from a bang against the windshield. Through her fog, she heard someone open her car door. Gentle hands pushed her back in her seat, away from the deflated airbag. A familiar voice spoke.

"Oh, God, Dani, I was afraid it was you when I saw the car."

Dani slowly blinked her eyes open to see an angel hovering over her. Or at least it looked like an angel. Dressed in white, her eyes were the kindest eyes she'd ever seen—like Liz's. Dani attempted to turn her head and focus.

"Don't move. The ambulance is on its way."

"Liz?"

"Shh. Try to stay calm." Liz's voice quivered. Sirens drew closer and died down right outside the car. Dani heard doors opening and muffled speech.

"Ma'am, you can step back now," a male voice said behind Liz.

Two firemen put a brace around Dani's neck. They pulled her out of her car and set her on a gurney. Rain pelted down on her as they carried her toward the ambulance.

"Can you tell us your name?" a female medic asked who walked beside the gurney.

"Dani Roberts."

"Dani, are you experiencing pain anywhere in your body?"

"My left wrist. Head and neck are a little sore, too," Dani managed to mumble. They started to lift her in the back of the ambulance. "Where's Liz," she asked frantically. "Did you see her?" Dani tried to sit up.

"What?" the medic asked as she gently, but firmly, pushed Dani back down.

"Dani, I'm right here. Don't worry. I'll follow the ambulance to the hospital."

"What's your name, ma'am?" the medic asked Liz. "We'll make sure the staff knows you're coming in."

"Dr. Liz Springer." When the medic's eyebrows rose, Liz said, "I'm a veterinarian."

"Right. We'll see you there." The medic placed a blood pressure cuff over Dani's arm and took stock of her injuries.

The ambulance arrived at the hospital, and the medics pushed the gurney through the emergency room doors. Other faces hovered over her, and a man in scrubs Dani assumed was a nurse fired questions at the medics. The female medic rattled off her vitals. Dani didn't know much, but it eased her mind to hear it didn't sound like anything major was wrong.

As the nurse manipulated her wrist, Dani winced.

"It doesn't feel broken, but we won't know for sure until we get an X-ray."

Another man's face appeared to her right. "I'm Dr. Van Nuys. We're going to keep the neck brace on until we get a CAT scan. Any pain in your neck or back?"

"There was in the car, but it's eased up."

"Good."

He leaned over her and probed her face. "Any pain?"

"There." Dani jerked as he pressed her right cheek.

"I don't feel any bone displacement, but again, a CAT scan will show us any problems. You do have some swelling there." He glanced across the gurney at the nurse. "CAT scan first. X-ray second."

"Will do." The nurse stepped away for a few minutes and returned with a woman. "Sharon here will take you to the CAT scan, then we'll take care of the X-rays."

Sharon tried some small talk as she wheeled Dani down several hallways, but Dani wasn't in the mood.

"Here we are." Another technician joined Sharon, and in no time, the CAT scan was complete. Sharon took her for X-rays. Dani had to stifle a groan as the radiology technician manipulated her wrist in different positions for the film. When she was done, Sharon returned and wheeled Dani to a large room cordoned off by multiple curtains. A few minutes later, the curtain drew back, and Dr. Van Nuys reappeared.

"Good news. No concussion, no fractures of your cheeks, and no sign of any trauma to your neck or spine." He reached up and carefully removed the neck brace. "You won't need this." He handed the nurse the brace. "More good news. No fracture of the wrist. Looks like a severe sprain. We'll give you a brace to wear, but when you get home, you'll need to ice the wrist to get the swelling down." He gave her instructions for icing at home.

"How long will I need to wear the brace?"

"Should only be four weeks, but your wrist will let you know. You should also follow up with your regular physician." He motioned to her right cheek. "I know you might get sick of the ice, but that cheek could use some, too, when you get home. It'll cut down on the swelling and bruising." He gave her a half smile. "Although you're already sporting a shiner."

Dani heard voices on the other side of the curtain and recognized one of them as Liz's.

Another nurse led Liz to Dani's gurney. "Is it okay if she visits now, Doctor?"

"Yes. I'm done here." Dr. Van Nuys patted Dani's leg. "All in all, you're very lucky, Ms. Roberts."

The nurse followed the doctor and pulled the curtain closed behind her. Suddenly, Dani and Liz were alone. Dani looked up into those green eyes that had taken her breath away the first time they'd met. The rain had drenched Liz's hair. She'd removed her white lab coat, but the rain had managed to soak into her polo shirt, drawing Dani's attention to the outline of her bra.

I will not look at her nipples. I will not look at her nipples.

Liz moved closer to the bed. She raised her hand, and her fingers hovered over Dani's cheek, but Liz didn't touch her. Dani felt the heat as if she had.

Liz pulled her hand back and lowered her head. "I'm so glad you're okay," she said in a hushed tone. "I saw your car and I... I..." Liz swallowed hard. "I was so afraid of what I'd find when I opened your door."

Dani reached out and took Liz's hand. "Hey. I'm okay. No concussion. No issues with the neck or spine." She held up her wrist. "Severe sprain that I'll get a brace for." She gingerly touched her cheek. "And I guess I have a black eye."

Liz allowed a small smile. "It's already bruising. Should be quite colorful by morning." She quickly sobered. "Thank God you can walk away from this."

The nurse returned with paperwork, a package that held a wrist brace, and instant cold packs. She set the wrist brace and cold packs on the side tray. "You need to sign these, and you're ready to go."

Dani signed the forms.

The nurse pulled the brace out of the bag and carefully wrapped Dani's wrist. Dani noticed she loosely tightened the Velcro straps. "Once you get the swelling down at home, you can tighten this as needed. Also, I'm giving you a few instant cold packs. Be careful when you use them and wrap them in a towel. You don't want to risk any freezer burn. For pain, Dr. Van Nuys suggests ibuprofen. If you find you need more than that"—she handed Dani a card—"call his office to get a prescription for pain medication."

Dani sat up a little more on the bed, anxious to leave.

"I believe the firemen gathered whatever personal items you had in your car before it was towed away. They'll be at the front desk. You'll need someone to take you home, though."

Liz spoke up. "I can do that."

Dani's heart skipped a beat, and it wasn't from the unwanted trauma of the day.

"Good. I'll send for a wheelchair."

Dani slowly swung her legs over the side of the gurney. Liz kept her hand at Dani's back to steady her. Dani looked down at her shirt and noticed she was just as soaked as Liz.

"Damn." She fingered the material.

"Wait here, Dani. I'll get a dry one out of your bag."

Liz returned with Dani's suitcase. She pulled out a T-shirt and handed it to Dani. She turned as Dani started to pull off her wet shirt. Pain shot through Dani's wrist when she attempted to tug the shirt over her head.

"Liz, I hate to ask you, but—"

Liz spun back around. "Here, I'll help you." She stretched the collar out wider and lifted the wet shirt over Dani's head, setting it aside. She grabbed the dry T-shirt. Before she started putting it on Dani, their eyes met. Liz's face reddened as they locked gazes for what seemed like minutes. Liz pulled the shirt over Dani's head.

Dani tugged it down the rest of the way over her body. Her hands touched Liz's, and Dani could feel that Liz was trembling. Again, they stared at each other before Liz broke away from the gaze and leaned down to get Dani's wet shirt and her suitcase.

"My car's just outside the emergency room doors," Liz said in a soft voice.

As the words left her lips, a volunteer zipped in with a wheelchair. "Hospital policy," she said in a chipper voice.

"I'll pull the car into the round-a-bout." Liz hurried away.

The volunteer cheerfully talked to Dani as she pushed her down the hall. Dani saw one of the nurses who'd treated her, and she thanked him.

Liz's Outback stopped in front of the ER doors. She got out and helped Dani into the car. They pulled out of the hospital parking lot and onto the state road toward town. They sat in silence for a while. Liz spoke first.

"I really don't want to take you home to be alone. Is there a friend you can stay with?"

"Tina and Barb, but I didn't call them before I left Nashville to let them know I was headed back early."

The miles to town churned under the car before Liz spoke again. "Why were you in Nashville?"

"A conference," Dani answered a little too quickly. *Do I really want to tell her the other reason?* "I also went there to see C.J." She glanced over at Liz. The dashboard light illuminated her enough that Dani could see her face. Liz was biting her lower lip. *Great, Dani. What the hell were you thinking?*

"She was performing there? I guess she would be. I knew she went there to record."

Dani took a deep breath. "It's over. Actually, it never should have been 'on' between us. I knew what I was dealing with, but I..." Her voice trailed off as she felt tears come to her eyes. She turned away to stare out the window, watching as the rain rolled slowly down the glass. "She was with someone else." There was a finality to the words, as if there was never a question where this had been headed all along between Dani and C.J.

Liz turned briefly to Dani. "I'm sorry, Dani. I'm sorry you got hurt."

Dani was about to speak, but Liz stopped her. "I don't think I can talk about this right now. My ex hurt me in the same way, and I—"

"Liz, you don't need to explain."

"Do you understand why?" Liz glanced over long enough to Dani so that Dani could see the mixture of emotions zipping across her face. "I remember what I went through when my ex cheated on me. You need to work this out. Work through what you're feeling. When you're done, and when you're ready, then we can talk."

Dani wanted to say more, but she simply nodded.

They didn't speak again until Dani gave Liz directions to Barb and Tina's house. By the time they pulled into the drive, the rain had stopped. Liz walked over to help Dani out of the car. She got Dani's bag out of the back and led her to the front door.

Dani knocked lightly. She heard Frodo's "German Shepherd" bark. His nose pushed back the blinds. Then his bark changed over to an excited yipping—well, as much as beagles can yip.

The outside light flicked on, and Tina's face appeared at the glass after she pushed the blinds aside. "Jesus Christ!" Dani heard Tina's muffled exclamation before she swung the door open.

Tina helped Liz bring Dani inside. Frodo circled Dani's legs and jumped up on her, practically knocking her over. Dani reached down to pet him and felt a little lightheaded with the move.

"Barb! Honey, can you put Frodo out back?"

Barb rounded the corner of the kitchen, took one look at Dani, and said, "Shit. Yeah, sure."

Liz and Tina got Dani seated on the couch. Barb joined them in the living room after she let out Frodo.

"Dani got caught up in this afternoon's storm," Liz said. "Someone ran her off the road where she hit a tree. I happened to be driving home from the office when I spotted her car."

Tina looked like she was about to cry.

"Tina, I'm okay. No concussion, no neck or spinal injuries. Just a black eye and this." Dani held up her wrist. Before Tina could ask, she said, "Not broken, only a sprain."

"Oh, that reminds me." Liz left and returned shortly with the cold packs. "She's supposed to ice the wrist and her cheek tonight. The doctor said icing the cheek would help with bruising, but I think we might be past that point. He suggested ibuprofen for pain, but if it gets worse to call his number for a prescription."

Tina took the cold packs from Liz and sat down by Dani. "Why were you coming back today? You weren't due back until tomorrow afternoon."

Dani glanced up at Liz who stared at the floor. "One of the reasons I went there, well, let's just say it didn't work out."

Tina's entire body tensed, and her face flushed with anger. "Don't tell me that bitch was with someone else."

Dani smiled weakly. "Okay, I won't."

"It's not funny."

"Don't you think I know that?" Dani's whole head throbbed with the statement.

Barb walked over and sat on the other side of Dani. She looked across Dani to Tina. "None of that shit matters right now, Dani. What matters is you're okay. I'm glad Liz was there to help you."

Liz met Dani's gaze. Liz's eyes reflected kindness. Pure kindness. What had I ever seen in C.J.'s eyes except for electricity and that nagging feeling of danger? Dani wondered.

Liz motioned toward the door. "I'd better be getting home. I'm sure Melanie's wondering where I am."

Dani felt disappointment in the pit of her stomach. She knew Liz had to go, but she'd secretly hoped she could stay longer.

Barb and Tina stood up. Dani got ready to try, but they both said at the same time, "You sit!"

Dani couldn't help but laugh. "I see what a weekend with Frodo has done to you two." Liz joined Barb and Tina in laughing, breaking the tension in the room.

"Thank you, Liz, for everything," Dani said softly.

Liz smiled. "I'm just glad you're safe." Barb and Tina walked Liz to the door. "Please keep an eye on her tonight."

"You don't have to worry about that," Tina said.

After she left, Tina sat on the sofa with Dani, appearing very much like she wanted to dissect the weekend's events. Barb quickly put that to rest.

"Tina, Dani's going upstairs to lie down with these cold packs. She can talk to us in the morning."

"I'll help get you to bed," Tina said.

Dani held up her hand. "Not before I see Frodo again."

"You sure you're ready for that?" Tina asked.

Dani nodded. At least her head wasn't throbbing as much this time with the action.

"Be prepared for a bouncing, baby beagle." Barb headed to the back door. Frodo bounded into the room. With a running start, he seemed to leap from about halfway into the living room onto the couch.

Dani didn't care how much she hurt. Frodo was here. Her best friends were here.

And the promise of something else had just walked out the front door.

Chapter 19

"Dr. Springer, your two o'clock is here."

Liz stopped writing in the chart and raised her eyebrow at Mary. "Two o'clock? I didn't think I had another patient until two-thirty."

"It was a last-minute appointment."

Liz stifled a sigh. "Very well. Exam Room 2."

Mary handed her a chart. Liz flipped it open and was surprised to see "Brutus Richards," plus that he was an eight-year-old Great Dane. She didn't think it was coincidence that she was seeing this particular patient.

Rex, one of the clinic's technicians, met her at the door that led into the exam room.

"Let me go in first to talk to the client," she told him.

"I saw where it's a Great Dane. You sure you don't need help lifting him onto the table?"

"I'll call you in when I need you."

"Whatever you say, Dr. Springer."

Liz schooled her expression before opening the door. Michelle had her back to the door. Brutus, a tan-colored, gorgeous Great Dane, was busy sniffing the floor. Michelle turned.

"Michelle, hello. I assume this beautiful, big guy is Brutus."

Michelle patted Brutus's side. "Yes."

Liz set the chart on the exam table and opened it. "And what is Brutus here for today?" She had a feeling it had nothing to do with Brutus, but she wanted to hear Michelle's answer.

Michelle kept her head lowered. "Really, um, he's okay. He has a small rash on his right hind leg. I have pills from his vet in Atlanta that help with his scratching. I wanted to get those refilled. And..."

"And?"

Michelle blushed. "And I couldn't get you to answer my calls, so this was kind of a last-ditch effort on my part to talk to you."

Liz closed the chart and crossed her arms. "Michelle, please don't take this the wrong way."

"Uh-oh. It's never good when someone starts a sentence like that."

Liz smiled. "I enjoyed our date a few weeks ago."

"But?"

"But I'm not in a good space right now." *God, how many clichés can I use in one afternoon?*

"It was the woman at Carl's Cavern, wasn't it?"

Liz's stomach clenched, but she didn't answer.

"Dani something?"

"Dani Roberts."

"Right, Dani Roberts. There seemed to be a connection between you two."

"No." *Not that I don't want there to be,* Liz thought.

"But you wish there could be?"

Liz let the question hang between them.

"I thought she was with C.J. James, from what I could tell."

Liz wasn't about to get into that discussion with Michelle. Even though she might be interested in Dani, she was being truthful with her in the car. Dani needed time to sort things out.

"Michelle, like I said. I did enjoy the date. Thank you for taking me to the concert."

"That sounds pretty final. Like I won't get a second chance."

"I'm sorry."

Michelle leaned down and scratched Brutus's head. "I am, too. But I get it."

Liz motioned to Brutus. "Would you like me to at least check out his rash?"

"Sure."

Liz let Brutus sniff her hand before she knelt down and examined his hind leg. The rash was healing nicely. Probably one more round of the allergy medication should do it.

Liz glanced up at Michelle. "Looks good. I'll get that refill for you." Liz rose to her feet and was almost to the door when Michelle spoke.

"I wish you the best, Liz."

Liz glanced over her shoulder. "Thank you. I wish you only the best, too." As she left for the pills, she wondered how Dani was doing.

* * *

"And that's all she could say? 'Dani. You're here'?" Tina asked.

It was the Thursday night after Dani's accident. She still felt a little banged up, but she'd recovered enough that she agreed to go out with Tina to Carl's Cavern.

"Then she said she hadn't been expecting me so soon." Dani swirled the ice in her glass of Coke. They sat at the bar while Barb worked.

Tina snorted. "Fucking bitch. Like she had to prepare for you to be there." Tina took a sip of her beer. "I blame her for your accident, too."

Dani squeezed Tina's arm. "That wasn't her fault, Tina. That was from an idiot driver who was flying like a bat out of hell to pass a semi—in a freaking monsoon."

"But if she hadn't been screwing around with that chick in the dressing room, you would have stayed the weekend and you wouldn't have even been on that road Saturday."

Dani shook her head. "It happened when it was supposed to happen."

She felt Tina looking at her. Dani glanced her way. "What?"

"You, my friend. You truly amaze me sometimes."

"That doesn't mean it still doesn't hurt." Dani took a drink from her Coke. "Whatever. It's over."

"What about Liz?"

"I don't know," Dani murmured.

"What do you mean you don't know?"

"She's sorry for what happened with C.J. I guess she went through something similar with her ex. She wants me to take time to figure things out, but I think she's still interested in me."

"Duh." Tina motioned Barb to their end of the bar. She jabbed her thumb at Dani. "Dani said she thinks the doctor's still interested in her."

Barb rolled her eyes. "Why don't you call her?"

Dani shook her head. No. She was going to give Liz time, and she'd take Liz's advice and give herself time.

A customer called Barb away.

"You stubborn lesbian," Tina said with a smirk. "Don't wait too long. Liz is a keeper, just as you are." She held her bottle up in the air. "To you and the doc."

Dani clinked her Coke glass against the bottle. "I'll drink to that."

* * *

Music blared from the bowling alley speakers. Two weeks had passed, and for two days, Dani had been gathering her courage to contact Liz. Tonight, Dani was filling in for someone on Barb and Tina's bowling team. She wasn't a great bowler. She told them that repeatedly. She even tried to use the excuse of her sprained wrist, although she was no longer in pain. They reminded her that she bowled right-handed and still insisted she join them. Dani suspected it was because they wanted to get her out of the house.

"Nice pickup, hon," Barb shouted to Tina as Tina walked back to her chair.

She leaned over and gave Barb a quick kiss. "Why thank you, my love."

"Okay, Dani, you're up after Fran," Barb said.

Dani checked the scores on the overhead screen. She was bowling an eighty-seven in the eighth frame. *I suck,* she thought miserably. Why had she agreed to do this?

Fran from the other team bowled a strike. Of course. Her team cheered as Fran joined them and accepted their high fives.

Barb pointed at Dani. "Okay, chief, no pressure. None whatsoever." Dani detected the teasing tone in Barb's voice. Dani wasn't amused.

She approached the lane and picked up her bowling ball. She toed the arrow where she liked to stand and started her motion. Just as she was about to release the ball, the DJ's voice crackled over the speaker.

"Now, here's an early release from C.J. James's upcoming debut album—'Dani's Eyes.'"

Dani promptly dropped the ball which landed in a loud thud and slowly—painstakingly so—rolled into the left gutter.

"Fuck!" Dani exclaimed. When she whirled around, she saw Barb and Tina's shocked expressions. The women from the other team stared at her with their mouths gaped open. Dani retrieved the ball that had rolled back from its slow trip down the lane.

She toed the same spot again. She first tried to block out C.J.'s voice as she concentrated on the ten pins at the end of the lane. Then she let the music seep into her brain. It was pissing her off. Maybe this was a good thing.

Dani approached the line and flung the ball out hard. It rolled at a fast clip down the lane and slammed into the pins, knocking them all down.

As she took her seat beside Tina, Tina patted her on the back. Dani bowled out of her mind after that. A 173 for the second game. And 189 for the final one. The best she'd ever bowled was a 132, and that had been years ago.

The night ended with Barb and Tina's team on top. Dani hadn't been a detriment like she'd feared.

As they walked to their cars, Tina spoke. "You okay, Dani?"

"Yeah. At least I think I'm on the way to being okay."

"You want to come back to our place for a beer?" Barb put their bowling balls in the back of the Explorer.

"I'm going to head home, but thanks for having me join you. You were right. It was what I needed." Dani gave them each a hug.

Barb slapped her on the back. "Go home and get some rest, okay? You've been through a lot lately."

"I'll see you tomorrow at work, Tina."

Tina waved at her as they drove away.

Dani got into her new MINI Cooper. Her other one had been totaled in the crash. She'd debated about getting a different car but decided she still deserved to have some fun.

When Dani made it home, she took Frodo for a long walk. Taking a deep breath, she tried to enjoy the neighbors' flowers and lilac bushes along the way. She waved at Mrs. Dickinson who watered her petunias in front of her house.

She thought about Liz and how right Liz had been when she told Dani to take some time. It allowed her to step back and let her heart take a break. Even though she wanted very much to look up Liz's home number and give her a call, she didn't. A part of her wished she would run into Liz walking Melanie, but the other part of her was glad for the solitude.

"Come on, Frodo, let's go home and get you food."

His ears perked up at the word "food."

Dani laughed. "Sometimes, you're just too damn smart."

When they got to the house, Dani unlocked the door and let Frodo go. He flew into the kitchen and pranced by his bowl.

"I know, I know. Mommy promised." She dropped a cup of his food in his dish and hung his leash on the hook. She rubbed the back of her neck. "Man, I think I pulled something on that spare I fired down the lane," she mumbled.

A hot shower sounded like heaven. After the shower, the pain subsided. She toweled off and padded naked into her bedroom. She put on a pair of boxer shorts and a sleeveless T-shirt. She had left the kitchen light on for Frodo, but she was too tired to go down to turn it off. As she lay back on the cool sheets, Frodo's collar jingled as he came up the stairs. She felt him hop up lightly onto the bed. He gave her his customary good-night lick on the side of her face, went into his circling routine, and settled down with a sigh.

Maybe she'd contact Liz tomorrow.

Chapter 20

It was morning. Aware that someone was staring at her, Dani blinked her eyes open. Frodo was within inches of her face. As soon as she could focus, he licked her cheek.

"Frodo, I get the hint. You have to go potty."

Dani got out of bed and took a quick trip to the bathroom. She headed down the stairs with Frodo flying in front of her. After letting him out back, she turned on the Keurig machine. She peered at the clock. Eight-fifteen. Shit! Eight-fifteen! Dani never overslept. When she let Frodo out, she hadn't noticed the sky had lightened.

Dani ran to shower. She threw on a pair of jeans and one of her "Dani's Den of Book's" short-sleeved cotton shirts. After pulling on her sneakers, she hurried back downstairs.

She searched for Frodo in the backyard. "Come on, boy!" Preoccupied with barking at something in the front of the house, Frodo ignored her. "Frodo, come on. I've got to get to work."

He trotted into the house and waited for his morning food. Dani dropped a cup into the dish and filled his water bowl with fresh water. She grabbed her shoulder bag on the way to the door. When she opened the screen door to leave, she didn't think she had to be careful because she thought Frodo was still in the kitchen. She felt him brush against her leg as he dashed out the door. She saw a flash of gray as a cat zipped through the neighbor's front yard across the street.

"Frodo. No!"

He'd already started for the front porch steps and attempted to leap from the second step to the ground below. Just as Dani had a horrible image of him running into the street, he yelped and came to an abrupt halt at the base of the stairs. He held up his left hind leg and continued yelping.

"Shit." Dani threw her bag aside and sprinted down the stairs. He stood still while she touched his back leg, fearful that he'd broken something. He flinched and tried to put his weight on it but yelped again. "Frodo, what did you do?"

Despite her wrist brace, Dani scooped him into her arms, taking care not to press into that leg. She set him on the living room floor. He sat down and stared at her, as if begging her for help. Dani grabbed the portable phone and made a call to the vet's office. Dr. Patterson wasn't in, but Liz was. Mary said she'd let Liz know Dani would be bringing him in. Dani hung up from that call and phoned to Tina.

"Hey, boss. You usually beat me into the office."

"Tina, Frodo's hurt his back leg. I need to take him to see Liz. Can you handle opening up?"

"Absolutely. Call me when you find out something."

Frodo hadn't moved from his spot on the floor, which told Dani how much pain he was in. She gingerly lifted him and took him out to the car. She set him in the backseat and returned to the porch to lock up and grab her bag. On the drive to the vet's office, Frodo whimpered when she hit a bump.

"I'm sorry, little guy. I'm trying to miss them."

She pulled into the parking lot. They must have been on the lookout for her. Jake met her at the car and carried Frodo inside directly to an exam room. He set him on the exam table and stood on one side while Dani stood on the other. She kept petting Frodo while they waited for Liz.

As she stood there worrying, she was transported back in time when Frodo was a puppy and she brought him home for the first night. He was so frightened of his new surroundings. She stayed up with him that night and held him as he trembled on her chest while she sat in her overstuffed chair. He'd inch his way up to her neck the instant she fell asleep. She'd push him back down so she could breathe a little easier only to wake up to find his face against hers again.

The other door opened, and Liz entered the room.

"Dani, what happened?"

Dani explained how Frodo had gotten past her to chase a cat but had hit the ground hard. "He lifted his left back leg. I thought he broke it at first, but I couldn't see anything wrong. It seems loose, though, if that makes sense."

Jake held Frodo in place while Liz maneuvered his back leg. Frodo jerked.

"No, it makes sense."

Dani watched Liz's expression for any answer to how serious the injury was.

"It feels really loose, like you said. I'm pretty sure he's torn his ACL."

"ACL?" Dani didn't even know dogs had ACLs, let alone could tear one.

"Unfortunately, yes."

A sudden cold fear shot through Dani's body. Her eyes filled with tears. "He's going to be okay, isn't he? You don't have to... have to..."

Liz must have noticed her panicked expression. "Oh, no. It's serious, yes, but not serious in the way you're interpreting it. He'll probably need surgery."

Dani almost collapsed with relief. "You'll do that?"

"No, but I can give you recommendations for some surgeons who specialize in joint repair." Liz nodded at Jake who left the room. "Jake will bring you a sheet with the names and locations of the surgeons. You can make the decision."

"I'll go with whomever you recommend."

Jake returned and handed the paper to Liz. Liz indicated a clinic that was located halfway between Francis and Atlanta. "They're all good at what they do, but if you want someone close by, Dr. Stanton is excellent." Liz pointed out his name.

"Okay. Sure. I'll call him right away." Dani's lower lip trembled, and she swiped away a tear rolling down her cheek.

"Jake, could you give us a minute?"

He left the room again.

Dani kept her head lowered while she continued to pet Frodo. She stopped her petting when Liz placed her hand on top of hers. She raised her head.

"Dani, I won't lie to you. It's a serious injury, just like it would be to a human. But just like humans, we have surgeons who can fix it." As Liz spoke, she stroked the back of Dani's hand with her thumb. "It's expensive—"

"I don't care," Dani said forcefully. "I don't care what it costs."

Liz smiled. "I know that about you."

Dani stared down at their joined hands and then met Liz's eyes. Liz didn't say anything, but in that moment, Dani sensed this was about much more than Frodo.

"How have you been these past few weeks?" Liz asked softly.

"Better. Thank you for suggesting I take the time to work things out."

"And did you?"

"Yes." They were both petting Frodo as if using him as a buffer. Even in his pain, Frodo seemed to sense there was something more going on. He licked Liz's hand then Dani's.

"If you don't mind, I'd like to keep in touch to see how Frodo is doing." Liz hesitated for a moment. "And you."

"The clinic has my home number. Let me give you my cell."

Liz pulled out her cell phone and typed in Dani's number. "I'll text you mine."

Dani's phone dinged in her pocket. "Got it." They stared at each other for a long moment until Dani cleared her throat. "I guess I should take Frodo home."

Liz shook her head as if to clear it. "Right. Sorry. Let me get you some pain medication that should tide him over until you get in to see the surgeon. It'll also help keep him quiet until his appointment. I'll have Jake come back in to help you with Frodo to your car." Liz leaned over and scratched Frodo's ears. "I'll be thinking about you, Frodo. Dr. Stanton will make you good as new." She started for the door.

"Liz?"

Liz turned. "Yes?"

"Thank you for seeing Frodo on short notice. I know Dr. Patterson is his vet, but I'm glad it was you."

"You don't need to thank me. Call me once you get that appointment. I want to know how he's doing, too. Maybe even come by." Liz's cheeks colored.

"I'd like that very much." Dani put her arm around Frodo. "We'd like that."

After she left, Dani bent over and nuzzled her face next to Frodo's. "You're going to be okay, little guy." He licked her nose.

And your mommy is, too.

* * *

Dr. Stanton was able to schedule Frodo's surgery two days later. He explained the procedure, complete with informational pamphlets and a model of a dog's knee. Frodo's recovery would be similar to a human's—about eight weeks until he could start using stairs. He'd remain overnight. Dr. Stanton explained the steps Dani needed to take to set up her home for Frodo's return. She'd already decided to let Tina run the store for the first two weeks until he came back to have his stitches removed. Full recovery was six months.

Dani returned home that night, her head spinning with everything Dr. Stanton told her. She understood now what Liz was trying to tell her in the clinic. It really was a serious injury.

Dani set up a place to sleep in the spare bedroom on the main floor. No, it wasn't her king-size bed, but it was the best solution until Frodo could again take the steps. She'd carry him down the back steps and walk him on his leash when he needed to do his business. She couldn't risk him trying to chase after a squirrel or any other critter he might spot.

The first night home after his surgery, he was miserable. Dani would be, too, if she had a cone wrapped around her neck. She hated the e-collar, but it was necessary to keep Frodo from licking his incision. After his second dose of pain medication, he settled somewhat but would wake up whimpering. Dani finally made up a bed for herself on the floor. He tried to nuzzle her, but the e-collar kept getting in the way.

The next day, Liz called to check on his progress. Dani explained the issues he had with the e-collar.

"Maybe I can help with that. Can I come by tonight?" Liz asked.

"Yeah." Dani chided herself for being excited at the prospect of Liz in her home. She should be focused on Frodo. She gave Liz directions.

At seven-thirty, there was a knock at the door. Dani, who'd been keeping Frodo on a leash in the house for just this reason, grabbed his leash to keep him from sprinting to the door.

When Dani opened the door, Liz smiled and held up what looked like a small life preserver. Dani stepped aside for her to enter.

"Hi, Frodo." Liz leaned over to pet him. Frodo wagged his tail a couple of times. "Why don't we see if it's okay with your mommy if we can take this e-collar off and replace it?" Liz glanced up at Dani.

"If it'll help his state of mind and make him more comfortable, I'm all for it."

Liz untied the e-collar and slipped it off Frodo's head. She fastened the soft collar on with the Velcro straps. "There. Better, Frodo?" He licked her face, and she giggled. "I thought so." She rose to her feet. "We find that these work for some dogs who really struggle with the regular e-collars. You'll need to be a little more vigilant to make sure he can't reach his incision site. I've inflated it all the way, though, so he should be fine."

"Thank you, Liz."

Liz rubbed her hands on her thighs and wouldn't meet Dani's gaze. That's when Dani realized she was nervous.

"Would you like a cup of coffee? Or tea?"

"Tea would be lovely."

Liz followed her into the kitchen area and slid onto one of the stools at the island. "Your home is beautiful. It's a little larger than mine. Four bedrooms?"

"Yes." Dani filled a kettle with water, set it on a burner, and turned on the flame. She joined Liz at the adjoining stool.

Liz couldn't seem to keep her hands still on the island counter in front of them. Dani covered her hands with her own.

"Hey. You don't need to be nervous. We're already friends. At least I hope we are."

Relief flooded Liz's face. "We are."

Frodo entered the kitchen and circled a few times before curling up between them. Liz stared down at him.

"He seems to be getting around okay."

"He is. I walk him out in the backyard when he needs to do his business. I'm not sure how happy he is about it."

Liz laughed. "I bet his beagle nose isn't happy at all. They love to investigate every square inch."

The kettle whistled. Dani got up and prepared their tea bags and water. She slid Liz's mug to her.

"Sugar or milk? Sorry. I don't have any cream."

"I like it plain, so you're fine."

Liz doused her tea bag until the water darkened. "This smells great. Chamomile?"

"Yup. Only tea I like."

"We have something in common."

They sipped their tea in comfortable silence. Dani's heart warmed with the knowledge that being in Liz's presence brought her peace. Her lips slipped into a smile.

"What's that smile for?"

"I was thinking about how easy this is." Dani motioned between them. "How peaceful."

Liz returned the smile. "It is, isn't it?"

For the next few minutes, Dani leaned her chin on her open palm and listened while Liz explained the rehab period for Frodo. She stared at Liz's sensual mouth while she talked, caught up in how much she wanted to lean over and kiss her. She suddenly realized Liz had stopped speaking.

"Dani?"

"Hmm?"

Liz's mouth quirked, obviously catching Dani in the act.

Dani straightened on her stool. "I'm sorry. Did you ask me something?"

"I asked if you'd like to go for coffee once Frodo returns for his check-up and you're reassured he's progressing well."

"I'd love to."

"Why don't you call me after his visit?"

"All right."

"Well, I'd better go. I need to get home to Melanie."

For the umpteenth time, Dani was so relieved that Melanie was Liz's dog and not a woman waiting at home for her.

Dani followed her to the door. "Thanks for stopping by and helping out with Frodo." They both watched him as he joined them in the living room. "You've lifted his mood. Believe me." Impulsively, Dani leaned over and kissed Liz's cheek. "And you've lifted mine."

Liz parted her lips and looked surprised. She touched her cheek. "I'm glad."

"I'll call you soon," Dani said as Liz walked toward her car.

"I look forward to it."

Chapter 21

Two weeks later, at Frodo's first post-op appointment with Dr. Stanton, he received a glowing report. He also had his stitches removed. When Dani brought Frodo home, she had a little talk with him as if he completely understood. He sat in front of her in the living room as she sat on the couch.

"Frodo, I'm going to remove the soft e-collar Liz gave you, but you have to promise me that you won't make any moves to lick that site. Dr. Stanton told me to keep an eye on you, and I will." As she was talking, she released the Velcro snaps. He shook his head. "Better?" He licked her hand. "I'm taking that as a yes. Now, remember, you can't go flying through the house, and you're on leash duty until at least another four weeks when you go back to see Dr. Stanton."

He shook his head again.

"Yeah, I didn't think that'd make you too happy." She reached for the portable phone. "What this also means is I can have that coffee date with Liz." At the mention of Liz's name, Frodo wagged his tail. "You like her, too, huh?" His tail thumped harder against the floor. Dani chuckled. "Believe me, I get it. But I can't leave you home alone. I'm calling Tina and Barb to see if they can babysit you." Frodo nudged her hand with his nose. "I know. Not a hardship at all."

Dani hated imposing on her friends, especially Tina, after she'd not been into the store in two weeks. Tina kept assuring her that everything was running smoothly and she should quit apologizing.

"Yo," Tina answered. "How's our nephew, the flying beagle."

Dani snorted. "Here's hoping he never tries that stunt again." She scratched his head while she talked. "Listen, I hate to ask this after all you've done these past two weeks."

"Dani, I told you to let that go. Everything has been great at the store. You needed to worry about Frodo. What is it?"

"I was wondering if you and Barb could watch Frodo. I'm thinking Saturday, but I have to call Liz first and see if it works for her."

"Ohhh, a date with the good doctor."

Dani could hear her smile behind the words. "It's not really a date. It's to have coffee."

"Technically, that's a date."

Okay, Dani admitted. Tina was right. "Fine. It's a semi-date. We haven't had a chance to really get to know each other. I'm thinking it'd be a good place to start."

"We'd love to watch him. Would it be easier if we came over there?"

Dani hadn't thought of that. "If you don't mind."

"Nope. Let me know what time on Saturday if it works for Liz."

"Will do."

Dani hung up and immediately called Liz before she lost her nerve. Liz told her Saturday worked fine.

"There's a little coffee shop in town," Dani said. "The Better Brew. It's on—"

"Maple. I pick up a coffee from there most mornings."

"Would four be okay?"

"Works for me."

Dani hung up with a big grin on her face. "Your mommy has a semi-date with Liz." His ears perked up, and he cocked his head. "Not you, too. I refuse to call it a date. I don't want to jinx it."

* * *

Saturday afternoon at three-thirty, Liz finished getting her second shower for the day. She realized she didn't really need to but, out of nervousness, decided to anyway. It was time to make a decision on clothes. Which was silly. This was only coffee, right?

"Right, Mel? It's only coffee." Dressed in her panties and bra, she stood in front of her bedroom closet. She pulled out a pair of jeans then hung them back up. "No, shorts make more sense." She flicked through her hangers until she stopped at a light-green sleeveless blouse. She tried to ignore the voice in her head that said, "You're only picking that one because Dani said something about the color of your eyes." She went to her dresser and pulled out a pair of khaki shorts. After she dressed, she turned to Melanie, who sat on the floor at the foot of the bed.

"What do you think?"

Melanie gave a little bark.

"Well, alrighty then. I have the approval of the beautiful Melanie. That counts for something."

She snatched her keys off the table in the entryway.

Dani's leg shook nervously under the table she'd chosen by the front window of the coffee shop. *Damn it. Get a grip.* She literally did just that when she reached below the table and pushed hard on her denim-clad leg. She began tapping the table with her fingers. The woman at the table in front of her turned away from her laptop with a frown aimed at Dani.

"Sorry," Dani mumbled.

She scanned the sidewalk for any sign of Liz and glanced at her watch. She was ten minutes early. *Silly to be nervous about a no-show.* As that thought bounced around in her head, she saw Liz step out of her car on the other side of the street. Dani swallowed hard. Yes, she was dressed simply in khaki shorts and a light-green blouse. But Liz could have just as easily have been wearing a slinky gown and walking down a runway at a fashion show. She looked that amazing.

Liz crossed the street and smiled at Dani when their eyes met through the large plate-glass window of the coffee shop. The bell on the door to the shop jingled. Dani shot to her feet as Liz approached the table. Something about Liz Springer made her want to exhibit all the manners of a southern gentleman courting a debutante.

"Hey, Dani. I'm sorry. Have you been waiting long? I tried to get here a little early, but it seems like you had the same idea."

"I've only been here a few minutes. Can I get you a coffee?"

"You don't need to treat."

"I'd like to, if you don't mind."

"That's sweet of you." Liz scrunched up her face in thought.

"I can see you're debating about getting a coffee with calories."

Liz laughed. "I'm that obvious, huh?"

"Well, if you're worried, you shouldn't be. You look perfect just the way you are." Dani closed her eyes as she felt her face heat. "I mean—"

"That's such a sweet compliment. Please don't take it back."

Dani relaxed.

"How about an iced caramel macchiato?" Liz said.

"No fat content there."

"Absolutely none."

"Right. One non-fat iced caramel macchiato for you, one black house blend for me."

"Don't tell me you're not joining me in the decadence."

"Have you ever tried their house blend? It's excellent."

"I order that when I'm on my way to work, but I felt like throwing caution to the wind this afternoon."

"Sounds like a great plan. I'll be right back." As Dani left for the counter to place their orders, she couldn't tamp down the giddiness bubbling inside.

Liz let her gaze drift down to Dani's ass that fit oh-so-nicely in those jeans. Jesus, she thought. Was she really the kind of woman who blatantly stared at another woman's ass? Apparently she was. She also was apparently the kind of woman who entertained thoughts of what she'd like to do with that body.

While waiting on their order, Dani turned. Liz jerked her eyes back up but not fast enough it seemed, if the crooked smile that graced Dani's lips was any indication. Liz stared down at the table, finding infinite interest in the wood grain and coffee stains.

"Here you go."

Liz took the plastic cup from Dani. She didn't wait to see if Dani had started drinking. She dove right in. Closing her eyes, she groaned with pleasure. She glanced up to find Dani staring at her with her cup halfway up to her mouth. "Everything okay over there?" Liz enjoyed the effect she had on Dani. She needed some boost to her ego, knowing whom Dani used to date.

Dani took a sip of her coffee. "Everything's great."

They drank in silence for a couple of minutes. Liz decided to confront the elephant in the room.

"So... you and C.J."

Dani sat back in her chair and blew out a breath.

"I'm sorry. Maybe you're not ready—"

Dani held up a hand to stop her. "No. You're right." Dani started at the beginning, about how her gut kept trying to keep her in check, but that she didn't listen. She stopped and stared at the ceiling before continuing. "Being with C.J. was like getting smacked in the head by flying debris while walking outside during a Category 5 hurricane."

"That's quite a visual."

"It's the best way to describe her." Dani finished by telling her what happened in Nashville.

"Like I told you before, I'm so sorry you had to go through that." Liz hesitated. If she was asking Dani to open up, she needed to share. She told Dani about that horrible day when she walked in on Therese and Rachel. "Not only was my partner cheating on me. She was cheating on me with my best friend."

"Oh, man, Liz. That's horrible."

"No more horrible than what you walked in on in Nashville."

Dani seemed to be debating about saying more.

"What?" Liz asked.

"A year ago, my girlfriend broke up with me."

Liz waited, thinking there had to be more.

"On Twitter."

Liz's jaw dropped. "You're kidding."

"Nope. In a tweet. She couldn't even finish apologizing. Apparently, she ran out of characters."

"Well, you're only allowed 140."

Dani scowled at her.

Liz burst out laughing. "Oh, my God. I wish you could see your face. I'm sorry. I didn't know if you knew how many characters made up a tweet." Liz was relieved when Dani joined in the laughter.

"I've had this discussion with Tina. Social media isn't my favorite thing."

"Join the club."

They talked for another hour. Dani glanced at her watch.

"I'm sorry, Liz. I should probably go. Even though I trust Tina and Barb with Frodo, I'm an overprotective mommy."

Liz reached across the table and placed her hand on top of

Dani's. "That's something I love about you, so please don't apologize."

Dani walked Liz to her car. "I've really enjoyed this."

"Me, too." Liz stared down at her keys as she waited for Dani to say more.

"I'd love to get together again."

Neither made the move to set up another date, much to Liz's disappointment. She wondered if Dani was reticent because of her experience with C.J. James. She hoped Dani wouldn't put her in the same heartbreaker category.

"You're going back to work next week?"

"Yes. I feel better with Frodo's progress. Barb works nights at Carl's, so she'll watch him during the day. I'm such a worrier, though, I'll spend all my lunch breaks with him."

"Like I said. That's something I love about you." Liz decided to be the braver of the two. "I might stop by this week at the store." She knew she made the right move when she saw Dani's relief.

"Good. I'd like that."

Liz rose on her tiptoes to plant a soft kiss on Dani's cheek. She enjoyed the blush the kiss caused. She opened her car door and slid inside. "Hope to see you soon."

Dani shut the door and waved as Liz pulled away. On her way home, Liz replayed the coffee date in her head. She'd give Dani one more chance to ask her out. Then she'd take the initiative. Liz nodded once.

"You get one more try, Dani."

Chapter 22

"So, how's our nephew?" Tina asked as Dani entered the store, back from her lunchtime visit.

"Pampered." Which wasn't an exaggeration. Barb bought a new dog bed with memory foam. Hell, it looked more comfortable than Dani's bed. He also had his choice of treats whenever he wanted them. When Dani had asked Barb to show a little restraint to how much she fed him, Barb told her she needed to quit fussing.

"Hell, yes, he's pampered. He's Frodo, and he's had a traumatic injury."

"He's getting around better now. Not as tentative." Dani waved toward the office. "I'm going to get some paperwork done. Let me know when that shipment of new books comes in. We had some moms order a couple of the best-selling children's books."

"You got it."

Dani settled in behind her desk and dove into the mail that had stacked up in her absence. Tina freely admitted that she "hated doing that paperwork shit," which worked out fine. While Dani could rifle through the mail and check on any bills they received, Tina could tend to customers out front.

An hour later, Tina hollered to Dani that the UPS truck had pulled up. Dani was ready to take a break. She directed the delivery man where he could wheel the boxes of books and signed off on the shipment.

She sat on the floor as she pushed books to one side of the shelf. The front door jingled open. When she reached back and grabbed another stack of books, she felt someone standing over her. Dani instantly fixated on a pair of familiar, gorgeous legs. Her gaze slowly traveled up to find Liz who looked down on her with a smile.

Dani jumped to her feet.

"I was headed back to the clinic after a short break, but I wanted to see how Frodo's doing," Liz said.

"He's doing great. Pampered like all get out, though."

"He deserves it!" Tina shouted from the counter.

"Barb and Tina must think I torture him at home." At Liz's upraised eyebrows, Dani added, "I'm kidding."

A lock of hair had fallen onto Liz's forehead. Dani had an overwhelming urge to reach out and push it off her face. Her face warmed as she realized she was staring at Liz's lips.

"Thanks for checking on him, Liz. I appreciate that you stopped in." Dani almost asked her if she'd like to have dinner, but a part of her was still gun-shy over her C.J. James experience.

"I won't keep you." Liz lingered for a few seconds and turned to leave.

"Liz." Dani walked up behind her.

Liz spun around.

"You'll never know how much your kindness with Frodo has meant to me."

Dani wasn't sure, but she thought she saw disappointment in Liz's eyes.

"You don't need to thank me. I care about you, and I care about Frodo."

Dani caught the emotion on her face. She reached out and impulsively gave Liz a hug. She felt a surge of desire fire through her body. Liz relaxed in her arms and uttered a soft sigh. Dani reluctantly ended the embrace, and Liz left the shop.

Tina came up behind her as they watched Liz walk to her car.

"I'm not a femme, and I'm not the best at reading them," Tina said. "But even I could tell she was waiting for you to ask her out."

"What?"

"I wasn't trying to eavesdrop." Tina shifted her weight. "Maybe I was. But when she said she didn't want to keep you and stood there waiting for you to say something? That was a big clue."

"Damn it. I'm so dense. I'm so fucking worried about doing or saying the wrong thing that I make it worse by saying nothing."

"You've already had that coffee date."

"Yeah. I didn't count that as a date date, though."

"As opposed to a date."

Dani rolled her eyes. "You know what I mean."

"After watching you not ask her for a date date, I think we need to send you to a Reading Femmes 101 course."

"Ha-ha."

Tina craned her neck around Dani to look out the window. Dani followed her gaze. Liz had her purse on the hood of the car, rummaging through it in an obvious search for her keys.

"You still have time to catch the doctor before she drives off," Tina said.

"Do you think—"

"Damn, woman. What more do you need me to do? Shove you out the door?" Tina grabbed Dani's arm, dragged her to the door, and opened it. Then she pushed Dani outside. "There. Now go."

Dani stumbled leaving the store but righted herself and crossed the street. She approached Liz.

"Liz," Dani said, but she didn't think Liz had heard her. She grabbed Liz's shoulder. Liz wheeled around and, in one swift motion, whacked Dani in the face. Dani staggered sideways into the SUV parked in front of Liz's car.

"Oh, my God, Dani. I didn't know it was you. It was a self-defense reflex. I'm so sorry."

Dani felt a little woozy, so she sat down on the bumper of the SUV. She moved her jaw around and checked for damage. Liz gingerly pulled Dani's hand away from her face. She looked like she was about to cry.

"Don't," Dani said.

Liz dropped her hand. "I was trying to see—"

"No, you can touch me. Just don't cry. If you cry, I might lose it here. You have no idea what your eyes look like when you cry."

Liz lightly brushed her thumb along Dani's cheek. "It's red here, but I don't think I bruised you. Thank God. You don't need another black eye, and you sure don't need one coming from me."

"You got your money's worth wherever you took those self-defense classes."

Liz seemed uncertain of what to say. She relaxed when she must have caught on that Dani was teasing her. She laughed and sat down beside Dani on the bumper.

Dani took Liz's hand. "I'd like to ask you out. On a proper date.

Not that going to the coffee shop wasn't nice. I mean it was." Dani closed her eyes. "God. I'm such a klutz at this."

Liz squeezed her arm. "Yes."

"Yeah?"

"I'd love to go out on a proper date." Liz's eyes twinkled in the sunlight. She lifted her hand and softly caressed Dani's cheek. "But I promise I'll no longer abuse you." She stood up and brushed off the back of her skirt. "I really need to get to the clinic. My afternoon appointments start in half an hour." She didn't look up when she spoke as she continued to brush her skirt. When she raised her head, she caught the full brunt of Dani's stare.

Dani's gaze dropped to Liz's mouth. A flicker of uncertainty passed over Liz's face, but she gave a slight nod. Dani cradled Liz's face in her hands as their lips touched for the first time. It started as a soft kiss, but it deepened with each passing second. Dani dropped her hands to Liz's hips and pulled her in tight. She parted Liz's lips with her tongue. Liz responded by pressing her tongue into Dani's and went limp in Dani's arms. Dani didn't know how long the kiss lasted, but it felt like it was over too soon.

When they pulled apart, they were both breathing heavily. Liz swallowed hard. She cleared her throat. "Call me?"

"I'll call you tonight."

Liz turned around and fumbled in her purse again that sat on the hood of her car. She raised the keys in the air. "I'm such a ninny sometimes," she said with a goofy grin as she jingled the keys. Her face flushed as she backed up and bumped into the side mirror of her car. She groped behind her, pulled the handle, and hurried to get inside. In her haste, she dropped the keys to the floor. She bent over, held them up in triumph, and started the engine. She merged into traffic and waved at Dani before driving away.

No one could've wiped the smile off Dani's face no matter how hard they tried. Her cheek still hurt a little where Liz struck her, but it didn't matter. She'd managed to fluster Dr. Liz Springer with a kiss. Dani started to whistle but winced with the effort. So she hummed "I'm in Love with a Wonderful Guy" from *South Pacific*, silently changing it to "Girl" in her mind as she headed back to the store. She pictured Mitzi Gaynor dancing in the sand by the ocean. And that cartwheel Mitzi did in the middle of the song? Yeah, she could pull it off. She might fall on her ass in the middle of the street, but it would be worth it.

When she walked into the shop, Dani heard a noise behind the counter. She didn't see Tina until she reached the back. Then she spotted her. She was crouched behind the counter, doubled over in laughter.

"I guess you saw the WWE Smackdown, huh?" Dani asked.

Tina laughed harder and fell on the floor to rest against the wall.

"Oh, my God. I wish I had a video of that. You have no idea how funny it was."

"Shut up." Dani sat down on the stool and moved the mouse to take the PC out of sleep mode.

"How's your face?" Tina snickered as she stood up. She touched Dani's cheek. "Eh. No black eye this time. Liz sure seems capable of taking care of herself."

"Tell me about it."

Tina's eyes sparkled with amusement. "I do have to say that your kiss was one for the movies."

"Jesus Christ, Tina. Did you watch everything?"

"Um, yeah. Damn. You can kiss when your heart's in it. I mean, I've seen you kiss Katie before, but this was different. It was..."

"Magic," Dani finished for her.

"I was going to say 'fucking awesome,' but I guess 'magic' will do."

"You're too much."

"Yeah, I am, huh?"

Dani remembered she had been in the middle of stocking new books when Liz entered the store. That kiss did an even bigger number on her than she thought. "I need to finish stocking those books." While she sat on the floor and slid books into place, she heard Tina on the phone.

"God, Barb, you should've seen it. It was so damn funny. What's that? No, she's okay. What? I'm pretty sure it went fine considering it ended in a kiss." Tina laughed. "Yeah, it's about time, huh?"

Dani smiled. They were right—it was about time.

"'I'm such a ninny'? God, Liz. And you *hit* her. You're lucky she still wants to go out with you." Liz turned into the clinic's parking lot. When she got out of the car, she leaned against the door and relived the kiss. The out-of-this-world, mind-blowing kiss. She brushed her fingertips across her lips. If she felt this way after one kiss, she couldn't wait for another preview of coming attractions.

Chapter 23

Dani spun Liz on the dance floor at Carl's and tugged her back into her arms. Liz giggled.

"Having fun?" Dani asked.

Liz couldn't remember the last time she enjoyed herself this much. Maybe it was the music. Maybe it was the dancing. Dani winked at her as she spun her again. Who was she kidding? It was definitely the woman.

They'd gone out on three dates now. Each one left Liz wanting more. She'd felt herself falling for Dani a little the first time they'd met at Frodo's exam. The more she got to know Dani, the closer she wanted to be to her. Everything led up to this time in her life. Their walks with Melanie and Frodo. The night of Dani's accident with the mutual understanding they needed to give each other time.

The caring side of Dani melted Liz's heart. Dani was the opposite of Therese. Not dangerous. Or risky. Yet, Liz held back a little when Dani would take her home. Each time, she could tell Dani waited for her to ask her inside. With what Liz was feeling tonight, her reluctance was breaking down like a fifteen-year-old used car.

The music slowed, and Dani pulled Liz close. Liz loved the way they fit together. She would say like a hand in a glove, but it was too much of a cliché. She tried to come up with something else.

Dani leaned back and searched Liz's eyes. "What are you thinking so hard about? You're having fun, right?"

"I can't remember the last time I enjoyed a night like this." Liz stroked the hair at the nape of Dani's neck. "It's because of you, Dani. As for what I was thinking so hard about, I was trying to come up with something other than we fit like a hand in a glove. Too much of a cliché?"

Dani caressed Liz's cheek and gave her a gentle kiss. "How

about we fit together like two hearts beating as one?" She raised her eyebrow.

Liz laughed and slapped Dani lightly on the shoulder. "You're a smooth talker."

"Is it working?"

"Kiss me again, and I'll tell you."

* * *

Dani was in the kitchen microwaving more popcorn. After she and Liz dated for a while, they decided to stay in on Saturday night to watch a DVD. Dani left on the stereo radio while she was out of the room. She hummed to the tune she heard playing and waited for the popcorn to settle down in the microwave.

Liz shouted to her, "How many times have you seen this movie?"

"I don't know," Dani said in a loud voice from around the wall. "Enough to where if I wanted to, I could irritate the hell out of you and recite each line." Liz laughed. "Do you need another Coke?"

"No. I'm good."

Dani poured the popcorn into one big bowl. She reached for a Coke from the back of the refrigerator. When she walked around the corner, she stopped short. Liz didn't notice she was watching. Liz sat on the couch in her shorts and tank top with her legs curled up under her. With one hand, she was reading the back of the DVD box. Her other elbow rested on the back of the couch while she ran her fingers through her dark hair.

God, she's beautiful, Dani thought. And she doesn't even have to try. Dani felt her breath catch. Liz must have heard her. She turned her head to where Dani stood in the dining room.

"Are you okay?" Liz looked genuinely worried.

"Ye-yeah. I'm fine." She sat down next to Liz and set the bowl of popcorn onto the coffee table in front of them.

Frodo raised his head from his bed next to the couch. He sniffed the air but settled back into the bed cushion.

"The music's so beautiful in this movie," Dani said as she picked up the remote to the stereo, ready to turn off the radio.

Dani's stomach erupted in flutters. Not from fear, like she felt deep in her gut with C.J. It was a feeling from her past. It was like the anticipation she'd get in the backyard in Peabody with her dad and brother as they waited for a falling star. She remembered being on edge as she scanned the black starlit sky above her. Then, there it would be, out of the corner of her eye, and her heart would pound harder as she watched the star begin its quick descent.

Her heart pounded now in anticipation of what this night held. She realized she still had the remote in her hand but hadn't turned off the radio. She got ready to hit the button, but Liz placed her hand on her arm.

"What were you thinking about? You were far away, but you were smiling."

"It was a memory from my childhood." Dani cleared her throat. "But the same happiness I felt then? I feel it now." She set the remote down and reached up to brush Liz's hair back. It was so thick and sensual. She ran her fingers through the strands until she entwined her fingers at the nape of Liz's neck. "It's you, Liz." She lowered her lips to Liz's and whispered against her mouth, "It's you." She parted Liz's lips with her tongue and waited for Liz's tongue to meet hers. Then she opened her mouth wide to bring Liz inside. Heat surged deep in her core as she pushed Liz back onto the couch. Dani trailed kisses to Liz's throat and felt the vibration on her own lips when Liz let out a soft moan.

Liz cradled Dani's face in her hands. Liz's eyes answered the question that Dani was about to ask. She pulled Dani close so she pressed against her full length. Liz was the one who pushed her tongue hungrily into Dani's. Liz was the one who brushed her thumb against Dani's nipple until it hardened. Liz was the one... It was Liz.

The music playing on the radio swirled into Dani's brain. She was lost in the kiss and in Liz's touch, but the words to the song prickled Dani's ears, not unlike trying to understand a foreign language. Then Dani knew. The words rang in her head like clashing cymbals:

Your eyes to me were like a pool of light,
They shimmered and took me to another world.
Where I knew everything would be all right,
'Cause you opened my heart to let my love unfurl.

Liz tensed underneath her. She lifted her hand away from Dani's breast, and she pulled her mouth away. Her eyes met Dani's, but they didn't reflect hurt. They reflected resignation. *Those damn words.*

Dani wanted to shout that Liz was wrong as Dani slowly sat up. She wanted to shout that it was just a song. But it was more than that. The song was a reminder. And Dani sure as hell didn't need that image in her head when she was trying to make love to Liz.

Liz joined Dani in sitting up. Dani snatched the remote from the table and flipped off the stereo before the song reached the chorus where C.J. spoke Dani's name. She tossed the remote onto the table where it rattled against a coaster. Dani stared straight ahead for a long moment. She turned to Liz to find her staring at the far wall, too.

Dani reached for Liz's hand.

"Look, Liz, I'm sor—"

Liz entwined her fingers with Dani's and squeezed. "Dani, please don't say you're sorry. There's nothing to be sorry about." She turned so that their eyes met. Dani attempted to swallow the lump in her throat when she saw the regret etched on Liz's face.

"She means nothing to me. You know that, right?"

Liz brushed her fingertips alongside Dani's cheek. "Yes. I do know that."

Dani wanted so much to pull Liz close and kiss away what had happened, but the moment and the mood were gone. "We can still watch the movie," she said hopefully.

"I think I'm going to head home. It's getting late."

Dani glanced at the clock and saw that it was only nine-thirty, but she didn't argue with Liz.

Liz stood up. Dani did, too, but a little too quickly. Her knee bumped the bowl of popcorn and sent the white fluffy stuff flying onto the floor. Perfect, she thought. That pretty much tops off the evening. Liz started to help pick up the mess, but Dani stopped her.

"It's okay. I'll take care of it." Frodo munched on the popcorn that had fallen by his bed. "Or Frodo will."

"You sure?"

"Yeah. It's fine."

Dani walked Liz to the door. Liz kissed Dani gently on the mouth. "Don't beat yourself up about this, okay?" She tucked Dani's hair behind her ear.

Dani nodded, but she knew it was too late for that. She opened the door for Liz, and the warm Georgia night air swept into the house. Liz descended the porch steps, waved, and got into her car. Dani stood there until the red taillights were out of view. She shut the door and locked the deadbolt. She leaned her back against the door. Frodo walked over and stared up at her as if he knew something was wrong. Anger rose up like bile into her throat until she could no longer tamp it down.

"God damn you, C.J. James." She slid down the door and slumped onto the floor. Frodo laid his head on her lap and licked her hand. "Sorry, little guy. I'm not mad at you." He nudged her hand. She stroked his soft fur. "Let's hope this doesn't scare Liz away."

* * *

"How have you been, stranger?"

Liz glanced at her sister Laurie and turned her attention back to Tucker and his brothers playing with Melanie. Laurie had called Liz to see if she'd like to join them for an outing in the park. She watched while Eric and Tucker played a game of keep-away from Melanie with a ball. "I've been fine."

"We've not heard from you for several weeks. Sometimes that can be a bad thing. Anything going on that's kept you from us?"

"What are you fishing for, Laurie?"

"Well, there was that certain Amazon from the family barbecue."

"Michelle?"

"Yeah. How'd your date go?"

"Oh, that."

"Uh-oh. What happened?"

"Nothing happened. We went to Carl's Cavern to hear C.J. James sing on her last night."

Laurie sighed. "C.J. James."

"Please don't start again. You freaked me out enough last time."

"Oh, all right. Party pooper." Laurie whipped her head toward the kids. "Tucker Marcus McKinley, what did I tell you about excluding Tanner from your play?"

Tanner sat with his legs crossed, elbow planted on his knee with his chin on his fist in the classic sulking pose used by kids for generations.

"That it was mean and to remember I was four years old once," Tucker mumbled.

"Right. So you and Eric let Tanner play with Melanie, too."

Tucker motioned Tanner over. "Come on, Tanner."

Tanner sprang to his feet and hustled to join his brothers.

Liz was glad for the reprieve that she knew would be short-lived. Here it comes...

"Back to you," Laurie said. "Let's forget about C.J. James for a minute. How was your date with Michelle?"

Liz told Laurie about the evening at Carl's. She surprised herself when she included the encounter with Dani.

"The same Dani you're attracted to?"

"Yeah."

"Is she still dating C.J. James? I wondered about that when she left for Nashville."

"No." Liz told her about their breakup.

"That's good, right?" Laurie twisted on the bench to face Liz.

"Mm hmm."

"You're dating her now, aren't you?" Laurie smacked her lightly on the arm. "You little devil. You swooped right in."

"It's not like that." Liz talked about Dani's accident and the time they allowed each other before their first date. She also told Laurie about what happened Saturday night.

Laurie cringed. "I wondered about that song. It's really about Dani?"

"Yup."

"Kind of ruined the mood, didn't it?"

"Yup."

They watched the kids still playing with the ball. Melanie had stretched out in the grass, obviously tired from her running.

"Sooo..."

"So, we've not talked since then."

"Elizabeth Ann Springer, get over yourself and call her."

"I know, but..."

"But what?"

"How the heck do I compete with C.J. James? You, my supposedly straight sister, even thinks she's hot."

"From what you told me of your date Saturday night, Dani was sorry the song interrupted your hot and heavy make-out session."

"Yeah, she was sorry."

"Like I said, get over your damn self." Laurie's voice softened. "Dani obviously makes you happy. What else are you afraid of?"

Liz shrugged. "Maybe that it's too good to be true and the song was a sign we should stop before we really get started."

Laurie put her arm around Liz and pulled her close. "I know Therese did a number on you, but I also know you're too kind and beautiful to go the rest of your life without allowing love back into your heart. You deserve to be happy, and you deserve to be with a woman who puts that smile on your face."

Liz couldn't help it. She couldn't stop her lips from slipping into a slow smile when she thought of Dani Roberts.

Laurie tapped her nose. "There it is. There's the smile. Promise me you'll call her? Or better yet, go see her? I think she's a little skittish right now, too, and probably thinks she's run you off."

Liz thought how disappointed Dani looked when Liz left Saturday night. "You might be right."

"Of course I am. I'm your big sister. We know all things."

"Ah, yes, oh omnipotent one. How could I ever doubt you?"

"Hell if I know," Laurie said and laughed.

Liz joined her in the laughter. "I'd better get my poor, pooped pup and head home." She stood up.

"Don't wait too long in calling her or seeing her."

"I won't."

"Promise?"

"Promise." Liz leaned over and kissed her sister's cheek. "Thanks, Laurie."

"You're very welcome. Good luck with that bookstore owner."

Chapter 24

All week long, Dani hesitated to call Liz. Deep down, she had a fear she'd notice a change in Liz's voice and would know that things were different between them. She didn't want to hear it, so she decided to wait before calling. Now, she wondered if she'd waited too long.

She talked to Tina about the incident. Tina's first reaction was to hunt C.J. down in Nashville and "kick her ass." Her second reaction was to tell Dani to get over herself and "call the good doctor."

Dani decided Saturday afternoon she would do just that after she got home. They closed the shop late due to a surge of customers at five. She picked up Frodo from Barb's. About six weeks had gone by since his surgery, and he was healing nicely. Time to get back into the routine of the high school girl coming over to walk him and check in on him. After seven, Dani and Frodo entered the house.

She threw her keys in the dish by the door, flipped through her mail, and felt her stomach growl in protest, a reminder that she hadn't taken time for lunch earlier in the day. Frodo got his food first, and Dani was encouraged to see him prance in front of his dish again. She lifted a box of Chicken and Broccoli Medley from the freezer and tossed it in the microwave. "Frozen Dinner City, here I come," she muttered. She watched the dinner spin slowly in the microwave and thought about what she'd say to Liz. Her mind felt like the cold dinner on the spinning glass plate.

The microwave dinged, and Dani carefully removed the dinner and set it on the table to cool off. As she watched the steam rise from the mixed concoction, she thought she'd ask Liz to drive to Atlanta next Saturday for a day trip. She'd wait an hour before calling so Liz would have time to relax after work. Dani shook her head. *Yeah. Right. You're afraid to call her.*

After she finished dinner, she glanced up at the wall clock and saw it was eight. A hot shower sounded good. She placed her foot on the first step of stairs and stopped when she realized Frodo was on her heels.

"No, Frodo. You can't go upstairs yet." She nudged him back and slid the child's gate in front of the bottom step. He whimpered, which just about broke her heart. "I'm sorry, little guy. It's for your own good. We still have a few more weeks before you can take the stairs." At the tone of her voice, he slinked back into the living room and slumped down on his bed in a huff. "Yeah, yeah, yeah. I'm a horrible mommy."

Once in the bathroom, Dani stripped and ran the water as hot as she could stand it. Despite the heat outside, once she stepped out of the shower, she'd cool down in the air conditioning of her home. It was one of her favorite things to do.

She finished but barely toweled off before donning a pair of boxer shorts and a white tank top. She wanted to be wet enough for the air to cool her body. As she headed downstairs, the front doorbell rang.

Who would stop by to see me at this hour, she wondered, as her bare feet slapped across the hardwood floor. She squinted her eye to look through the peephole. *Liz.* Dani glanced down at her boxer shorts and tank top. She was braless and the shirt clung to her still damp body.

Shit. Shit. Shit. Taking a deep breath, she opened the door.

Oh good, she's home, Liz thought as the door swung open.

"Hi, Dani, I—" She stopped as she took in Dani's appearance. She first noticed Dani's slicked-back hair, then her damp tank top where Dani's nipples pressed enticingly against the white material. Her gaze dropped to tan, muscled thighs and calves, all dripping wet as if Dani just stepped out of the shower.

Dear God.

Dani crossed her arms in front of her chest.

Liz wanted to tell her, "Don't do that on my account." Instead, she tried to keep her voice steady and her focus on Dani's face. "I'm sorry I dropped by without calling."

"No, no. It's fine." While keeping one arm across her chest, Dani motioned at her body with her other hand. "I just got out of the shower. Obviously."

Yup. Quite obviously. "I can come back another night."

"Liz, please come in." Dani pulled the door open farther and moved to allow Liz to step inside.

Frodo jumped up from his bed and trotted over.

Liz knelt down and stroked his back. "He seems to get better each time I see him." She gingerly felt his incision. "And this is healing quite nicely." She giggled as Frodo licked her face. "I'm glad to see you, too, boy." She tried to regain some of her composure before she chanced turning back to Dani. She rose to her feet. "You're probably wondering why I stopped by."

Dani motioned to the couch. "Why don't we sit down?"

After they had settled next to each other, Liz reached for Dani's hand. "It's taken me all week to come over, and it shouldn't have. What happened last Saturday wasn't your fault. You can't control the music on the radio." Liz gave a small laugh. "Although that night I wish you could have."

"You and me both," Dani muttered.

"It made me think of C.J. James. Her looks. Her sex appeal." She tossed her hand up in the air. "Her everything. And I thought I fell short."

"Liz—"

Liz squeezed her hand. "No, let me finish. Please."

Dani gave a slight nod.

"I also had to get over being skittish because of Therese. Being afraid that maybe what we have going is too good to be true." Before Dani could object, Liz said, "But I realized this week, after some talking to by my older sister, that I'm pretty special and you're not Therese. We deserve this, what we have going on between us."

As Liz awaited Dani's response, she thought back to how she'd practiced her speech on the way over. In her mind, it sounded like a self-help pep talk: "Hi, my name is Liz, and I'm pretty special." But saying the words out loud were empowering. She really was special, and she was worthy of love again.

Dani's response was to lean over and touch her lips to Liz's in a light kiss. She pulled back and cupped Liz's cheek. Her dark-brown eyes swirled with emotion. "You are more than special, Liz. I've known that since the first time we met. You're kind and gentle." She brushed her thumb against Liz's cheek. "And beautiful. C.J. James? She's like a quick fix to a junkie. I'm sorry I was pulled in by her charms. It never felt right. Or real."

Liz searched Dani's eyes and looked for honesty there. "And us?"

"You're everything I've hoped for in my life. I'd like to think we have something magical together."

"Yes," Liz whispered. "Oh, yes."

Dani stood and held out her hand.

When Liz clasped Dani's hand and rose to her feet, her gaze dropped to Dani's legs, still damp from the shower. She slowly worked her way up to Dani's boxer shorts and then to her breasts. Again, Dani's nipples grew hard against the cotton material, but it wasn't from the air drifting over her body. It was from the want in Liz's eyes that shifted color in the light of the room. They were the deep forest green of desire.

Liz brushed her fingernails lightly along Dani's side until Dani shivered. She ran her hand to the small of Dani's back and pulled her closer. Her eyes suddenly became playful. "We're leaving the radio off this time," she said in a low, throaty voice—one that Dani hadn't heard before, but one that Dani hoped to hear for the rest of her life.

Liz sought out Dani's mouth. Their tongues met, and Dani opened her mouth farther as the kiss deepened.

Dani broke away from the kiss, her heart pounding. "Bed?"

"Yes," Liz said in a hoarse whisper as she grasped Dani's hand. "You'll need to lead the way, though."

Frodo started to follow them down the hall to the guest room. Dani stopped. "Sorry, bud. You need to sleep out here tonight." He plopped his butt on the hardwood floor and sighed. "And that's not going to work." With that, he stood up, huffed, and marched back to his bed in the living room.

Liz was shaking, obviously trying to hold her laughter in.

"Sorry this isn't as romantic as I hoped."

This time, Liz didn't hold in the laugh. "It's perfect. Now, take me to your bed."

Liz's command caused Dani's center to throb with need. "Yes, ma'am." Dani led her into the bedroom. The bright moon streamed in through the windows and cast the bed in a soft blue light.

"It's not the king-size bed upstairs, but—"

Liz placed two fingers against Dani's lips. "Dani?"

"Hmm?"

"Shut up and kiss me."

Dani tilted Liz's chin upward. The moonlight shone in Liz's eyes, and they changed into yet another color—turquoise. Hypnotic. Dani dropped her mouth to Liz's and brushed it lightly. She trailed her lips to Liz's neck and kissed her softly there. She slid her hands along Liz's sides and thrilled at the shudder her touch caused. Dani grazed her fingertips across Liz's bare arms and slowly undid each button of Liz's cotton blouse. She continued to nibble Liz's throat and felt the vibration of her moan. She pulled the shirt off Liz's shoulders and cupped each breast in her hands, rubbing Liz's nipples until they hardened against the material of her bra. Liz stepped back and unsnapped the bra. She let it glide off her shoulders and slowly fall to the floor.

Dani let out a small gasp as she gazed at Liz's bare breasts. "God, you're beautiful." Dani wasn't sure she spoke the words out loud until she caught Liz's shy smile. It was Dani's turn to tremble with desire. She stepped forward and lowered her head to one breast. She took the nipple in her mouth and softly sucked it. Liz pulled Dani's head even more into her. Fire shot down Dani's belly, and she was instantly wet. Dani caressed the other breast while continuing to lick the nipple until it was rock hard.

Liz gasped. "Please, Dani. Please take me to bed. I don't think I can stand any—"

Dani broke away from Liz's nipple and brought her mouth back up to Liz's, thrusting her tongue inside. Dani pushed Liz back onto the bed to lay across its width with her legs off the side. Dani unzipped Liz's shorts and pulled them to the floor. She pressed her hand between Liz's legs to her mound. Her panties were soaked. Another surge of wetness hit between her own legs when she felt the effect she was having on Liz. Dani reached down and tugged Liz's panties off, almost ripping them in her haste.

Dani left Liz's mouth and dropped again to Liz's nipple. She pushed her fingers into Liz's wet folds and moaned as she felt her slick center. She plunged her fingers deep inside until Liz cried out.

Dani moaned when Liz closed around her fingers. She kissed her way back up to Liz's mouth as she thrust in and out, faster and faster. Liz's hips moved in synchronous rhythm, as though they were making love to a silent symphony that only they could hear.

Liz broke away from Dani's mouth. "Oh, God, Dani. Oh, God!" Dani pushed her knee hard against her hand when she knew Liz was close to climax. "Dani, please." With one more thrust, Liz tensed, squeezed Dani's shoulders, and shuddered.

As Liz lay there with her chest rising and falling with each hard breath, Dani rose up and removed her tank top and boxer shorts. When she stood nude in front of Liz, she almost fell to her knees, seeing the love there on Liz's face.

She lifted Liz onto the pillows so she lay completely on the bed now. Dani lowered her body on top of Liz and pressed against her.

"Dani, let me—"

"Shh," Dani whispered into Liz's ear. She knew Liz wanted to make love to her, but Dani couldn't stop even if she wanted to. She wanted to discover and worship every inch of Liz's body. Trailing her kisses down Liz's body, she pushed her lips to her breasts and sucked softly on each nipple before continuing her descent. She gently pulled Liz's legs apart and began at her ankles, pressing her lips to first one, then the other. To the inside of one knee, then the other. She kissed each thigh, lingered there, and enjoyed the scent of Liz's essence. She looked up to see Liz's eyes full of desire and wonderment staring back at her. Dani let out a soft cry. She couldn't wait any longer. She parted Liz's soft folds with her fingers and pressed her mouth into Liz's wetness. She licked the length of Liz's lips, then captured her clit and gently sucked.

Liz's legs began to tighten around Dani's head, but before they tightened completely, Dani slipped her fingers inside of Liz until she felt Liz pulse around her.

"Oh yes. There," Liz cried. "Don't stop!"

Dani didn't know which "there" Liz was referring to, but she knew she wasn't going to stop either movement. She pressed her tongue hard into Liz's wet folds and plunged her fingers deep inside. Liz cried out and tightened her legs around Dani's head even more. The spasms fluttered against Dani's fingertips. The muscles in Liz's thighs trembled, and Dani was lost. Lost in the sensation of knowing the pleasure she'd given Liz.

Liz's legs went limp. Dani withdrew slowly from her. Liz grabbed Dani's hair as she tensed up again and then relaxed back onto the bed. Dani kissed the inside of each of Liz's thighs and lifted herself up onto the bed to lie beside Liz. Liz rested her head on Dani's shoulder.

"Please hold me," Liz whispered.

"You don't have to say please." Dani pulled Liz close to lie face to face. She wrapped one arm around Liz's waist and draped her leg possessively over Liz's. Dani's eyes grew heavy and she heard Liz's soft, even breathing beside her as they both fell into a deep sleep.

Dani woke first in the same position as when she fell asleep. Liz's hair spilled onto Dani's bare chest. Pushing her hand through it, she was amazed at how sensual it felt as she let the silky strands fall through her fingers.

Liz stirred awake. She looked up at Dani and smiled. "Hi," she said in a soft voice.

"Hi." Dani kissed her forehead.

Liz lightly touched Dani's nipple until it hardened beneath her fingertips. "God, I can feel how wet you are on my thigh."

Dani started to pull her leg away, but Liz grabbed it and tugged it up even higher onto her hip. "Don't go away from me," she said in a hoarse whisper. Liz lowered her hand between Dani's legs. She pressed her palm into Dani's wetness and moaned. She dragged her fingers through Dani's lips. Dani pushed her hips up to meet them.

Liz lowered her body enough to lick Dani's nipple as she began a rhythm with her right hand.

"Go inside," Dani said through ragged breaths. "Please go inside." She felt Liz smile against her nipple as she plunged two fingers into her slick center. Dani gasped. "Oh God, Liz. *Please.*" Liz thrust deeper inside and pressed her palm against Dani's lips. Dani rocked with her, and Liz stayed in perfect rhythm. Dani tightened her leg around Liz until she felt like she'd explode. Liz licked faster, and her hand kept pace. "Yes!" Dani exploded into her orgasm.

Liz kept her hand between Dani's legs and raised her head to kiss Dani. Liz had stilled, but as soon as she kissed Dani, she started moving again.

Dani gasped. "Oh, God, Liz, I don't think I can—"

"Yes, you can, Dani. Do it for me." Liz's voice was a hushed whisper. Dani fell into Liz's eyes as Liz's desire swallowed her. "You can do it. You can do it." With each word, Liz pushed her hand harder. Her thumb found Dani's clit. She tweaked and probed until Dani cried out. "There? It's there isn't it, baby?" Her green eyes darkened even more. "Come for me, Dani. Let go. Just let go." Liz's thrusts deepened, and she rubbed Dani's clit faster and faster. Dani closed her eyes tight, and she literally saw stars.

She surrendered her last shred of self-control. She trusted Liz with her heart, with everything that Dani was. The pleasure built until Dani screamed out into the night. Liz lowered her lips back to Dani's nipple and thrust in and out of her. Dani's whole body shook as she climaxed for the second time.

Liz slowly removed her hand. Tears streamed down Dani's cheeks, but she didn't have the strength to wipe them away. Liz pulled her close.

"I could get used to this," Dani choked out. Liz smiled against her cheek.

"I could, too." Liz wiped away Dani's tears, Dani's scent still on her hand.

Dani's whole world had shifted. What they shared this night was something holy. Something pure. Something she could never relinquish. She could spend the rest of her life in the arms of this woman, safe in her warm and loving cocoon. With that knowledge, Dani fell asleep with a smile.

Chapter 25

"What is it that they say? Read 'em and weep, suckers." Tina spread out her cards.

Dani threw her cards into the middle of the table when she saw the four aces. "Damn it."

"And y'all thought I was losing my touch." Tina raked the chips toward her.

Liz reached over and grabbed her hands. "Wait. I'm not sure, but doesn't this beat four of a kind?" Liz, who now accompanied Dani to poker nights, laid down her hand. A straight flush.

The women at the table laughed.

Barb snickered. "Uh, I think Liz has you there, hon."

"Yeah, Tina, I think you spoke too soon," Monica said. Alice, the woman she'd been dating steady for several months, laughed. It was great to see Monica so happy and with someone who treated her right.

At the sound of loud laughter, Frodo rose from his spot in the living room and trotted into the dining room. He sat down by Barb and pawed at her leg.

"What's wrong, my little nephew? Are Dani and Liz not giving you enough treats?" Barb headed to the top of the refrigerator where she pulled down a jar of doggie biscuits. Frodo was right on her heels. "Hear you go, my poor starved and mistreated Frodo."

"Oh, good Lord, Barb. He has you so whipped."

"Don't tell him that, Dani. He thinks he's fooling me each time he visits. I have to continue the ruse."

Frodo had healed even more in the weeks since the surgery, and Dani could leave him home alone, but she felt more at ease if he was close by. She and Liz took turns on whose house they stayed in overnight. Except for that first night when Liz had her sister check in on Melanie, she'd bring Melanie over to Dani's house if she stayed all night. Dani did the same with Frodo when she stayed with Liz. They'd established a rhythm to their relationship. Dani had even met Liz's family at several outings. But she'd been scared to say the words "I love you," although she felt them deep in her heart. Liz seemed to be hesitant, too. Ghosts from the past haunted their present. Dani hoped to banish those ghosts... soon.

Barb sat down again. "Let's get back to business."

Tina shuffled the cards and dealt them out with a flourish. Liz won yet another hand.

Tina smacked the table with an open palm. "Liz, you cannot tell me that you've never played poker before. That's bullshit."

"My dad might have taught me a thing or two. He was a dealer at a Las Vegas casino in his younger years."

Tina had just taken a sip of her beer. She sputtered. "What?" She stared at Liz. "You're telling me your dad was a dealer in Vegas?"

"Yeah," Liz said with a sly grin.

"Well, shit."

Barb laughed. "Way to go, Liz. Way to go."

The evening ended with Liz the big winner. Tina, shoulders slumped, walked to her mantel as if she were walking to the guillotine. She picked up the trophy, kissed it once, and handed it to Liz.

"Thank you, Tina. I know that was extremely hard for you," Liz said in a solemn voice, but the corners of her mouth twitched in amusement.

"Oh shut the fuck up." Tina was obviously trying to look upset, but her playful expression gave her away. "Come here and give me a hug." Liz embraced her.

Dani hugged Barb and Tina and waved to the others. Everyone else decided to stay and watch a movie. Dani clipped on Frodo's leash. "Say goodbye to Aunt Barb, Aunt Tina, and everybody."

Barb patted his head. "You be a good boy."

Tina walked them to the door. "You three stay out of trouble, you hear?"

"We'll try," Dani said as she led Frodo outside. She took Liz's hand and squeezed it tight.

They didn't say anything for a while. The night air was perfect.

It was the last week of August. They had been enjoying unusually cool nights for that time of year.

Liz broke the silence. "You know you keep telling me this is the happiest you've ever been, Dani," Liz said in a soft voice. Dani glanced over at her, but Liz kept her head lowered as she walked. "I've never felt anything like this before, and sometimes it scares me. I'm almost afraid it's a dream."

Dani stopped. She waited until Liz looked up. Even in the moonlight, Dani could see the green depths of her eyes.

"I'm sometimes scared, too, Liz. But the more time that passes, the more it sinks in that I've started living the best years of my life. And nothing is going to happen to change that."

Liz pulled Dani in for a quick, gentle kiss. "I know," she whispered. "Just keep reminding me."

Dani kissed her again. "I will. Every day. But how about I remind you even more when we get home?"

"Sounds like a perfect plan."

Frodo interrupted their embrace by tugging them toward a tree.

"All right, all right, I get the message, Frodo," Dani said. They chuckled.

Liz linked her fingers through Dani's hand again as they continued on home.

Chapter 26

"Where do you want me to put this shit again, Dani?"

Dani tried to hold in her laughter as she watched Tina struggle with a display. With a huff, she staggered and carried it to the center of the store. Displays were never Tina's favorite thing to do, but Dani needed to work in the office to place some orders.

Dani led her to a table of bargain books. A lesbian group from Biloxi, Mississippi, that arrived in town on a tour bus had almost wiped out the entire stock. Dani wouldn't have known their hometown, but they all wore denim shirts with "Butches from Biloxi" stitched on the pocket. After their visit, the stock of bargain books went from three tables to one table with a row of two.

"Here," Dani said as she removed the books. "I want it to be at the front of the store."

Tina picked up one end of the table while Dani lifted the other. They set the table down by the entrance. Dani headed back to the office after showing Tina how she wanted the display to look.

"I hate doing this shit," Tina mumbled under her breath.

"What?" Dani asked as she continued walking. She'd heard Tina but wanted to give her a hard time.

"I said I *hate* doing this shit!" Tina shouted.

Dani laughed.

"It's not funny."

Dani sat down at the desk and clicked onto the website. She scrolled through the listings and began ordering what she needed. She was at it for about an hour when she felt someone watching her. Without looking up, she said, "Tina, just bite the bullet and finish the damn job." She didn't get a response. "What? No colorful retort?" Dani looked up. Her stomach did a quick turn when she saw who stood in the doorway.

C.J. James.

Dani sat back in her chair. She didn't know what she was feeling, but it wasn't good. For one thing, she couldn't speak.

"Hello, Dani," C.J. said softly. She looked great as always—even in torn jeans and a paint-stained, blue T-shirt. Her eyes were still the mesmerizing crystal blue that Dani remembered.

"Hello, C.J." Her own voice sounded so far away—like drifting up from a deep abandoned well.

C.J. moved closer to Dani's desk. "I'm sure I'm the last person you were expecting and that you don't even want to talk to me."

Dani nodded her head in agreement.

"But I came here to apologize. I'm sorry. There's nothing I can say except I'm sorry. I made a mistake in Nashville. A big one. I know that—believe me I do." She paused. "It's taken me these last months to realize what a fool I've been."

Dani sat there for a few seconds before she could find her voice again. "C.J., it's over."

"Please know I didn't mean to hurt you—"

Dani couldn't help it as she laughed sarcastically. "Wait. Let me get this straight. Fucking a teenager on your dressing room table wasn't meant to hurt me?"

C.J.'s face reddened. "She wasn't a teenager."

"You're going with that? She wasn't a teenager?" Dani tamped down on her anger. "It doesn't matter. Don't even try to justify it because it does *not* matter."

C.J. stepped closer to Dani's chair. Dani stood up. C.J. tried to touch her, but Dani yanked her hand out of reach.

"I always fuck stuff up, Dani. When I let someone inside, I—"

"I don't want to talk, okay? I'm in a very happy relationship now. What we had is over. It was probably over before it even had a chance to get started. You've said what you needed to say. I'm asking you to leave."

C.J. took a step back. "I didn't know."

"Well, now you do. So please go."

As Dani moved forward to show C.J. the door, C.J. suddenly pulled Dani to her and kissed her. Her lips felt cold against Dani's. What the hell did I ever see in her? flashed through Dani's mind. She grabbed C.J.'s arms to shove her away. Before she made the move, she heard a gasp from the doorway. She caught a quick glimpse of Liz as she hurriedly left.

"Liz! Liz!" Dani shouted. She roughly pushed her way past C.J. Liz ran out the door. Dani chased her toward her car. "Liz. Stop." Before Dani could reach the car, Liz pulled away. And she was crying. "Liz!" Dani shouted after the car.

Dani stood in the middle of the street. She felt like she'd been sucker punched. She stood there watching Liz's car until a horn blared behind her.

"What are you doing?" the driver yelled.

"Sorry." Dani moved out of the way. She walked back to her shop, her blood boiling a degree higher with each step she took.

She pushed open the door. Tina's eyes were wide with shock. "Dani, man, I'm so sorry. I was in the backroom getting the books for the display. I didn't hear the door when either one of them came in."

"You don't need to apologize, Tina. It's okay." Dani turned her attention to C.J. who still stood in the doorway of her office. "You." Dani hurried toward C.J. Tina moved fast to jump in front of Dani.

"What the hell is the matter with you?" Dani shouted. "What part of 'I'm in a relationship' didn't you get?"

"Dani, I'm sorry—"

"You're sorry? Sorry?" Dani made a move toward C.J. She wasn't sure what she wanted to do. Shake her until she came to her senses? Hit her? She wanted to do something, and none of it was good. Tina kept her hand pressed against Dani's chest.

Tina looked at C.J. "You need to go. Now," she said in an even tone.

C.J. opened her mouth to say something but must have thought better of it. She moved past them to the front door.

"And you know what, C.J.?" Dani shouted at her back. "You can take that song and shove it up your ass."

C.J. stiffened at the words. She turned to give Dani a long look before leaving.

Dani suddenly felt weak. Letting loose all of the anger bottled up inside of her had siphoned off her strength.

"Come here, Dani." Tina led her to the office chair and helped Dani sit down. "Take some deep breaths."

Dani took her advice. After the third deep breath, she said, "Liz didn't see me shove her away. She just saw me kissing her, and I wasn't even returning the kiss."

Tina knelt and placed her hands on Dani's knees. "You need to explain what happened. Liz is a smart lady. She'll understand."

"I'm not so sure about that, T. She was just telling me how she was having a hard time accepting how great everything is going for us. We've both had something like this happen. And now?" Dani shook her head trying to rid herself of the cold fear that shot through her gut. "Now I'm sure she's thinking that—" Dani ran her fingers through her hair in desperate exasperation. "Fuck."

"You have to go to her, Dani."

Dani drew in a breath and blew it out. She tried to will her heart to stop racing and her insides to stop roiling. "You're right. I'm not waiting. I'm going after her right now."

Tina rose and patted her on the shoulder. "Good girl."

"T?" Dani said as Tina reached the door.

Tina stopped and turned back at Dani. "Yeah?"

"Thanks." Dani managed a weak smile.

"No problem, boss."

After Tina left the office, Dani hurried out to her car, punched in Liz's cell number, and started the engine. Liz didn't pick up, which was rare. She usually answered after the second ring. Dani hung up and tried it again as she pulled out onto Main Street. When she didn't get an answer this time, she left a message to explain what happened.

"Where would she go?" Dani wondered out loud. Her eyes darted back and forth as she approached each intersection. As she drove, she began to get angry again. Why would C.J. think she could just march into her bookstore, say she was sorry, and everything would be okay? Dani's first thought was that maybe that tack had worked before. Her second thought was that C.J. was truly sorry and knew what she had lost. "I don't care about that. I only care about Liz," she whispered.

She drove past Liz's house but didn't see her Subaru. She searched each street but had no luck so she turned her car onto the state road. *I'll try the vet's office.* When she got there, she again didn't see Liz's car. As she drove back into town to her own home, thinking Liz may be there, she spotted the Subaru in the lot at the park. Dani searched the grassy, tree-lined area and saw Liz walking with her head down at the far end of the park. Dani pulled into the lot next to Liz's car and headed toward her.

"Liz," Dani said as she got closer.

Liz stopped. She turned and Dani slowed her steps when she saw her tear-stained face.

Dani's heart jumped to her throat, and she had to swallow hard. "God, Liz, please believe me. It wasn't what it looked like." Dani closed her eyes for a second and shuddered at her words, knowing she had watched so many scenes in movies where the actor or actress uttered those exact lines... and it was always what it looked like.

Liz swiped her cheek with the back of her hand. "Dani," she said in a choked voice.

Dani stood in front of her. "You weren't there to see me push her away. She kissed me. I didn't kiss her. I know this might bring back bad memories, but—"

"Can you give me some time? Please. Seeing the two of you..."

"But—"

Liz placed her hand on Dani's chest. "Please, Dani," she said in a pleading voice. Her eyes again welled up with tears.

"Okay," Dani whispered. "Okay. Just know that I would never intentionally hurt you."

Liz nodded and bit her quivering lower lip. She motioned toward the trail that lined the park. "I'm going to walk awhile."

Dani watched Liz walk away. It took every ounce of self-control not to run after her, but she loved Liz enough to let her go. She only hoped she'd get a chance to tell her that she loved her.

Chapter 27

"Think about what you're doing, Liz."

Liz pulled more clothes out of her closet and folded them into her suitcase. She'd made the mistake of calling Laurie, but only because she wanted her to watch Melanie while she was out of town.

"I need to clear my head."

"You can't do that here? You know? In Francis? Why fly all the way to Colorado? Wait. Isn't Grand Lake where you took off to when you and Therese broke up?"

Of course Laurie would remember that little tidbit of information. "I broke up with her. She didn't break up with me."

Laurie grabbed one of the shirts Liz had thrown on the bed near where Laurie was sitting and folded it. "Remind me again why you broke up with her."

Liz spun around. "You know very well what happened."

Laurie set the shirt in the suitcase and crossed her arms over her chest. "Say the words."

Liz felt her face flush with anger. "She was sleeping with my best friend," she said through clenched teeth. "I caught them in bed together."

"Okay." Laurie dragged out the word. "And what happened with Dani?"

Liz stared down at her sneakers. "I walked in on her kissing C.J. James."

"No. You walked in on C.J. James kissing *her*. You told me Dani explained what happened. Don't you believe her?"

"It's not that." Liz pulled a pair of jeans off a hanger.

"Really? Then tell me why the hell you're willing to fly across the freaking country rather than stay here and get this sorted out."

"Yoo-hoo. Where are you guys?" Lacey shouted from the front

of the house.

"We're in the bedroom," Laurie shouted back.

Liz glared at her. "You called Lacey?"

"Well, yeah. I figured if you were so adamant about being foolish, I needed reinforcements."

Lacey stomped into the room. She thrust her fists to her hips and gave Liz a hard stare. "Liz. What. The. Fuck?"

Liz threw her hands up in the air. "Oh, my God. I can't believe you two are going to tag-team me." She went to her dresser and pulled out underwear and bras.

Lacey grabbed a pair of panties from her as she walked by. "Victoria's Secret? Nice."

Laurie clapped her hands. "Lacey. Focus. God, you're just like my kids, who I swear have the attention span of a gnat."

Lacey handed the panties back to Liz. "I can't help it. It's been awhile since I bought something that fancy to wear for Ray."

"TMI," Laurie said.

"Oh, and what? You saying you're a wanna-be lesbian isn't too much information?" Lacey snapped.

"Stop. Will you both stop?" Liz grabbed her head. "You're making my head hurt. I can't think."

Lacey put her hands on Liz's shoulders. "Yeah, I kind of figured that if you're getting ready to hightail it out of town over a misunderstanding."

"It's not like I won't be back," Liz mumbled as she zipped her suitcase.

Laurie popped up from the bed and joined Lacey to stare down Liz.

"Will you two stop with the freaky eyes shit?" Liz said. "I feel like I'm in a Wes Craven movie."

Laurie looked at Lacey. "First she accuses me of being an alien. Now a freaky character in a horror flick."

"Hey, if it fits," Liz said.

"All right. We"—Laurie motioned between her and Lacey—"don't understand why you can't stay here and actually talk this out with Dani. You know. Like an adult? But if you're going to go through with this, please tell us it's only for a few days."

"I'll be back by the weekend. Laurie, you're sure you don't mind watching Melanie?"

"My kids are already excited about it. I can't back out now."

Liz grabbed her suitcase and popped the handle to wheel it to the door. Laurie and Lacey followed on her heels like two puppies. She stopped suddenly, and they bumped into her.

"Change your mind?" Lacey asked.

"Nooo. I want you both to know that I appreciate your concern." Liz softened her tone. "And your love."

Laurie pushed Liz's hair behind her ear. "Hon, we don't want you to give up on such a good thing. We've met Dani, remember? She treats you like a queen. She obviously lo—"

Liz raised her hand. "Don't say the word."

"You have to know she does. Just because I don't say the word doesn't make it not true."

"That was such a double-negative."

"You know what I mean."

"We haven't told each other that yet." Liz knew that it was coming, though. It scared her. Thrilled her. Made her feel like acrobats were turning backflips inside her stomach.

"You will," Laurie said emphatically. "But only if you quit running anytime something a little bit scary pops up."

Liz moved toward the door. "Like I said, it's only for the week. When I get back, I'll talk with Dani. I told her I needed some time, and she's respected that so far."

"You're simply leaving town before she quits respecting it," Lacey said, her voice dripping in sarcasm.

"Why did you two want to talk to me? Because this little pep talk isn't helping."

Laurie patted her on the back. "Oh, it will. Probably when you're flying over Kansas on your descent into Denver."

* * *

From her window seat on the airplane, Liz stared at the farmland stretched out below her. *That's probably Kansas*, she thought. She really, really hated that her sisters were right. Because at that moment, she was questioning the logic in flying over 1,000 miles to "clear her head."

The plane landed at Denver International Airport. She followed the rest of the passengers to the tram that carried them to the baggage claim and sliding glass doors that led to the rental car shuttles. She was glad she'd packed light enough to carry her suitcase on board. The only thing left to do was pick up her car. She landed at noon Denver time and was anxious to drive up to Grand Lake before it got dark in the mountains. The shuttle dropped her off at one of the rental car sites located near the airport. In no time, she had the keys to an eight-cylinder Tacoma.

As she drove, she thought about Dani, and she thought about the conversation with her sisters. Unfortunately, their advice was ringing so true to her now. Funny how sobering a three-and-a-half-hour flight can be when questioning her decision.

A light mist started outside of Denver and picked up in intensity the farther she drove to her destination. She debated pulling off into one of the towns along the way, but thankfully, the rain abated as she drove into the heart of the Rockies. The scenery was just as breathtaking as the last time she'd made this trip. When she attempted to leave her heartache behind after her relationship ended with Therese, she'd found the lodge she was driving to during an online search. The name alone—Rainbow Lodge—had promised new hope for her tattered life. What was she looking for this time?

Two-and-a-half hours later, she pulled into the gravel parking lot. Here, the sun was shining brightly off the mountain peaks. She grabbed her suitcase out of the trunk and wheeled it behind her as she ascended the stairway to the lodge entrance. She grimaced with each thump of the wheels along the steps.

Liz was pleased to see the same older woman at the front desk. Her name escaped Liz at the moment.

The woman raised her head from her paperwork. "Hello. Welcome to Rainbow Lodge. I'm Tess. Would you like to check into a cabin?"

Liz smiled at the friendly greeting. "Yes."

Tess reached under the counter and pulled out a form. "How many nights?"

"Only four. I'd like to check out Friday."

"You're in luck. We have some cabins open. I don't know if you're aware that we close down after Labor Day weekend. So, you made it in when most of our guests are checking out."

"Good to hear."

The beautiful blonde Liz had met on her last visit walked around the counter. "Aunt Tess, have you seen Corey?" She glanced at Liz. "Sorry I'm interrupting."

"That's fine." Liz definitely remembered her. She'd flirted with Liz, but Liz was in no mood at the time for any kind of dalliance. The other woman had backed off immediately.

"No, Erin. Corey didn't see fit to give me her itinerary today."

Liz couldn't help but chuckle at the sarcastic answer.

"Funny, Aunt Tess."

"A major credit card and we're set," Tess told Liz.

Liz pulled out a card from her wallet. After Tess ran the card, Liz signed the form. She could feel Erin watching, and she wondered if Erin remembered her.

"Here you go." Tess handed Liz a key. "Cabin Four on the trail on the other side of the walkway you used to come up here. My niece will show you the way." Tess motioned at Erin.

"Sure," Erin said. She came around the counter and bent over to pick up Liz's suitcase.

"You don't need to—"

"No problem. You look a little beat. Drive in from Denver?"

Liz quickened her step to keep up with Erin. "How could you tell?"

"I remember you checking in before, and I know you're from out of town. Out of state if my memory serves me right."

Liz blushed as she recalled her last visit and Erin's flirtatious ways.

Erin noticed her reaction. "Don't worry. I won't flirt with you this time." A handsome butch with dark-brown hair strode toward them. "I'm happily married now, and here comes my wife."

Liz couldn't help but notice the butch's resemblance to Dani. Not in looks as much as the purposeful stride and short, dark hair. Her heart skipped a beat. She was already missing Dani.

"Hey, Erin." The woman nodded at Liz. "Ma'am."

Oh, my Lord, Liz thought. She called me ma'am. Either she's incredibly polite, or I look incredibly older than I think I do.

Erin kissed her briefly on the mouth. "Corey, meet... I'm sorry. I don't remember your name."

Liz held out her hand. "Liz Springer."

Corey shook her hand. "Corey Banner."

"What've you been working on today, hon?" Erin asked Corey.

Corey hooked her thumb past her shoulder. "Fixing some of the flooring in Cabin Seven. Now, I'm heading up to catch a bite to eat at the restaurant."

"Great. I'll join you once I show Liz her cabin."

"Nice to meet you." Corey shook Liz's hand again before leaving for the lodge.

"Wow." Liz didn't realize she'd spoken the word until Erin laughed.

"She's really as nice as she seems."

They reached the porch of the cabin. Erin let Liz step in front of her to open the door. The interior was how Liz remembered but seemed brighter with what appeared to be a new coat of paint.

"Corey's been steadily renovating all the cabins. This is one of the finished ones." Erin set the suitcase by the door. "Do you remember where everything is?"

Liz walked in and poked her head around the kitchen doorway. "I believe so."

"Let us know if you need anything. Glad to have you back at Rainbow Lodge." Erin stepped out on the porch and started up the pathway to the main lodge.

* * *

It was Thursday morning, and Liz was thankful she'd be leaving late tomorrow. The past several days reinforced what she already knew and what she should've been able to tell Dani. Liz was in love with her. She'd thought about catching an earlier flight home, but as each day dawned, the scared part of her decided to stay the week. She just hoped she hadn't blown it by leaving Francis and not staying to talk.

Sitting on a large boulder by the shore, she stared out at Grand Lake and marveled at the reflection of the mountains on the placid surface. She heard footsteps behind her. She glanced over her shoulder and saw Erin headed her way.

"Looks like you've found my thinking rock. Do you mind if I join you?"

Liz patted the cool stone beside her. "Not at all."

They sat in silence for a few moments before Erin spoke. "Can I ask you something?"

"Sure."

"Is everything okay?"

Liz wondered if her emotions were that transparent.

Erin touched her arm. "Don't worry. It's not obvious. I remember the last time you were here, you were going through a difficult time." She gave a sly grin. "Believe me, I tried my best to get your attention."

Liz laughed. "It wasn't you."

"Normally, I'd be wounded with that statement."

"But now you're happily married to Corey."

Erin lit up at the mention of Corey's name. "Yes, I am. She's everything I could ever dream of in a life mate. I'm blessed that we met. Back to you, though. I was going to say that this time you're different. It doesn't seem like you're grieving the end of a relationship."

"You figured that out?"

"I went through the same thing with an ex. I knew the signs after I quit flirting with you long enough. It feels like this trip for you might not be strictly a vacation. You've been very quiet and have kept to yourself." She patted Liz's knee. "Please stop me if I'm being too forward."

"You're fine. I came here to think things over. I'm in another relationship now. Something happened, and I started questioning everything."

"She didn't—"

"No, no. She didn't cheat on me." Liz told Erin what happened at the bookstore.

"Let me see if I understand. You walked in on this other woman kissing your girlfriend, but your girlfriend told you what really happened. That the woman had kissed her."

Liz nodded slowly. Maybe the 1,000-plus miles were finally hitting her, but hearing Erin using the same words as her sisters had a completely different result.

"God, I'm so stupid. I can't believe I flew all the way out here."

Erin bumped shoulders with her. "Don't beat yourself up. Corey kind of did the same thing at the hospital when I was injured in a car accident. She lost her previous partner the same way, and the accident scared her so much, she couldn't face me." Erin stared off at the mountains. "Aunt Tess set her straight. When she came back to the hospital room, we had a good talk about how you can't run away from your fears. How we needed to face things together as a couple, especially if we wanted a lasting relationship together."

Liz leaned over, picked up a rock, and flipped it over in her fingers. She cringed a little more with each word Erin spoke. Now, she truly felt foolish.

"I'm not saying all of this to make you feel bad, Liz. I'm just telling you that talking it out is the way to go."

"And that maybe flying over 1,000 miles was a bit of a kneejerk reaction?"

"Um... maybe?" Erin winked at her.

Liz laughed. "You're right." It was time to go home and face the music, whatever song it played.

Chapter 28

Almost a week had passed, and Dani still hadn't heard from Liz. She was giving her the time and space that Liz requested, but it was tearing Dani apart inside.

When Dani couldn't take another day, she walked down to Liz's house. She decided to knock and stay there if no one answered. If she had to camp out on the front doorstep until Liz left for work in the morning, then so be it.

Liz's car wasn't in her drive. There was one light on in the front room of the house, and the porch light was on. Dani knocked on the door again, but there was no answer—not even from Melanie.

Did Liz leave town? No, she could be out for the night. That had her mind racing. If she was out for the night, who the hell was she with?

"Stop it, Dani. Just stop it."

On her walk back home, she debated contacting Liz's sisters but didn't want to involve them if she could help it. Instead, she would drive to the vet's office in the morning on her way into work. She hesitated doing it before. She still wanted to respect Liz's space to work things out and definitely didn't want to cause any problems at Liz's office.

But now, Dani was at a loss. She longed to see Liz.

* * *

Dani pulled into the clinic parking lot but still no sign of Liz's car.

Not good, not good, not good, Dani thought with each step to the door. As usual, Mary was behind the counter. Dani stood back until Mary finished her phone call and hung up.

"Hey, Dani, how's Frodo?" Mary asked. "I know he had ACL surgery."

"He's doing great." She hesitated. She wasn't sure what she was going to say or how she was going to say it. So, she winged it. "I'm looking for Dr. Springer. I want to discuss Frodo's diet since his surgery." That sounded lame, but Dani kept talking. "Do you know how I can reach her? I've been trying her home, but there hasn't been an answer."

"Dr. Springer left Monday for Colorado. She decided to take a last minute vacation and said she got a good deal on the Internet."

Dani's heart sank to the floor.

Mary leaned forward. She had a conspiratorial look on her face, like she was about to divulge the whereabouts of all the hidden missile silos in the United States. "Do you want to know where she's staying?" she asked in a hushed tone.

Dani nodded.

Mary pulled out a Post-it with writing on it and copied the information onto a piece of paper. She handed it to Dani. Dani looked down and read, "Rainbow Lodge, Grand Lake, Colorado." There was a phone number.

"Sorry, but the only address I have is a PO Box number. I'm sure you can get more information off the Internet, though."

"Thanks for this." Dani waved the paper.

"No problem." Dani started to leave. "Oh, and, Dani?" Dani turned back. "Good luck." Mary sported a knowing smile.

Dani stared at the information on the paper as she walked to her car. Grand Lake freaking Colorado. Could she travel any farther from Francis, Georgia? *Well, yes, I guess there's Nevada, then California. And of course, Alaska and Hawaii.*

* * *

"Colorado?" Tina asked in a surprised tone.

"Yeah," Dani mumbled. She was counting the money from the day's sales. She arrived at work in the morning and hesitated telling Tina until right after closing time—mainly because she feared Tina's reaction.

"Well?"

Dani didn't stop counting the twenties. "Well, what?"

"What do you mean 'well, what?' When do you leave for Colorado?"

Dani completely lost count of the money with the question. "What the hell are you talking about?"

Tina rolled her eyes. "Hello. Earth to Dani Roberts. This is the woman of your dreams. The woman you plan to spend the rest of your life with, and you haven't thought about going to Colorado?"

"She told me she needed some time to think about things. I want to give her space—"

Tina cut her off by whipping off her Braves cap and slamming it onto the counter. Her face reddened like she was about to explode. "Argh!" She grasped her curly hair and looked every bit like she would pull out a clump of it as her fingers tightened around the curls.

"Tina, I—"

"No." Tina held up her hands. "I don't want to hear excuses. I don't want to hear 'I want to give her space.' Remember that Reading Femmes 101 course I said you needed to take? Well, I'm going to find one somewhere, somehow, and I'm going to fucking enroll you in it."

"Calm down."

"No, no, no." Tina paced in front of the counter. She whirled around to face Dani. "You want to know why I won't let you screw this up?" Dani could only nod. "Because Dr. Liz Springer is the best thing that's ever happened to you. You don't see your face when you're with her. You just light up. Like from the inside out. It's amazing."

Tina walked around the counter and took Dani's hands in hers. Her dark-brown eyes were wet with tears. "Don't let her get away, Dani. She wants you and needs you." Tina squeezed Dani's hands. "And you want and need her. The love between the two of you, it's so plain."

Dani ducked her head. "That's just it, Tina. I haven't told her I love her."

"Well, guess what? You can fly out to Colorado to tell her. Think about how romantic that'd be. Listen to your best friend. Have I ever steered you wrong?"

"No."

"Right answer."

Dani grabbed Tina for a long embrace. "You're such a good friend. I love you, T." Dani choked back her tears.

Tina patted her on the back. "If you really love me, you'll sit your ass down in front of that computer and find a cheap flight to Denver. Then make sure you rent a car with GPS because this Grand Lake place definitely sounds like it's in the mountains."

"I'll find it. Don't worry."

* * *

"Frodo, sit."

Frodo looked over at Dani who was driving him over to Barb and Tina's house. They agreed to dog sit while Dani went to Colorado. Ignoring Dani's command, Frodo tried to climb over the gearshift again to get into Dani's lap. It was obvious he knew something was up. Maybe the suitcase gave it away.

"Frodo, sit. I'm driving here." Dani gently pushed him back into the seat. "Mommy has to take a trip, but when I return, your other mommy will be with me." He cocked his head. "I know you're missing her, too." Dani was still unsure of herself, and she needed to feel some confidence before she got on that plane. Talking to her beagle was a start.

It was five a.m. when she pulled into Barb and Tina's drive. Her flight was scheduled to leave at seven-thirty-five. They were at the door ready for Frodo. Barb took the leash and practically shoved Tina out the door.

"You better get going. You know how much crap you have to go through before you get on a plane," Barb said. "Dani, hon, good luck. Bring your woman home."

"Thanks, Barb. I'm going to try."

"Pull your car up there in the front, Dani," Tina said. "I'll take you in the Explorer."

Dani got back in her car and swung the MINI Cooper around the SUV to pull into the space in front of the fence. She opened the hatchback, grabbed her suitcase, and threw it into the backseat of Barb's Explorer.

"Don't worry. I'll get you there in plenty of time, Dani."

Tina backed out of the drive. When she drove out of town and onto the Interstate, she made good on her word. Dani wasn't worried about arriving at the airport late considering they were going about twenty miles over the speed limit.

"Tina, you really don't have to hurry like this," Dani said through clenched teeth.

"We're cool, we're cool." Tina zipped in front of a semi then over into the fast lane.

Dani reached for the handle above her door and held on for dear life. "I have to say I've never seen this side of you."

"You never had to rescue your girlfriend before."

"I'm not sure you could call it rescuing."

"Whatever you want to call it, you're getting to the airport on time and on that plane to Denver." With that, Tina cut across the highway to get off at the airport exit.

"Jesus Christ, T!"

"Don't worry. That was only six lanes."

They stopped at the passenger drop-off. When she got out of the Explorer, Dani had to suppress the urge to kneel down and kiss the sidewalk. She reached in to get her bag.

"Take care, Dani. Don't worry about the pup. He's in good hands."

"Thanks, Tina." Dani shut the door.

Tina powered down the passenger window. "Dani?"

"Yeah?" Dani turned back to the SUV.

"If you pull this one off, you've successfully moved on to Reading Femmes 201."

Before Dani could respond, Tina merged into the lane to leave. Dani checked her watch. *Damn. It was five-thirty.* Tina had cut thirty minutes off what should have been an hour drive.

After boarding, Dani walked down the narrow aisle of the plane. She pulled her iPod out of her bag and lifted the bag into the overhead compartment. She sat down in her window seat. After the plane took off, she listened to the flight attendants' spiel. When they finished, Dani plugged in her earbuds and settled back in her seat. She fell asleep to Mary Chapin Carpenter's "The Calling."

Dani woke up from a dream when the flight attendant announced the temperature in downtown Denver. In the dream, she and Liz were walking Frodo and Melanie. Dani swore she could still hear Liz's infectious laugh. In another twenty minutes, they were taxiing to the gate. Even with the three-and-a-half-hour flight, it was only a little after nine a.m. with the time difference.

Dani took the shuttle out to the rental car facility and asked if they had any Jeeps.

"Can you drive a stick?" the attendant asked. He was maybe nineteen at the most. He popped his chewing gum in his mouth while he stared at Dani through watery eyes.

"Yes, I can drive a stick," she answered, resisting the urge to yank the gum out of his mouth.

He gave her a once-over that screamed, "Yeah, I guess you could." He handed her the paperwork to fill out and pulled the keys down from the hook.

Dani took the keys and mumbled her thanks. As she walked to the Jeep, she started thinking about what she'd say to Liz. She only hoped that Liz would be glad to see her.

She tossed her bag into the passenger seat of a Jeep Renegade. After tugging the slip of paper with the address to the lodge out of her wallet, she programmed the GPS. She would catch US-40 off I-70 and then up to US-34. That should take her directly into Grand Lake.

The drive time was supposed to be around two-and-a-half hours if the traffic was light. Dani familiarized herself with the Jeep and then pulled out onto the Interstate. She breathed a sigh of relief at the lighter traffic. She hadn't been sure what to expect.

As she drove, her mind drifted back to the first night of passion that she and Liz shared. They had many nights like that since, but the first was the one so vivid to her. Their passion ebbed and flowed like the tide, as they each took their time to pleasure the other until they collapsed in each other's arms at three in the morning, sweating and exhausted.

Dani merged onto US-34 and thought she'd try to ease her worries by listening to some music. When she flipped on the radio, Metallica immediately pounded her eardrums. She pictured the previous drivers of the rented Jeep as a heavy metal group stuffed in the vehicle on their way to a gig.

She adjusted the sound and used the button on the steering wheel until she came to a suitable station. If she heard C.J.'s song, she'd pull over to the side of the road and pummel the Jeep with her bare fists. It was a possibility since "Dani's Eyes" had moved into the top ten on the alternative rock charts.

She took the risk, though. She needed to hear something. Eventually, a Lucinda Williams tune came on. Dani had heard "Are You Alright" once before, but she listened to the lyrics with a new understanding. Williams's raspy voice, pleading with her lover to talk to her, drifted up from the speakers and filled the Jeep. Dani felt a sharp pain in her chest as the words flowed into her heart about a lover who leaves without saying a word.

Tears rolled down her cheeks. She brushed them away with the back of her hand and sighed. "I can't lose her. I just can't."

The beauty of the Rockies was truly mesmerizing as Dani drove higher and higher into the mountains. She made it to the lodge shortly after noon. She parked the Jeep, stepped down from the driver's seat, and leaned against the side of the car. She took in a deep breath of clean mountain air and what she hoped was a breath of   courage.

Leaving her bag in the Jeep, she made her way up the path to the front of the lodge. At the bottom of the stairs to the large porch that ran the length of the lodge, she paused to take in the magnificence around her. Lush, green mountains, with a sprinkling of aspens, surrounded Grand Lake as if cradling a baby in their arms. The clouds hung low—almost as though Dani could reach out and touch them. She could see why Liz chose to come here.

She went up the steps to the lodge. When she reached the long porch, she checked the large swings hanging there to see if Liz was enjoying the warm weather. No such luck. She entered the lodge and approached the front desk. An older woman with a warm smile greeted her.

"Hello. Welcome to Rainbow Lodge. I'm Tess." She glanced down at Dani's feet. "I was about to ask if you needed a cabin, but it doesn't look like you're staying."

"Uh, I'm not sure how to ask this. I have a feeling lodgers' information is probably confidential."

Tess's warm smile slipped a little. "You'd be right."

Dani moved to the counter and leaned on it. "I hate to beg, but I'm desperate."

Tess gripped her arm. "It's not an emergency, is it?"

"It depends on what you mean by emergency. I'm looking for my girlfriend. She should've checked in on Monday."

"Aunt Tess, I got this," a soft feminine voice said behind her.

Dani turned and met the startling, light-blue eyes of a blonde woman about her age.

"Erin, you know I don't like giving out lodger information. We don't—"

"Aunt Tess, you have to trust me on this one."

Tess didn't seem happy about it, but she nodded. Someone else approached the counter, and she left to assist them.

"Thank you so much," Dani said.

"Let's go out on the porch, and you can tell me who you're looking for. I have a feeling I know who it is."

Dani joined Erin in sitting on one of the big, wooden swings. Dani sat on the edge, ready to spring into action once she found out where Liz was staying.

"She's my girlfriend, Liz Springer. She arrived here on Monday. I'm not exactly sure when she's coming home. I hope she's still here."

Erin's smile was as bright as the sun pouring on the lake below them, and it filled Dani's heart with hope. "You're in luck. She leaves later this afternoon for an evening flight."

"Do you know where—"

Erin stood up. "I'll walk you down."

As they walked along the trail to the shore of the lake, Dani was at a loss as to what to say. Erin said she thought she knew who Dani was. Did that mean Liz talked about what brought her out here?

As if sensing Dani's thoughts, Erin glanced over at her. "Don't worry. Liz has only told me a little of what happened and how's she's feeling."

And that was it. Erin said no more. Dani wanted to stop their descent and bombard her with questions. Then she reminded herself the person she needed to speak to was at the end of this trail.

Erin stopped before they reached the very end. She motioned in front of her. "You'll find Liz sitting on what I think of as my rock. I shared it with her this week, though." Erin squeezed Dani's hand. "Go to her." With that, she headed back up the trail to the lodge.

Dani continued on the path. She stopped suddenly when she saw Liz on the rock, her knees drawn to her chest. Dressed in a pair of khaki cargo pants and a green short-sleeved T-shirt, she had her neck bent back so she faced the sun. She was... stunning. Dani's heart raced even faster as she thought, *she's wearing green. Those eyes I've missed will be amazing.*

Liz's dark hair flowed over her shoulders. It shone like burnished ebony in the sun. She stared out at the water and appeared to be deep in thought.

Dani walked slowly to the large rock. Almost there, she stepped on a twig. Liz turned at the sound. Dani hadn't been sure what to expect, but if Liz looked at her with any kind of disappointment, Dani's heart would shatter in two.

Liz's eyes filled with tears when she saw Dani. "You came," she whispered.

Dani could only nod as she drew closer.

"You came 1,500 miles to see me," Liz said in a choked voice.

"Honey, I would travel the world over to see you. Don't you know that?" Dani struggled to speak around the lump in her throat.

"Dani, I've been so... so..."

Dani sat down beside Liz and took her hand. "You didn't give me a chance to tell you this before you left." She stroked the back of Liz's hand with her thumb. "I love you, Liz Springer. I think I fell a little in love with you that first day at Frodo's exam. It just took awhile for my brain to catch up to my heart."

"Thank God," Liz choked out. "Because I love you, too." She sniffled and laughed without humor. "I know leaving Francis isn't the best way to show you."

"It doesn't matter." Dani thought her heart would burst with hearing Liz say she loved her. She tried to draw strength from the splendor around them before she spoke again. She held both of Liz's hands and locked gazes with her for several seconds before speaking. *God, these eyes. I could fall into their green pools and never come up for air.* "I'd never hurt you intentionally," she said carefully, but with a strong voice. "I didn't kiss C.J. She kissed me. I only wish you could've seen me push her away."

"I believe you. It just... it brought back this flood of memories for me when I saw the two of you together. I couldn't stop them even if I tried." A silence passed between them, only broken by the wind that rustled through the tall pines. "I got scared. And when I get scared, I run." She gazed toward the lake, the sun reflecting off her beautiful face. "I came here to think. Once I cleared my head, it didn't take me long to question flying all this way. I can be a little impulsive."

"Good to know," Dani said with a laugh, trying to lighten the mood.

Liz gave Dani an incredulous look. "And, God. You came all this way?" She shook her head in wonder. "But you need to know I still get frightened. I shouldn't, but I do. It's like I told you before, that you're too good to be true. *We're* too good to be true."

"You have to trust me, Liz. To trust us. I'm not going anywhere. I'm only running to you. Wherever you go, I will run to you. Do you understand?" She squeezed Liz's hands. "I love you, and I can't lose you. I just can't." Dani's voice broke, and she tried to choke back her tears, but a couple still escaped.

Liz brushed away one of them from Dani's cheek.

"Then you have to promise me something, Dani. You have to promise me that when these doubts creep up for me, you'll understand, and you'll tell me just what you're telling me right now. I know that may sound insecure, but—"

Dani kissed Liz's hand. "It's not."

A small smile crept across Liz's lips. "And you have to promise me one more thing."

"Anything."

A twinkle appeared in Liz's eyes. "We will never ever own any C.J. James music."

Dani laughed. "Okay, okay. That's a reasonable request."

"The woman wrote a song about you. I mean, how can I compete with that?"

"You don't have to compete, because there's no competition." She leaned in and gave Liz a soft kiss, a reconnection to what they shared after the time spent apart. She pulled back and caressed Liz's cheek. "Don't you know our love means so much more than a song?"

As the words left Dani's lips, tears welled in Liz's eyes. A low rumble of thunder sounded above, and a gentle rain began to fall. The sun pierced the clouds with heart-stopping clarity, and a rainbow dropped down into the lake before them. Dani stared at Liz's face glistening with tears and rainwater, and she was overcome with Liz's beauty. Liz met Dani's gaze and smiled.

Just as on the first day they met, Liz's eyes whispered to her of hope and promise for the days ahead. Caught up in the joy that drummed a staccato beat inside her chest, Dani smiled back and pulled Liz close for another kiss.

This time... this time Dani would hold onto that promise and never let it go.

Photo credit: Phyllis Manfredi

Author Chris Paynter with Buddy the Wonder Dog, June 2013

About the Author

Chris Paynter is the author of eight novels, including the *Playing for First* baseball series. Her *Survived by Her Longtime Companion* was a 2013 Lambda Literary Award Finalist and winner of the 2013 Ann Bannon Popular Choice Award. Her short stories have appeared in Regal Crest's *Women in Uniform: Medics and Soldiers and Cops, Oh My!* (2010) and Cleis Press's *Love Burns Bright: A Lifetime of Lesbian Romance* (2013). After earning a Bachelor's degree in journalism, Chris worked as a general assignment reporter and sportswriter until accepting her current position as the editorial specialist to a law journal. A sports junkie, you can find her screaming at the TV during a Colts game or living vicariously through her Cincinnati Reds. When not writing or editing books, Chris loves to get lost in a good romance. She resides in Indianapolis with her wonderful wife, Phyllis.

Visit her website: www.ckpaynter.com
Email her at: ckpaynter@ckpaynter.com
Visit her Author Page on Facebook: www.facebook.com/
ChrisPaynterAuthor
Find her on Twitter: @ckpaynter

If you enjoyed the characters of Erin and Corey in *More Than a Song*, be sure and check out their story in *And a Time to Dance* (2013) from Companion Publications...

They parked in the lot at the dude ranch and followed couples strolling hand in hand to the corrals in the back. Overhead lights draped over a stage set up to the rear. To their right, several long tables overflowed with buckets of iced beer and bottled water for those not inclined to drink alcohol.

"If I remember right, you like Coors." Erin reached in a bucket and lifted out an ice-cold bottle dripping with water. She handed it to Corey and grabbed one for herself.

The band played the open notes of a fast country tune, and couples took to the dirt dance floor.

Erin challenged her. "Ready?"

Corey grimaced and held up her bottle. "Can I at least down this to get some courage?"

"Then no backing out, ya hear?"

"Oh, I hear all right." Corey sipped her beer as she watched the dancers.

Erin watched, too, tapping her toe to the beat. By the time the song ended, Corey had finished her beer.

"Nervous?" Erin asked, with a smile.

Corey opened her mouth to answer when something behind Erin caught her attention.

"Erin, how are you?"

Erin turned to see Lee ambling over. She was wearing a short jeans skirt with a denim shirt tied at the bottom over a white ribbed top. Her full breasts filled out the top, showing plenty of cleavage. She wore her cowboy hat low, cloaking her face in shadow.

"Lee. Hi."

Lee raised her chin at Corey. "What was your name again?"

"Corey," she answered with an even voice.

The two women stared at each other like gunslingers ready to draw their six-shooters in the middle of town.

"Corey and I were about to dance. She's never two-stepped before."

"Why don't you and I show her how it's done, Erin?"

Erin was about to protest, but Corey silenced any refusal. "I'll wait, Erin. Go ahead."

Lee didn't need any more incentive. She grabbed Erin by the hand and pulled her toward the center of the dance area.

"You know, you were kind of rude," Erin said as the music started.

"She's a big girl. Besides, she needs to let two pros show her the moves."

Erin didn't say anything as she concentrated on following Lee's lead. She had to give Lee this much. She was good. Erin got lost in the music, not paying much attention to who she was dancing with. She searched for Corey who had drifted into the shadows. She seemed to be following their every move. Erin couldn't tell if she was concentrating on getting the steps down or if it was something else.

The song ended, and the band quickly started on the next.

"How about another go?" Lee asked.

"No, I promised Corey I'd show her how to two-step." Erin pulled out of her embrace and walked toward Corey. "Got your courage up yet?"

Corey set her beer on a nearby table. "One-and-a-half beers gave me enough gumption."

Erin held out her left hand and Corey took it. She placed her other hand loosely on Corey's shoulder.

"Since I'll be leading, put your left hand on my arm here. You'll be able to feel which direction I'm headed when I squeeze your other hand."

"Okay." Corey lifted her head and gave a small sniff. "I smell lilacs."

"Uh... that's my perfume."

"Good. I mean it smells good."

"Thanks. Did you catch on any to the dancing?" Erin asked in a rush.

"Not much."

"First of all, don't let the experienced dancers scare you." She nodded toward couples doing fast spins around the dance floor. "I'll teach you the basics. Watch my feet at first. I'll lead. It's two quick steps forward. That's two quick steps back for you." She moved forward. "And then two slow steps. The beat is quick-quick-slowslow, quick-quick-slow-slow."

Corey's brow furrowed, and the tip of her tongue stuck out of the side of her mouth.

God, she's adorable, Erin thought as they moved haltingly with the other dancers. Corey uttered an occasional "damn it" when her steps faltered.

"Now, don't look at our feet," Erin said.

"Are you crazy? If not, I'll fall on my ass."

"No you won't. Trust me. Raise your head and focus on me."

Corey met her eyes as another fast song drifted through the night air. The face lined in concentration had slipped away, and a much more heated expression had replaced it. This time, Erin stumbled. She quickly righted her steps.

They moved now with a smoother gait, almost as if they'd been dancing together for years. The music ended, and they stopped as the band led into a slow song. A lot of the couples left the dance floor. Erin still held Corey's right hand in her left with her other hand on Corey's shoulder.

Without thinking, she drew Corey closer and dropped her hand around Corey's waist. They swayed gently to the mournful country ballad. Eventually, Erin rested her cheek against Corey's. Corey trembled at the move. Erin wanted the song to last forever but had to settle for a few minutes of bliss in Corey's arms.

She reluctantly withdrew from the embrace when the song ended. "That was... nice."

"It was," Corey said in a soft voice. She shook her head slightly as if to regain her composure. "Do you mind if I sit the next one out? Lee's coming this way. I think she'll want to dance with you again."

Erin was about to say she didn't want to dance with another woman, but Corey had already drifted from under the overhead lights and into the darkness.

Make sure to check out these other <u>C</u>ompanion <u>P</u>ublications titles by Chris Paynter:

From Third to Home	978-1-942204-12-1
To Love Free	978-1-942204-00-8
And a Time to Dance	978-1-942204-09-1
Survived by Her Longtime Companion	978-1-942204-07-7
Two for the Show	978-1-942204-05-3
Come Back to Me	978-1-942204-03-9
Playing for First	978-1-942204-01-5

www.ingramcontent.com/pod-product-compliance
Lightning Source LLC
Chambersburg PA
CBHW050521190726
48284CB00003B/893